WINTER'S TALE

ABOUT THE AUTHOR

Geoffrey Lewis was born in Oxford, in 1947. Educated at the City's High School, and Hatfield University (then a polytechnic), he has since followed a varied career, including spells as a research chemist, security guard, and professional photographer. After many years in the motor trade, and eight years as captain of a canal-based passenger boat, he is now semi-retired, and concentrating upon writing.

Photographer, bell-ringer, beer-drinker, and American car enthusiast, he lives in a narrowboat on the Grand Union Canal.

OTHER TITLES FROM GEOFFREY LEWIS:

FLASHBACK   The First David Russell Novel
STRANGERS   The Second David Russell Novel

And *CYCLE* - the story which steps back in time to tell of the first collaboration between David Russell and Doug Rimmer, for release during 2005.

WINTER'S TALE

A D.I. David Russell novel

Geoffrey Lewis

SGM
Publishing

ISBN 0-9545624-2-9

Printed in Great Britain

First published in Great Britain in 2004 by

SGM Publishing
20 Alexandra Road, Gravesend, Kent DA12 2QQ
info@sgmpublishing.co.uk

For Phil: The friend and mentor who
kicked me out of my former complacency

CHAPTER ONE

'Roddie! Wait! I've got to talk to you!'

Roddie McKeenan turned with a resigned sigh as Lucy Cavendish ran up behind him; it was late, he had some business to attend to, and the last thing he needed was another confrontation with her.

'Roddie - please - let's talk about things, can't we?' She'd followed him from the downstairs bar, caught up with him in the back corridor; now, she took him by the arm and made him face her.

'There's nothin' ta talk aboat, Luce. Ah toald ye on Sonday, it's all oaver - whatever we had, it's all funushed.' His Belfast accent made itself known, as it often did when he felt stressed.

'You can't say that! You can't just write off three years of our lives - not just like that, after all we've been to each other!' By contrast, Lucy betrayed the clipped tones of her boarding-school education. McKeenan sighed again:

'Ah *can* - Ah *have* to.' He shook his head: 'Mebbe Ah did love ye, at the start - but no moare. Ye'll find yersel' someone else, someone better, in no time at all, you'll see.'

'I don't *want* anyone else, can't you see that? I love *you,* you stupid Irish bastard!' McKeenan shook his head again, making his long wavy dark hair bounce on his shoulders:

'No ye *doan't,* Luce. Ut's all in yer mind - ye'll soon forget me, if ye'll just let me be gone.'

'I *won't,* Roddie! And what about Freya? She worships you,

you know she does - how can you do this to her?' At this McKeenan rounded on her angrily:

'Now doan't troy *that* on me, Lucy! She's a crackin' kid, for sure, but *she isn't mine,* so doan't pull the oald guilt thing on me! Now:' He pushed her away, gently but firmly: 'I've got business te be dealin' with, outside, all right?'

Lucy stared after him as he turned and hurried away towards the door which opened into the back-alley behind the nightclub. He disappeared into the cold dark night, and a cold, empty feeling grew in her chest, as if her heart had left the building with him; she fled into the ladies toilet, tears of pain and frustration burning behind her eyes. At the handbasin, she spun the cold tap on, practically ripping it from its mounting as anger swelled in her, adding even more confusion to her mixed-up feelings.

Not bothering to remove her gloves, she splashed the ice-cold water in her face, shook her head as it ran from her chin, and stood gazing at her reflection in the mirror. *The bastard!* How could he just turn his back on her, after more than three years together? The image of her gun rose in her mind, the little hand-bag sized automatic Roddie'd acquired for her in the interests of self-protection after that bastard of a client had beaten her up a year or two ago - but whether the urge was to use it on him or on herself, she was too confused to know.

She closed her eyes, let her head fall forward to hang between her shoulders - either way, she knew as her flare of fury cooled, she wouldn't, *couldn't,* do it. Her mother's instincts took over: The protection of her child was the most important thing of all, and she would be no good to Freya if she was in the ground, or in jail for murder. And anyway, it was in her bag, in the hostess's changing room along the corridor.

She raised her head again, to look herself in the eye through the mirror. So - if it *was* all over? *You're not a bad-looking gal, even if you are getting on!* She tossed her head, watching her long, wavy auburn hair bounce, looked again into her dark green eyes: *You'll do, kiddo! And twenty-six isn't that old, after all.* But even as she thought it, she knew the bravado was hollow, that she would take a long time to get over Roddie - they'd been so *close,* seemed so right for each other... How *could* it all be finished?

As she stood, contemplating the collapse of her life, she became aware of some background kerfuffling. A few loud thumps - then the sound of voices in the corridor beyond her temporary world, voices raised in... what? Anger? No, shock, distress - what was going on? She roused herself, quickly towelled her face, shook her hair into place and opened the door.

Emerging into the corridor, she was confronted with a scene of confusion to match that which reigned in her head. Suddenly, one of the other hostesses grabbed her, pinned her by both arms against the wall:

'Stay here, Luce! Don't go out there!'

'What? What is it, Elsa, what's going on?' The other girl held her firmly, gazing into her eyes, shocked blue looking into her puzzled green:

'I don't know, not really, but... It's Rod, Lucy; he's been hurt.'

'What! Let me go, I must go and help him! *Elsa! Let go of me!'* But the blond girl held on, shook her head, the shock in her face turning to pain:

'You *can't* help, Luce - I... I think he's dead.' Her voice was no more than a whisper.

Lucy stared at her for a moment, shaking her head, her mouth forming a silent 'No!'; then she broke loose, fought her way through the crowd of bodies blocking her way, out into the alley, to fall on her knees beside the prone figure of her lover, sliding one arm beneath his head, feeling the limp unresponsiveness of him, taking in as if in a trance the bloodstained shirt.

'Roddie, Roddie, Roddie...' His murmured name became a dirge as she held him to her chest, her tears falling unheeded on his upturned face.

CHAPTER TWO

Alan Broadbent swung the tired Peugeot 406 off the High Street into Butcher's Lane. He glanced at the dashboard clock as he braked the car to a halt, a few yards on, picked up the microphone and called in to his control room to let the girl on duty know he was taking a break: Twenty past one - about time too!

He'd been driving taxis around Grancester for as long as he could remember; twenty years and more. Many a time he'd threatened to give it up, go and find a less stressful job; but the money was good, even if the hours were beginning to take more and more of a toll, as he got older. And anyway, at fifty-six, who'd give him another job? He turned off the diesel engine, reached for his sandwiches.

Munching on his cheese and onion, he opened the Stephen King novel he'd picked up in one of the local charity shops a few days before, carried on reading from the page he'd marked. He enjoyed the dark tension of King's stories, had read quite a few of them over the years; without taking his eyes from the page, he unscrewed the cap of his flask, poured a mug of strong coffee. Casting a quick look out of the windscreen, he smiled to himself; the pitch blackness of the alley had to be the best - or the worst? - place to be reading a horror tale!

Three loud reports made him snap to attention, his gaze focussed out in front of the car in the direction of the sound. He was quick enough to catch the flash of light which accompanied the last: His jaw dropped - gunfire? No, don't be daft! But even as he thought it, he knew he was wrong, those *had* been gunshots. He reached for the light switch, instinctively wanting to see what had happened; then stopped himself - if there was someone there with a gun, he didn't want it turned on *him,* next! Instead, he fumbled for his mobile phone, punched three nines.

* * *

Sergeant Ken Dixon had been a policeman for nearly twenty years. Jibes about 'Dixon of Dock Green' were long forgotten; indeed, the younger officers coming along today had probably never heard of that once-popular TV drama, a fact for which Ken was quietly grateful.

He was sat in the passenger seat of one of the town's patrol cars, parked to one side of Grancester's Victoria Square. The engine was ticking over, the heater running; a chill grey day had turned into a cold, dank night before either he or his companion had come on duty - but then, what else should you expect in late November? Beside him, WPC Faith Hallam tickled the throttle occasionally, if only to relieve the monotonous sound of the engine, as they conversed in a desultory fashion. An imposing figure of a woman at almost six feet tall, Faith was a very effective officer - it wasn't only her build, but an indefinable air of command about her that gave her the edge in many situations, along with perhaps a certain reluctance among her adversaries to use the same level of force or language that they might have employed against a male constable.

They had had a quiet evening so far. The highest excitement had resulted from the drunken brawling of two Scotsmen outside the Star and Garter in Fish Lane; a dispute easily settled, which resulted in the two combatants staggering off homewards, their arms about each other's necks in restored camaraderie.

When the radio suddenly crackled into life with the call to a shooting at Sweeney's Nightclub, Dixon turned startled eyes on Faith with the simple command 'Go!' as he grabbed the microphone:

'Delta 478 responding.'

'Roger, 478 - incident is outside the rear entrance of the club, in Butcher's Lane. Reported one man injured, no information about perpetrator. Ambulance is on its way.'

'Thank you, control - can you get another unit to the front entrance, tell them to stop anyone leaving the premises?'

'Roger, 478. 294 is coming in from Glebe Farm, will be there in a few minutes.'

'Thanks - 478 out.'

Butcher's Lane is a narrow alleyway, opening off the High Street, which runs behind some of the buildings in Midland Road before ending abruptly against the side wall of the new Sainsbury's store. The patrol car squealed around the sharp turn, braked to a halt close to the disarrayed group of dark figures clustered by the nightclub's back door, to be joined, seconds later, by the ambulance. Dixon and the WPC leapt out, urging people back to allow themselves and the paramedics to get to the prone figure and the girl who held him in her arms.

Lucy looked up, her shock and horror clear in her eyes, as Faith Hallam took her by the shoulders and gently pulled her away:

'Come on, miss, let these guys help your fella, okay?' Lucy nodded distractedly, let herself be eased away. The Ambulancemen checked Roddie over quickly, efficiently; one of them looked up at Dixon, shook his head. He rose to his feet:

'We'll take him into A&E, Sergeant - but there's nothing we can do for him. They'll have to confirm it, but he must have died instantly. Should we take the girl along?'

'I guess so - I assume she's his girlfriend or whatever. Just let me make sure we know who she is, all right?'

'Sure thing.' He turned away, helped his partner to lift the limp body onto the stretcher. Dixon put a hand on Faith's shoulder; she turned to him, her arm still around Lucy, as he spoke to the girl:

'Do you want to go with the ambulance, miss?' Lucy nodded:
'Of course - if it's all right?'

'You go - Faith here will go with you, okay?' She nodded again; Dixon addressed the WPC:

'Look after her - someone'll need to talk to her, at some stage.'

'Sure, Sarge.'

The two of them followed the paramedics, climbed into the ambulance. Dixon set about ushering the remaining crowd back inside the nightclub, as the best place to keep an eye on them until reinforcements could arrive; as happens under such circumstances, the members of the group fell into two categories - the ones who all wanted to talk to him at once, and the ones who were trying to keep their heads down and not be noticed. Gently, firmly, he guided them into the building, doing his best to make a note of the latter types as he did so; a uniformed constable appeared from within to help, and received a grateful smile from Dixon.

'Sergeant?' Dixon turned; a shortish, untidily dressed man with a noticeable paunch stood behind him.

'What is it, sir?'

'My name's Broadbent - I called 999.'

'Oh, yes, I see, sir. Were you in the club?'

'Nah - I'm a taxi driver, my cab was parked in the alley, at the end there. I 'eard the shots, and called you.'

'Oh, right! Where's your car now, Mr Broadbent?'

'I shifted it, parked just round in the 'Igh Street, so you could get down 'ere.'

'That was very thoughtful of you, sir. Could you join the rest of us, inside the club, do you think? Someone will need to take a statement from you, if you don't mind.'

'Of course, Sergeant.' He stepped past, went through the door to join the others inside.

Dixon told the constable to keep watch at the door, to let no-one out, and used his personal radio to call in:

'Delta control, 478.'

'Go ahead, 478.'

'We've got the injured man away to A&E, with the girlfriend and WPC Hallam. I've got everyone else confined inside the club, with a PC on both doors - except for the ones that had already sloped off.'

'Roger, 478. Mr Armstrong is on his way to take charge - how is the man?'

'The paramedics say he died instantly - but they need the hospital to pronounce when they get him there.'

'Roger. No sign of the attacker?'

'No - unless he's among the crowd.'

'Roger - I'll inform the Chief Inspector. He should be with you in ten minutes.'

'Thanks, Maisie. 478 out.'

Dixon himself entered the club and began to try to make sense of the crowds of people within, determining who were staff, who were patrons, and if any were outsiders who had simply been gathered in with the harvest. He was making some limited headway when the solid figure of Chief Inspector Armstrong strode in:

'Sergeant Dixon - what have we got here?'

'Good evening, sir. The injured man has been taken to the hospital; WPC Hallam and the girlfriend have gone with him. I've got everyone else who was on the scene here inside, unless a few had already departed before we got here. Mr Broadbent - the man over there, by the bar - dialled 999; he's a taxi driver, happened to be parked in the alley out back when the incident took place.'

'Very good! Did he see the attacker, do you know?'

'I don't sir - I thought it best to try to keep everyone together until you could get here rather than pursue any direct enquiries.'

'Good man! You know which of these people are staff, which are customers?'

'To some extent, sir - I was trying to sort them out when you arrived.'

'Okay. God, what a crowd!'

'Yes, sir - there must be at least two hundred people here, I'd estimate.'

'Right. We'd better concentrate on the staff, I think. Can you put two constables on to getting the names and addresses of all the customers, then let them leave? Tell them to check any proof of identity, try to make sure we don't get too many Donald Ducks. Best warn 'em we'll want to talk to them later, too. I'll talk to Mr Broadbent, and then we'll find out what we can from the manager and other staff.'

'Yes, sir.'

'Is there any suggestion of just what happened, or who the attacker was?'

'Not so far, sir. There's no sign of whoever it was - perhaps Mr Broadbent saw which way he left the scene?'

'Perhaps - I'll ask him. Thanks, Ken.'

'CID on their way, sir?'

'Yes - I called DS Rimmer, he's on standby tonight. I expect he'll grab a few DC's on his way.'

Armstrong turned to survey the scene of chaos in the ground-floor bar of the club. With a resigned sigh, he strode over to the bar, introduced himself to the nervous-looking taxi driver and led the man to a vacant table.

* * *

In Grancester Hospital, Lucy Cavendish sat silent and dry-eyed beside the WPC. A few minutes after they arrived, a solemn-faced young man in a white coat approached them:

'Er - miss?' God, he looks younger than me! Lucy thought:

'Cavendish - Lucy Cavendish.' He nodded nervously:

'The young man - your fiancé?'

'Boyfriend. His name's Roddie McKeenan.' The doctor nodded again:

'I'm afraid - there was nothing we could do for him. I'm so sorry.'

Lucy stared at him without responding, until he began to look really flustered; at last, she nodded slowly:

'Thank you. I think… I knew, already - but….'

'I'm so very sorry, miss.' He'd run out of words. The silence held for a moment, but then Lucy's composure failed - she turned to Faith, her face crumpling; the WPC drew her gently into her arms, held her as the tears came, held her as the sobs wracked her slender body. Over the heaving shoulder, the policewoman looked up at the young doctor, raised one hand to gesture for him to leave them; he nodded, gave her a quick, sympathetic smile, and hurried off to the next emergency.

As Lucy's tears began to subside, Faith whispered into her ear:

'Do you want to see him? Say goodbye?' The auburn head shook in refusal; but then Lucy looked up, contradicted herself:

'Yes - please. Can I?' Faith gave her a reassuring squeeze:

'Wait here, Lucy.' She stood up, walked across to the reception desk and asked the nurse on duty which cubicle they'd taken him to, to be directed along the corridor to their right. She returned to Lucy, gently lifted her to her feet and guided her along, a hand on each of the girl's shoulders. At the door, she paused:

'Are you all right, Lucy?' her charge nodded hesitantly; she pushed the door open, followed her inside.

Lucy stood still for a moment, gazing down at the still form under the white sheet, drawn up to his chin. Then she almost staggered forward, to fall on her knees beside the bed, leaning over Roddie, her arms encircling his head, her face buried in his chest. Her own shoulders began to heave again; Faith stepped up behind her, put one hand comfortingly on her arm, waited for her to give rein to her grief.

Eventually, the storm subsided once more. Faith encouraged the girl onto her feet again, led her gently out of the room to sit once again in a quiet corner of the reception area.

'Lucy?' Dark green eyes, red-rimmed with pain, lifted to hers: 'Faith - was that your name?' The WPC smiled, nodded:

'That's right, Lucy. How are you doing?' She was rewarded with a wan smile:

'Okay, I guess.' Faith slipped her arm around the girl's waist, gave her an encouraging squeeze:

'Good girl! Now - we need to find out who did this. And we'll need your help, Lucy.' The auburn head nodded, the look in her eyes almost childlike in its trusting innocence:

'I understand.'

'You work at the club?' Lucy just nodded, glancing down at her skimpy hostess outfit, suddenly surprised to realise that that was all she was wearing, that she hadn't even noticed the chill of the November evening.

'What about Roddie?'

'No - he just comes by, most nights.'

'To see you?'

'I... I thought so, but - he wanted to break it off, to finish it.'

'But he still came to the club?' Lucy nodded again.

'When did he tell you? About finishing?'

'Last weekend - Sunday. At home.'

'He lived with you?'

'Not exactly - he stayed with us most of the time, but he still had his own flat. In one of those big houses, down Midland Road.'

'Why did he want to break up with you, do you know?' The auburn head shook, puzzled:

'Not really - he said... he said he didn't love me any more, but... I don't know!'

'Who else lives with you, Lucy? You said 'us'?' The girl managed a brief smile:

'My daughter. Freya - she's nine. She loves - loved - Roddie, he treated her like she was his own kid. Why would he want to leave us?' Faith shook her head, sharing the girl's failure to understand the male species. Lucy went on:

'I think… maybe he'd just got itchy feet, you know? He's lived in a lot of different places before, I think he just… likes to move on. You know what I mean?'

'Yeah, sure! I know men like that, too! Unreliable, that's what they are!' Again, Faith was rewarded with a quick smile; she asked:

'What did he do - for a living?'

'He's got his own business - painting and decorating.'

'Successful?'

'Yes! At least, he's always got plenty of money!'

'Makes you wonder even more, doesn't it? I mean, why he'd want to pack in a good business, start again somewhere else?' Lucy just nodded; Faith felt a sudden change in the girl beside her, a sudden reticence, as if she'd caught herself on the point of saying something she shouldn't. Filing the thought for future reference, she changed the subject:

'Lucy - I know how difficult it is for you - but can you think of anyone who might have done this? Anyone who might want to hurt Roddie?' She shook her head:

'No - no-one. Oh, he wasn't an angel, he must have upset one or two people. But not so's they'd want to *kill* him, surely?'

'You can't think of any reason why someone would do this?' Lucy's eyes met hers - and again, the WPC felt that reticence, that uncertainty of what she should say. But Lucy just shook her head again:

'I can't imagine, Faith.' The sudden use of her name alerted the policewoman's senses further, made her almost certain that the girl was not telling her the truth - or not all of it, anyway. But she decided to let it go; after all, it would be CID's job to unravel the story from here. She'd pass on her feelings to whoever drew the short straw, and leave it at that. She gave Lucy's waist another quick, reassuring squeeze:

'All right, Lucy - thanks. I expect the boys from CID will want to talk to you, sometime; but now, let's get you home, shall we?'

This time, Lucy's smile was relaxed, grateful.

CHAPTER THREE

Daniel Russell had held the dubious status of teenager for just six weeks. And it seemed to his mother at least that having passed that notable milestone, he was trying to live up (or down?) to the expected attitudes of that transient if intransigent state.

Late last evening, once both Daniel and his little sister were in bed, she had tackled his father on the subject:

'I don't know what it is with him lately, David. He's always been so *good,* so thoughtful, you know what I mean. If I've asked him to help with anything, he's been there, no question - more often than not, he's just got on with little things for me before I've realised he's done them. But now - if I ask him to help around the house, or tidy his room, it's as if I'm putting upon him.'

'He does what you say, though, surely?'

'Yes, eventually. But it's with no good grace - I get that slump of his shoulders, the deep sigh - you've heard him! Can't you talk to him, find out what's got into him?'

David Russell slipped his arm around his wife's shoulders as they sat side by side on the settee, pulled her close and kissed her cheek. He didn't reply immediately - he understood the problem, but, in truth, didn't know how to deal with it. For a minute or so, he sat remembering his own adolescence, the way that, for several years, he hadn't been able to say a word to his father without them having a row. In his case, it had been his mother he could better relate to - now, with Daniel, it seemed to be working out the other way round.

Father and son had always been close, perhaps because they were so alike. Physically: Tall, slim, sandy-blond, hazel-eyed, Daniel could almost pass as his father at the same age. And mentally: Intelligent, quick-witted, he shared most of his father's interests, and had still an abiding fascination with Russell senior's job, growing to understand the complexities, the satisfaction of the work of a senior detective-inspector. And that closeness had been greatly reinforced the previous year, when the boy had found himself the unwitting target of a paedophile that his father had at the same time been tracking down. But now? In the winter months, their shared hobby of sailing radio-controlled scale model yachts had of necessity to be shelved until the weather improved again in the Spring, even if the preparation of boats and other kit would keep the two of them together, happily occupied in idle moments.

His relationship with his son didn't seem to have undergone any change - but, in the home, Tracy was the boss, and it appeared that that was what was at the root of the problem. He kissed her cheek again, turned her face to him with one hand cupped under her chin:

'Hopefully, it's just a phase, love. He's growing up; I suppose we've got to expect him to start to show more independence, and I guess that's going to mean he'll be less inclined to take orders from us old fogies. I'll try to find an opportunity to give him a nudge in the right direction, when the time's right, okay? And if you can try not to get grumpy with him when he's a bit slow off the mark; you know what I mean?'

Tracy smiled up into his eyes, nodded: 'All right, Davey. I'll go easy on him, but… Why can't bringing up kids be simple and straightforward? Perhaps we've been lucky, having it easy so far - they're both lovely children, really, compared to some other ones I know, so I shouldn't complain, should I?'

He shook his head, smiling back at her: 'Come on, let's go to bed, I want to get into the office early tomorrow, there's a mountain of paperwork waiting for me!'

* * *

But by the time he left the house the next day, he already suspected the paperwork was going to have to wait for another time. The early news on the radio had announced the drama of a shooting outside Sweeney's Nightclub in the town's Midland Road, so the message to report to his superior's office came as no surprise.

'Come!' Detective-Superintendent Harry Wilson was waiting for his knock. The head of local CID was popularly known (without his own knowledge, of course!) as The PM, sharing his shortish, rotund figure as well as his name with the one-time Labour Prime Minister.

'You'll have heard about our murder, David?'

'Yes, sir. You want me to handle it?'

'I do. Uniform have started things going, of course, they've been at the scene since the early hours, and your man's in charge of the CID contingent on the ground - Mr Armstrong's taken charge so far, but he'll be only too keen to hand it over to you. You'd best go and see him right away, get him to brief you on what they've got.'

'Doug Rimmer's already there, you say?'

'He is, David, with a few odd DC's, taking statements.'

'Right - who's the victim, sir, the radio news didn't give out the name?'

'A Roderick McKeenan, twenty-nine, Northern Irish born, lived here some years, I believe. Painter and decorator by trade.'

'What about suspects, anyone offering?'

'Clive will tell you - there's a girl-friend, it seems they've had a falling-out, but I don't know the details, whether there's any evidence.'

'All right, sir, I'll go and talk to him immediately, and bring you up to date later, if that's okay?'

'Indeed - go to it, David.'

* * *

Chief Inspector Clive Armstrong wasn't in his office. Russell caught up with him at the nightclub, where he'd been since just after two o'clock that morning.

At six foot two, the Chief Inspector was as tall as Russell, but much broader built, with a square, fleshy face. As forceful in manner as he was in appearance, he was universally known to his peers and subordinates alike as Strongarm, a fact which secretly pleased him. He emerged from the nightclub's front door just as the Inspector got out of his Jeep Station Wagon:

'Welcome home, chap!' Above the doorway, in huge, ornate letters, was spelt out the word 'POLICE', giving the clue to allcomers that the building had once been the headquarters of the local division of the Northamptonshire force.

'You copped this one, Russell?'

'Yes, sir. Mr Wilson's asked me to deal with it.'

'Right. Thought he would - If it looks tricky, get the medics on it!' The team of Russell and Rimmer were popularly known by that epithet, sharing as they did the initials D.R. The Chief Inspector went on: 'You'd better come through, take a look at the scene of the foul deed, so to speak. Dougie's about somewhere, already.' He led the way inside. As the twosome made their way through the ground floor of the building, Russell asked:

'What's it all about, sir, a mugging that turned nasty?' Armstrong glanced over his shoulder:

'Doubt it! The victim had over four hundred quid on him - no sign that anything else had been taken from him, either. Wallet, keys, mobile phone still in his pockets.'

'Oh! Any other ideas, sir?'

'Early days, David! There's hints that he and the girlfriend had fallen out, so you might want to keep an eye on her - but otherwise, no.'

'I see. You've got SOCO at work, sir?' Armstrong replied without turning around:

'Oh yes! The Mad Professor's in his element. Even forgave me for getting him out of bed at 3 a.m. when he saw what I'd got for him!'

They stepped out into the alleyway of Butcher's Lane to find the Forensic Sergeant kneeling down peering at the ground where McKeenan had lain. He leapt to his feet; clad in an all-encompassing white protective suit, his heavy spectacles and the wild grey tonsure around his shinily bald pate made him appear the very essence of the crazed scientist.

'Ah - Dave! Thought I'd be seeing you!' D.S. Terry Owen's lack of concern with rank was as well known as his appearance.

'What have you got for us, Terry?'

'Ah - well. Not a lot, yet, I'm afraid. Three spent cartridge cases - lightweight nine-millimetre of some sort. Tell you more later, once we've got 'em in the lab.'

'The victim was shot three times?'

'Well - yes, I suppose so. The autopsy'll tell you that, Dave.'

'Yes, Terry, thank you.' Owen grinned at the irony in Russell's voice, as Armstrong put in:

'Witnesses reckon they heard three shots, David.'

'Right. Is anyone searching inside, Sir?'

'I've got a team in there now, Dave.' Owen replied before the Chief Inspector could speak.

'Okay, thanks, Terry.' Armstrong interrupted their dialogue:

'I'd like to get away soon, before Mrs Armstrong gets too dischuffed - do you want to come back to the station, David, and I'll brief you on what we've got so far? Doug can take charge here.'

'All right, sir. Where is my Sergeant at the moment?'

'Inside - he's about done with the preliminary statements, I think; let's go and find him!' He led the way back into the building; they were met by the Detective-Sergeant, Russell's regular assistant, in the main lounge area of the club:

'Hello, sir - I heard you'd arrived.'

'How's it going, Doug?'

'All right, I think! It looks like there's a pattern emerging, from what the other staff have been telling us - the man seems to have had a row with his girlfriend, who's a hostess here, then later she follows him out of the bar, they argue again in the corridor near the loos, and the next thing he's been shot, in the alley out there.'

'You're saying she killed him?' Rimmer shrugged his shoulders:

'Too early to be categorical - but it looks that way to me.'

'Okay - but let's wait 'til we've got all the evidence in, Doug. How many people were here last night?'

''Bout two hundred, David.' Armstrong contributed.

'Damn! It's going to take us a while to get through that lot!'

'I've got the list of names and addresses of the customers for you. Doug's spoken to most of the staff, haven't you?'

'I have, sir - but I reckon we'll probably need to interview them again in detail when we've got more time.'

'Daresay you will! And the taxi-driver. I'm off now - the Inspector's coming to my office for a quick briefing, so we'll leave you in charge, okay, Doug?'

'Right, sir. I'll see you back here, boss?'

'Soon as I can, Doug.'

'It's all yours, then - Good luck, Dougie!'

Rimmer gave the retreating uniform a hard stare - he hated being called 'Dougie'.

CHAPTER FOUR

As the two senior officers stepped out into the cold, grey morning, a blindingly white BMW slammed to a halt behind Russell's Jeep. The solid, bull-necked figure of Charles Gidding, clad in a pale grey business suit, levered itself out of the driver's seat, slammed the door and strode over to confront them.

'What's going on, Armstrong?' If the Chief Inspector was annoyed by the abrupt form of address, he didn't let it show:

'Good Morning, Mr Gidding! You'll have heard, no doubt, that a young man was shot dead outside the back door of your establishment in the early hours of this morning?'

'Of course! My Manager tells me you've closed my club?'

'Temporarily, yes.'

'But the operative word, surely, was 'outside'? You expect my staff and I to forgo our right to earn a living because of something that happened *outside?*'

'Mr Gidding - the dead man was a customer of yours; his girlfriend is one of your staff; and from the evidence we have to hand at this time, it would seem likely that the killer, too, emerged from within your club. You will understand, therefore, that we need to be sure that we have obtained any evidence that might be relevant to our enquiries that might exist within your premises. We would hope to be done by tomorrow, so you should be able to open as normal then.'

'I should damn-well hope so! Tomorrow's Friday, our second

biggest night of the week! You're in charge, are you?'

'Oh, no, my boys only dealt with the incident overnight. The investigation will be a CID matter - Inspector Russell here will be in charge of that.'

Gidding's pale blue eyes, deep set under heavy brows, turned to blaze at the Detective:

'Russell?'

'Good morning, Mr Gidding.'

'Russell! If you expect any help from me, you can forget it! It's thanks to you that my son's behind bars!' Before either could respond, another voice spoke from behind them:

'Mr Gidding! Your son is in a young offender's institution as a result of his own downright bloody stupidity, as you well know! You should be grateful he didn't get what he *really* deserved, after what happened to little Hannah!'

Russell turned to look over his shoulder; Doug Rimmer had emerged from the front door of the club during their exchange with its proprietor. Now, his brown eyes were blazing with an unaccustomed anger; the Inspector was surprised, and even a little touched, by the vehemence of his Sergeant's defence of him. Before the row could develop any further, Armstrong intervened smoothly:

'I'm quite sure, Mr Gidding, that whatever your personal feelings, you will offer the Inspector the co-operation that he requires to conduct his enquiries, as an up-standing citizen? After all, it would look bad if there were to be a note on our files that you obstructed a murder investigation, the next time you come to apply for renewal of your licences, wouldn't it?'

The piggy little eyes glared round at them; but then Gidding backed down, with no good grace:

'Of course, Mr Armstrong, I would not wish to hinder justice in any way. I and my staff will assist *Mr* Russell as far as is necessary. All I am saying is' the eyes turned on Russell again 'you can expect no favours from me, that's all.'

Russell gave him the most charming smile he could summon: 'As a serving police officer, I couldn't accept any *favours* from you in any case, Mr Gidding!'

The man glared at him a moment longer, then he pushed past them and disappeared within. Russell turned to Rimmer:

'Did you want me, Doug?'

'Yes, sir - you'd best come and take a look at what we've just found.'

'I'll head on back to the station, David' Armstrong spoke up: 'I'll have the reports and so on in some kind of order for you, if you want to stop by shortly?'

'All right, sir. I'll take a look at what Doug's got, and then catch up with you, if that's okay?'

'Fine, David - soon as you can though, eh? Or I'll be on bread and water at home for the next week!' He grinned and turned away as the two detectives re-entered the club.

Rimmer led his superior into the corridor that ran from front to back of the building, to the right of the main bar area, and into the ladies toilet. Inside, a uniformed constable was standing next to a waste bin which had its flip-top lying on the ground by its side; Rimmer pointed within. Russell smiled at the young officer:

'Morning, Andrew!' P.C. Andrew Dorman smiled and responded with a polite 'Morning, sir!', as he bent to take a look in the bin. Lying on top of the usual collection of discarded tissues and make-up containers was a pair of gloves and a small hand-gun; the gun had been wrapped in a couple of tissues itself, but then disturbed in the course of the search:

'You found these, Andrew?'

'Yes, sir. I had picked the gun up, but I replaced it as soon as I realised what it was.'

'Did you touch it at all?'

'Only the tissues it was wrapped in, sir.'

'Very good. Would you go out the back and give D.S. Owen a call, please?'

The young officer hurried away. Russell looked at his assistant: 'Murder weapon, Doug?'

'Has to be, doesn't it? Too much of a coincidence, otherwise.'

'Indeed. Terry'll soon tell us for sure, I expect. And the gloves?'

'Worn by the killer?'

'That'd be a reasonable guess. Again, I expect…'

'What've you got for me, Dave?' The Mad Professor bustled up behind them, bent over the bin:

'Oh, goody! Just what I expected!' He reached in with gloved hands and carefully lifted the gun between thumb and forefinger:

'A nice little 9mm Walther. Woman's gun - big bang, lots of oomph, but it's nice and small, fits easily in the hand-bag, you see.' He slipped it into a plastic evidence bag retrieved from his pocket, put it aside on the worktop by the nearest handbasin, bent down to pick up the gloves:

'Mmm, nice! Pricey - calf-skin?' With one hand, he pushed his spectacles up onto his forehead, then held the gloves close before his eyes:

'Looks like powder residues - and…' he turned them over, examining the surface of the soft leather: 'Yes! I think so - tiny spots of blood!' He raised delighted eyes to Russell's, a huge grin on his face.

'So you'd say that could be the murder weapon, Terry?'

'Oh, yes, quite probably, Dave. And I'd guess that whoever killed your boyo was wearing these gloves, too.' The hint of his long-lost Welsh accent was a good indication of Owen's excitement. Russell grinned at him:

'How soon can you confirm that, Terry?'

'Oh, tomorrow, with any luck. I don't know if there'll be enough blood there to get a DNA match with the victim, but we'll do what we can. I'll let you know, okay?'

'Yes, please - soon as possible?'

'Of course! Soon as I can.' Owen pushed the gloves into another bag, sealed the openings and put them aside. He turned to peer once more into the bin, delved down and lifted out a small hand-bag, the kind of pretty, beaded item which had been all the rage in the flapper days of the 1920's:

'Hmm! Curioser and curioser!' Opening it carefully, he looked inside then closed it again, slipping it into a third envelope. Sealing this one, he hurried off again into the alley, where his scenes of crime van was parked. Russell raised amused and hopeful eyes to his Sergeant's:

'Looks like we're well on the way, Doug!'

'It does, boss. Fits in with the possibility that the girlfriend shot him, too. Shall I try the staff, see if I can get any suggestion who those things might belong to, if they might be hers?'

'Right! How many of them are still here?'

'Not many, I think. Uniform let most of them go earlier; I think the manager's still upstairs, though. Probably getting an ear-bashing from Gidding, right now!' Russell laughed:

'Quite probably! See what you can find out - I'd better go and talk to Mr Armstrong. Then, I suppose we'd better make the rounds of the staff who were on last night, and that taxi-driver. And the Cavendish girl. I'll get a team of DC's to go round the lists of last night's customers and interview them, over the next couple of days. I'll catch up with you in a while, Doug - I'll come back here, unless you're back at the station by then.'

'Right, boss. See you later.'

CHAPTER FIVE

Half an hour later, Russell knocked at the door to the Chief Inspector's office in the modern concrete-and-glass divisional police station. The new premises had, some five years before, replaced the old Victorian police station which now housed Sweeney's nightclub.

'Come in!' Russell pushed the door open.

'Come on in, David, grab a pew.'

'Thank you, sir. Sorry to have kept you waiting.' The Detective-Inspector did as he was bid.

'Not to worry - what was it that Doug had to show you?'

'The murder weapon, we think.'

'Really?' Armstrong's eyes betrayed a sudden excitement.

'Yes - one of those little Walther 9mm jobs. Terry Owen says it fits the cartridges they found - he's trying to get a positive match for me, for tomorrow.'

'Right! Where did the gun come to light, David?' Russell grinned:

'In a waste-bin, in the ladies loo!'

'Oh-ho! Lady's sort of gun, too, isn't it?'

'That's just what the Mad Professor said. And that's not all we found, sir.'

'Oh?'

'In the bin, with the gun, was a pair of lady's gloves - expensive ones, really soft leather, pale cream colour. Terry gave them a close look:' He mimed pushing up a pair of spectacles, holding something within an inch of his nose. Armstrong chuckled:

'Yeah! He's so short-sighted he barely needs a microscope, does he?' Russell joined in his amusement:

'Hardly! But he reckons there's gunshot residue on them, and some traces of blood. He's pretty certain that whoever killed McKeenan was wearing them when they shot him.'

'Hmm - I wonder if the girl-friend did do it? Several of the other staff have said he was trying to ditch her - revenge? Or just plain anger?'

'Has to be a possibility, sir - what we know of events could fit that way.'

'I'd think so. My money would have been on a connection with one of the more nefarious services offered in the club, but maybe I'm wrong.'

'What kind of thing did you have in mind, sir?'

'You name it, David!'

'I thought Gidding was at pains to keep the place clean?'

'Drug-wise, yes. But that man's cute enough to know that drugs would be the one thing we'd hit the place hard for, if we got so much as a sniff of them. He makes a big show of being anti-drug - not only keeps us off his back, but it's terrific PR for him and the club with the great unwashed out there.'

'I see, sir. So what else is he up to?'

'Well - we know he's not too choosy about the age of some of his customers, for a start. It's known that Sweeney's is the place to go if you want to be served alcohol at the age of fifteen or so. Oh, we've raided him a few times, given him a slapped wrist, but all that happens is he sacks a bartender or two, says he's sorry and he'll try not to let it happen again, pays his fine, and goes right back to his old ways. Do you know the layout in there, David?' Russell shook his head:

'Not really, sir - it's usually your boys who get the call to go there! And I've not had the time to take a good look around, as yet.'

'Yeah, sure! Well, as you saw today, the ground floor has that big central bar area, behind the cloakrooms and the doorman's station. To the right, the corridor we used to get to the back alley, right? Access from the doorman's spot, the door from the bar lounge, and another behind the bar itself - ladies and gents toilets together, opposite the door into the lounge, with changing rooms for the staff to front and back of the building, girls at the front, men at the back. Kitchens are off the bar to the left, where the old canteen used to be in our day - food's only served in the ground floor area. Both bars, ground floor and first floor, run across the back of the building, with the beer-cellar in the old cells, down below. Rest of the first floor is the main nightclub, if you like - dance-floor, stage, all that. Toilets to the right again, above the ones on the ground floor. Top floor's not supposed to be open to the public - Gidding has an office up there, and there's another, shared by the two managers. Rest of that level is three "courtesy suites".'

'"Courtesy suites", sir?'

'That's what they call 'em. Supposed to be for the use of staff, or customers who've had a few too many, and want to sleep it off. But we know full well that's not what they're really for.'

'You're talking about prostitution, sir?'

'Can't prove it, of course, Gidding's too cute for that. But he has a number of very attractive young ladies working as 'hostesses', and we're quite certain that their activities aren't confined to serving on the tables downstairs!'

'You've never found anything, when you've raided him?'

'No. he's got some kind of alarm arrangement up there. The moment a blue uniform appears anywhere in the neighbourhood, everyone runs for cover. And anyhow, we're not that bothered, frankly. There's never been any trouble, and we've got better things to do than stage an elaborate effort which would probably only result in the poor girls doing time and Gidding get off scott-free.

He's only got to say that he knew nothing about the use they were putting his "courtesy suites" to, and how do we prove he did?'

'Yes, I see.'

A friendly silence fell for a few moments. Russell liked and respected the big, bluff uniform officer; and Armstrong, for his part, admired the astute and self-confident detective. It was the latter who broke the silence:

'What about the staff who were on last night, sir?'

'I've got a run-down here, David.' Armstrong tapped the folder in front of him, flipped it open:

'Gidding wasn't there, of course. He usually leaves them to it, once the place is open and running smoothly. Both managers were in, Isaac Uris and Frank Duffy; Uris is the general manager, runs the club itself, Duffy is in charge of the bars. Uris, as you might have guessed, is Jewish - seems a decent enough character, even if the upstairs knocking-shop is part of his remit. Duffy can be rather prickly - he's an ex-jockey, takes himself very seriously, runs the bars like a military operation.'

'How many other staff were on, sir?'

'Let's see… Two on the downstairs bar, three upstairs… Two bouncers - doormen, Gidding prefers to call them. A girl on the cloakroom - and four hostesses.'

'That's it?'

'Yep. My boys have interviewed most of them - all of them, except for the Cavendish girl, Roddie's girlfriend. She went with the ambulance to Casualty; WPC Hallam went with them, too. You know Faith Hallam, do you?' Russell grinned:

'Fearsome Faith? Of course - how could you miss her?'

'Yes, well! She and Ken Dixon were the first on the scene last night - they can probably give you the best idea of the situation as they found it. Do you want to talk to them?'

'As soon as possible, if I may, sir?'

'Right - I'll have them come and see you as soon as they report in for duty today. Faith's a clever girl, she'll be able to give you a good idea of the girlfriend's state of mind, how she was feeling. If there's a possibility that the girl shot him, she might have picked it up from her attitude or her reactions.'

'I'll ask her. Who were the others, sir? Anyone known?' Armstrong grinned:

'One of the bouncers, a guy called Bruce Cartwright, has form for GBH. Otherwise, no. The other bouncer, Joe Haston, is a younger chap, built like the proverbial brick shit-house - probably never needs to lift more than a finger. Andrea Martin, the girl on the cloakroom, is a rather inconsequential little slip of a thing. The hostesses were Lucy Cavendish, the girlfriend; Elsa Jurgens; Diana Munson; Petra Sandwell. Barmen: Upstairs - Fred Collins, Peter Adams, Darren Chapman; downstairs - Karl Jurgens, Aaron Stevens.'

'Jurgens? Related?'

'Brother and sister, I gather.'

'I see. How about the kitchen staff, sir?'

'Oh, they don't serve meals after midnight. The chef, waitresses an' all had long gone home by the time Roddie was shot.'

'Right.'

'It's all here, David, everything we've got so far. Doug will have the preliminary statements, of course. You'll be talking to all these people again, will you?'

'I expect so, sir, once we've got a feel for what went on - and some results from Terry! And, hopefully, the Post Mortem report - is Iain Somerfield doing the autopsy, do you know?'

'I don't - but I'd expect him to do it, given the nature of the case.'

'I'll give him a call, find out. Er - has there been any other trouble at the club, which might have a bearing on the case?' Armstrong shook his head:

'Not that I can think of, David. It's pretty quiet, doesn't really cause us much grief, compared to some of the nightclubs elsewhere around - I'm glad one or two of the Northampton ones aren't on our patch! Just the occasional fracas, outside after chucking-out time mostly. Oh, there was that girl who died of an overdose, last year, wasn't it? She had been a hostess at Sweeney's, for a while, I think. Hardly likely there's a connection, though, is it?'

Russell nodded: 'I'll take a look at the file, but I expect you're right.' He tapped the file in front of him: 'Thanks for all this, sir - I'll leave you to get home.'

'Right - thanks, David. If you get a call to another murder, in Oakfield, you'll know Margie was a bit upset when I got there!'

Russell laughed dutifully, and ducked out of the office.

CHAPTER SIX

Russell took the dossier up to his own office on the third floor, leafing quickly through it as he mounted the stairs. He set it down on his desk, overcoming the urge to sit and read through everything in detail, and went down again to return to the scene of the shooting.

He left the Jeep in the street once more, and climbed the steps up to the front door, his memory flicking through some of the times he'd entered the building in years gone by, when he'd been the D.S., assistant to old Keith Foreman, his predecessor as senior Inspector in the local division. Inside the ground floor bar, Rimmer spotted his superior and hurried over:

'You get everything from Strongarm, boss?'

'Yes, all he had's in a folder on my desk waiting for us! Anything else new here?' He'd spotted that excited twinkle in the Sergeant's eyes; Rimmer laughed:

'You bet! The Mad Professor's found two of the bullets. But the bad news is they're pretty smashed up - must have gone right through Roddie and hit the brickwork behind him. He says he'll try to match them to the gun, but not to be too hopeful.'

'No sign of the third? Assuming there was a third, I suppose?'

'No sign. It seems pretty definite there were three shots fired, so with any luck the other bullet's still in his body. Might be in better shape for Terry to match it.'

'Yes - let's hope so. How's everything else going here?'

'Oh, pretty good. There's only Uris, the general manager, here now, Gidding's gone home and left him to it. Seems a bit rough; the poor sod's been up all night, and now the bastard expects him to keep an eye on us all day as well!'

'Par for the course, in Gidding's case, I'd say. Not a comforter of his fellow man, is he?'

'Hardly! Terry's gone, too, back to the lab with his latest playthings; he's left a few of his SOCO team here, they're still going over the ground for anything else that might turn up.'

'How about the victim's effects - what's happened to them?'

'The hospital have already handed over the clothes he was wearing, they're at the lab. I've asked Steve Campbell to go over the flat - he should be there by now, with a couple of PC's.'

'Okay, Doug. What about outside witnesses - was there anyone in the alley, in the surrounding buildings, who might have heard or seen anything?'

'It seems like the only person in Butcher's Lane was the taxi-driver, Broadbent. From what I hear, he reckons he'd been there about ten minutes before the shooting, and didn't see anyone else about. This side of the lane, the buildings that end' he gestured towards the High Street, left of the nightclub 'have no accommodation, and were deserted for the night.' Russell nodded; as he recalled, they were Barclays Bank, the Social Security offices, and the main Post Office on the corner.

'That way' Rimmer went on, waving an arm in the other direction 'there's only that little block of four shops before you get to Sainsbury's, where the lane finishes; I've got a pair of DC's knocking on the doors there at the moment. Over the back, the buildings on Drummond Street are a little way away, with back yards in between, but I've got another team going along there as well.'

'Okay, sounds good, Doug. Butcher's Lane used to go right along behind here, didn't it? Came out in Alperton Street, if I remember right?'

'That's right, sir. There was a hell of a fuss when Sainsbury's wanted to extend the store, if you remember - they'd bought those old properties the other side of the lane, and wanted to build right across. Went to an enquiry, but they got their way in the end.'

'Oh yes, that's right! Okay - have you got much more to do here yourself?'

'Not that the lads can't handle, sir.'

'Right - let's get back to the station ourselves, go through Strongarm's dossier, put it together with your statements. We'll need to get people on following up all the names on his list of last night's customers, get a statement from each and every one of them; and I want to talk to all of the staff who were in the place ourselves. Although I might leave that until tomorrow, see how much more we know after Terry's had time to play, and maybe got the PM report.' The two walked out of the building, continuing their conversation:

'Yes - might make sense to go over their stories when we've got our own ideas as to what really happened, see if they fit.'

'That's right. Oh, Doug - did you get any idea who the gun and the gloves might belong to?'

'Like I said, there's only the one manager here now. He says that Lucy Cavendish is in the habit of wearing gloves like those, over the wrist, soft leather - and always in that light buff colour.'

'Really? How about the gun?'

'He clammed up when I asked about that! I reckon he knows, or at least could make a good guess whose it is, but he doesn't want to say. I checked the number - doesn't show.'

'Illegally held, then?'

'Yeah, must be. Little thing like that, ideal for a woman as Terry said - if those are the girlfriend's gloves, it looks as though this might really be just the result of a lover's tiff.'

'Ye-es... Let's be certain before we jump to conclusions, though.'

'I reckon it's a pretty good bet - He tries to ditch her, she shoots him in a jealous rage - what do you reckon?'

'Could be, Doug. Let's see what our witness statements have to tell us, see if she might have had the opportunity to go with her motive.'

They climbed into the Jeep, Rimmer behind the wheel, and drove off.

* * *

Early that afternoon, following a quick lunch in the station's canteen, they were still going through the file covering the night's events. Occasionally, one or other would throw out a comment as he found something interesting; eventually, Russell pushed the now-empty folder aside, leant back in his chair and swung his feet up onto the corner of the desk - for once, Rimmer was seated in the other chair, facing him.

'Well, Doug, what do we know?' The Sergeant sat back, ran his hands over his hair and relaxed with his fingers interlinked behind his neck:

'Okay. Timewise: McKeenan arrived at the club a little after eleven. He took a table in the downstairs bar, ordered chicken and chips, had a couple of lagers while he ate. Lucy went over to sit with him at one point, but didn't stop long. He spent a little time standing at the bar, chatting intermittently with Jurgens, the barman. Then, about twenty past one, he left the bar, made his way out to the alley - and bang!'

'Right. The other barman, Stevens?'

'Yeah.'

'Stevens, says that the conversation between him and Lucy looked to be intense - not quite a row, but close to it. And after that, she seemed to ignore him. But then she follows him out into the corridor when he leaves.'

'Yeah - trying to talk to him away from everyone else?'

'Best guess, probably. But now Stevens is in the gents, with a customer he didn't recognise, and hears them talking in the corridor

- he's certain it's Lucy, knows her voice even if he can't make out the words. And he thinks it's Roddie she's talking with.'

'And again, he says she sounded heated. The talk stops - he hears a door slam, presumably McKeenan going out into the lane. He leaves the loo, with the customer, returns behind the bar, and moments later hears the shots from outside.'

'Okay. So - why was Roddie going out into Butcher's Lane? That's not a regular exit from Sweeney's, is it?'

'Nope. Fire Exit, and it's usually not secured while the place is open, so people could go out that way.'

'And get back in?'

'If they clipped the latch back, yes.'

'Hmm. Was he intending to return?'

'Can't be sure. The latch was clipped open, but almost anyone might have done that in the confusion that followed.'

'If anyone did, it would have to be staff, wouldn't it? Better ask if anyone remembers doing that, when we talk to them.'

'Right.' Rimmer leant forward to scribble a note on a pad.

'And there's no hint of a motive, other than the tiff with Lucy?'

'Not in this lot.' Rimmer tapped the pile of papers on the desk: 'But - you can't help wondering, can you? I mean, there has to be a possibility of something illicit there, with it being at Sweeney's - drugs, gambling, whatever?' Russell laughed:

'It's usually me telling you to keep your options open, Doug!'

'Yeah, well, I know, but... You told me not to jump to conclusions!' The Sergeant gave an embarrassed grin, shrugged his shoulders. He went on: 'Based on this lot, do you think we can assume that the killer came from the club, too?'

'Too early to be certain - but it seems likely, doesn't it? If the taxi-driver says he saw no-one else about, no-one enter the lane, then the murderer had to be there already, or have come from one of the buildings that back onto it.'

'Might have been there already, as you say, waiting for Roddie to come out.'

'But that would mean someone *knowing* that he was going to come out there.'

'Yeah - still possible though, if he was going to meet someone, or... whatever!'

Silence fell for a few seconds, until Rimmer asked:

'What about Lucy?' Russell sat in thought before replying:

'She could have followed him out, couldn't she? She wasn't in the corridor when Stevens and the customer came out of the toilet, and Jurgens doesn't mention her coming back into the bar. So where was she? Did she have the gun - is it hers, or could she have known where to find it? Was she mad enough with Roddie to want to kill him?'

'Maybe she didn't mean to kill, just to frighten him. Perhaps the gun went off while they were fighting over it?'

'Hardly likely. The sound would be muffled, then, surely? And *three* shots? No, that had to be deliberate.'

'Yeah, I suppose you're right, boss.'

A few moments more of silence, and then Russell said:

'There's only one way to find out where she was - let's go and ask her. We know where to find her?'

'Yeah - according to WPC Hallam, she'll be staying with this Mrs Hepple, over on Glebe Farm.'

'What's the relationship, do we know?' Rimmer shook his head:

'Dunno. Faith doesn't mention it.'

'Oh well - let's go and ask, shall we?'

CHAPTER SEVEN

Mid-afternoon - already the dank greyness of the day was fading into the sombre chill of the evening, the leaden skies leaning their weight ever harder upon the depressed landscape beneath.

Number 29, The Meadow, in the Grancester suburb of Glebe Farm, turned out to be a neat semi-detached house with a small but well-tended garden in front of the big picture-window which promised a light and airy interior - at least, when the weather permitted. The front door, set in a trim porch whose structure was shared between the two properties, was quickly opened at Russell's knock by a tall, spare woman of around fifty in a rather old-fashioned floral print dress. Fine lines radiated from the corners of faded blue eyes deep-set in her narrow, ascetic face; wavy hair which had once been golden-blond had faded also to a sandy grey. She regarded the two men on her doorstep steadily:

'Yes?'

'Mrs Hepple?' There was an almost aristocratic air to her nod of acknowledgement. Russell went on: 'I'm Inspector Russell, of Grancester CID; this is Sergeant Rimmer. I believe Lucy Cavendish is staying with you?'

'She is.' Russell glanced at his assistant - the woman was obviously not giving anything away voluntarily.

'We would like to speak to her, if she's feeling up to it?'

'Yes, I daresay you would, Inspector. She's doing remarkably well, all things considered - but she is terribly upset, none-the-less.'

'So may we see her?' The was a fractional hesitation before the woman nodded again:

'You'd better come in, then.' She stepped back to allow them across the threshold. As he stepped inside, Russell asked:

'Is her daughter here, too?'

'Yes - they're through here, in the lounge, if you'll follow me. The child is very shaken by what has happened, as well, you understand?' There was a warning tone to her voice.

'We understand, Mrs Hepple. I promise you, we'll try not to make things any worse for either of them - but we really do need to talk to Lucy right away, to try to find out just what did happen last night.'

She ushered them into the lounge, a big, bright room furnished comfortably but inexpensively. Lucy Cavendish and her daughter sat side by side on the three-seater settee. Russell felt momentarily taken aback as she looked up at the intruders - the reports had described her as good-looking, but the young woman who raised eyes the colour of dark emeralds to meet his was a real beauty. Catching his breath, he again introduced himself and the Sergeant; she rose to her feet and shook hands with them in turn - the figure within her plain white sweatshirt and well-faded denim jeans was as stunning as her face and the cascade of deep auburn hair which framed it.

She resumed her seat; the older woman joined her, sitting on the opposite side of the little girl who had remained in the centre of the settee, gazing with the frankness of childhood at the two policemen. Lucy slipped an arm about the child's shoulders as she introduced her:

'This is my daughter, Freya - is it all right if she stays here with me while we talk?' Russell smiled at the little girl, who responded with a rather fragile smile of her own, taking in her pretty face, eyes the same arresting deep green as her mother's, and hair which fell in heavy waves of russet gold, lighter in tone than Lucy's.

'That will be all right with me - but we need to talk about last night?' His tone left the decision to her.

'It's okay, Inspector, I've already told her what happened.'

'All right. Lucy - may I call you Lucy?'

'Of course, please.' Her smile was wan, but delightful none-the-less.

'You don't normally live here, do you, Lucy?' She shook her head, making her hair shimmer in the electric light.

'No, Inspector. I've a house of my own, in Buckingham Street, just off Midland Road. It's not very big, one of the old railway-worker's houses, but it does us, doesn't it?' She looked down at the child, who smiled up at her, nodding solemnly. She went on: 'Freya was staying here last night, with Granny Moo - she usually does, the nights when I'm working. Your policewoman dropped me here when we left the hospital, and we haven't gone home yet.'

'And you're to stay as long as you want to, you know that' interjected Mrs Hepple from the other end of the settee. Lucy turned to her, smiled and nodded.

'What about Mr McKeenan - he lived with you, I understand?'

'Not all the time. He'd always kept his own flat, in one of those big old houses on Midland Road, nearer the station. When I wasn't working, he would usually come and stay with us; on the nights when I was at the club, and Freya was here, he would use the flat.'

'That was the normal routine, was it?'

'Pretty much so. Sometimes, Granny Moo - Mrs Hepple - would stay at my house with Freya instead. But yes, Roddie would always go back to his flat if I wasn't home.'

'You two had been together a long time?' She nodded, her distress suddenly apparent in her face:

'More than three years. We were... so *good* together!'

'But - I believe he wanted to leave?' She nodded again, momentarily unable to find words; the deep emerald of her eyes took on a greater brightness as she held back tears. At last, she spoke:

'He said… it was over, he didn't love me - but - but - nothing had *changed!* We hadn't rowed, we *never* rowed, everything was just the same as before! But suddenly, he says he wants to go…'

The little girl was looking up at her mother, concern etched on her face. She reached across, took Lucy's hand in both of her own; at her touch, the tears began to spill down Lucy's cheeks. Her eyes still fixed on the Inspector's, she cleared her throat and went on:

'He's… he *was* the man I would have spent my life with, Inspector. I'm sure, too, that he did love me, whatever he said. We could have been…' she broke off, unable to go on. Freya looked up at Russell, still holding her mother's hand in her own; her voice was quiet as she spoke for the first time:

'Roddie was my Daddy. I've never met my *real* Daddy, but he was just as good as a real one…' She turned away as her own tears began to flow, buried her face in her mother's breast; Lucy held her tightly, raised apologetic eyes to Russell's and then returned her attention to her child.

The Inspector turned to the older woman, who was regarding him fixedly, mouthed silently the request 'Can we talk?' She nodded, beckoned him as she rose to her feet, moving carefully so as not to disturb mother and daughter. He followed suit, gesturing to his Sergeant to stay put and watch over them. She led him into the kitchen, turned to him with a look of concerned annoyance on her face; He raised his hands in a placatory gesture:

'I'm sorry! The last thing I want is to cause Lucy and the little girl any more distress.' Mrs Hepple held his eyes for a moment, then nodded, her expression relaxing. She sighed:

'I know. I wouldn't want your job, at a time like this.'

'Can I ask - Lucy called you 'Granny Moo' - is that just a kind of honorary title?' The woman smiled, her austere face taking on a sudden brightness:

'Oh no, Inspector! Freya *is* my grand-daughter, my son's child.'

'But - she said she'd never met her father?'

'Nor has she!' She seemed reluctant to elaborate, but at last gave way to the question which hung unasked in the air: 'My son, Inspector, is a no-account, good-for-nothing waster. He got that poor girl pregnant when she was still at school, and as soon as he found out, he turned his back on her, didn't want to know her or his own child! He'd been using drugs, as well - his father never found that out, mind, but *I* knew. He'd lost all respect for us, for himself, too, come to that - when he dumped poor Lucy, Arthur threw him out, told him to come home when he'd sorted himself out. But he never did.'

'Where is he now, do you know?'

'Last I heard, he was working as a porter at Northampton General Hospital. There's one of his old school friends, a lad by the name of Trevor Maggs, who sees him sometimes, and lets me know what he's doing. Alan's never managed to hold on to a job for more than a few months at a time - he's been unemployed more often than he's been working. We wanted to send him to college, give him the best start in life we could afford, but... He didn't seem to care, he just threw it all away. And the business over Lucy finished him, in his father's eyes. I used to meet him sometimes - I never told Arthur that, either - but in the end I gave up trying to influence him. He didn't want our help... Since then, Trevor has kept me in touch with what he's up to - he's a nice fellow, drives a van for one of those express delivery firms.'

'So your son - Alan?' She nodded in confirmation 'Alan, is living in Northampton?'

'Yes - Trevor tells me he's got a small flat in Kings Heath.'

'And in all this time, he's never seen Freya? Or Lucy?'

'Never.' Russell shook his head in disbelief, then asked:

'What about your husband, Mrs Hepple?'

'Arthur died six years ago, Inspector. He had a stroke; the doctors thought he'd pull through, but then he had another while he was still in hospital. They wouldn't confirm it, but it's my belief that the strain over Alan brought it on - or at least, hastened it along. So you'll understand that my love for my son is pretty limited, as horrible as it is to admit it.'

Russell nodded his understanding, changed the subject:

'You knew Roddie McKeenan, I assume?'

'Oh yes, of course! He'd come here sometimes, when Lucy and Freya were here, pick them up as often as not, on the days when Lucy was beginning a few nights off. He was a nice lad, had a real Irish twinkle in his eye, and enough charm to melt anyone's heart! This business is terrible, just terrible. Who could have done this, Inspector?'

'That's what I intend to find out, Mrs Hepple. You'd have no idea if anyone had anything against him, I suppose?' She shook her head:

'None at all - I can't imagine anyone not liking the boy, never mind... this!'

'I see. So - what can you tell me about Lucy?' The woman raised her eyebrows:

'What do you want to know about her?'

'You must know her pretty well - what's she like, in your view?'

'Oh - well, you've seen her, Inspector. She's a lovely girl, and not just to look at, either! She's bright, and considerate - and she's devoted to that kiddie of hers. Spends all the time she can with her, which is difficult, with her job.'

'Does she have a temper?' Mrs Hepple's eyes narrowed, a frown creasing her forehead, as she replied cautiously:

'We all do, to one degree or another, Inspector. Just because of her hair, don't think she's any more unpredictable than most people! She has a temper, yes - but she's the kind that will flash at you, and then cool right down again - she'll say what she has to say, but then it's forgotten, she's not the sort to hold a grudge.'

'She wouldn't have got into a rage with Roddie, because he wanted to leave her?'

'No - oh, no, Inspector! If you're thinking she might have… Oh, no, never! If he'd really made her lose her temper, she might have slapped him - good and hard, too - but to turn a gun on him… Never!' Russell raised his hands to ward off her tirade:

'Thank you, Mrs Hepple! Shall we go back in and see how they are?' She nodded, smiling in apology for her outburst; again, the smile softened the severity of her face, giving him a glimpse of the handsome woman that she could be. She gestured for him to precede her back into the lounge, quietly opening the kitchen door for him.

On the settee, they found Lucy and her daughter sitting arm in arm, talking quietly, their sorrow once more under control. Rimmer got to his feet as they returned; Mrs Hepple resumed her seat next to the little girl, the two policemen taking the two armchairs placed at each end of the room.

'Everything all right, Doug?' Russell asked.

'Yes, sir, fine.'

'How about you, Lucy? Freya?'

'We're okay now, thank you. Aren't we?' Lucy looked down at the little girl, who nodded up at her, smiling despite her reddened eyes and wet cheeks.

'Are you up to telling me about last night?' The auburn head nodded; she began to speak, quietly, thoughtfully, describing the events of the previous night at Sweeney's, from when she arrived for work just after nine pm, up to the time she had emerged from the toilet to discover that Roddie had been shot. Neither man interrupted her, letting her tell her tale in her own way; both noted in their minds how her story fitted with the other statements, as she spoke of joining Roddie at his table briefly, then giving up her attempt to talk to him in such a public place - and then, of following him out into the corridor much later and waylaying him in order to talk to him more privately. As she spoke of finding him slumped against the back wall of the building, coming close once more to breaking down, Russell reached across and put his hand over hers where it lay on the arm of the settee, gently stopping her:

'It's all right, Lucy. Can I just make sure I've got things clear - where were you, between talking to Roddie at his table, and then later in the corridor?'

'Oh, I was with this client. I slipped away from him for a moment, to go to Roddie's table, but then he wanted to go upstairs. We were up there for an hour, maybe a bit longer; then he left, and I went down to the bar again. I was pleased that Roddie was still there, and kept an eye open for a chance to talk to him until he went out of the room - I thought he was going to the toilet, until he said about having business outside.'

'Upstairs?' Rimmer asked.

'On the *dancefloor,* Sergeant! The man wanted to dance, and that part of the club is on the first floor.'

'Oh, right.' She gave him a look which said that they both knew this might be a little less than the whole truth, but implored him not to push the point in front of the child. He took the hint, letting it drop until a more appropriate moment, as Russell asked her:

'What sort of business did he have out there, do you know?' She gave him a level gaze, shook her head:

'No, Inspector. He's a bit of a wheeler-dealer, sometimes - it could have been almost anything. If you could find out who he was going out there to meet, they'd be able to tell you - but I suppose that must be who killed him, mustn't it? Perhaps they fell out over whatever it was...' She shrugged her shoulders hopelessly 'but - what on Earth could it have been to make them *shoot* him?'

'Hopefully, we'll find out, Lucy. One more thing - do you have the clothes you were wearing last night?' She nodded:

'They're in our room - do you want to see them?'

'Could we take them away with us, for testing? There might be traces you picked up in the lane which would help us.'

'Of course - if you think they might help.' Her acquiescence sounded puzzled but unconcerned. Mrs Hepple got to her feet:

'I'll get them for you, Inspector.' She left the room, as he asked Lucy:

'You always wear gloves at the club, is that right?'

'Yes - the customers like them. They look *classy,* Sergeant!' she responded to Rimmer's raised eyebrows.

'You have the ones you were wearing yesterday?' She nodded:

'They're with my other things. They're a bit… bloody, I'm afraid - thanks, Muriel.' Mrs Hepple returned, handed her a plastic bag; Lucy delved inside for a moment, withdrew a pair of cream-coloured gloves identical to the ones they had seen earlier in the bin at Sweeney's, except that these were heavily bloodstained. She held them out: 'Here.'

'Thank you, Lucy - if you just leave them in the bag with the rest, for now. Come on, Doug, we'll leave these people in peace for now. We will need to talk to you again, I'm afraid, and take a formal statement, but we can do that another day. Will you be staying here for a while?'

'They will, Inspector!' Mrs Hepple replied for her: 'I'll show you out.'

CHAPTER EIGHT

As the door closed behind them, Rimmer said:

'You didn't ask her about the gun?'

'No, not yet. I want a clearer picture from Terry before we lean on her, Doug. Now we've got her version of events, we can start to put things together, see how the stories gel - with some forensic information, any inconsistencies'll start to show themselves.'

'Doesn't sound like there are many. I mean, her story matches everyone else's, doesn't it?'

'Yeah, seems to. And she's got no alibi for that vital couple of minutes, has she? From their row in the corridor, until after he was shot. From the statements, the Jurgens girl met her coming out of the ladies at that point, and that's the nearest she has to any confirmation of where she was. No-one actually saw her go in there, no-one was in there with her, by her own admission.'

'She could be lying in her teeth, followed him out in a fury and shot him, then dashed back into the loo before anyone came.'

As he opened the car door, Russell nodded slowly:

'It's possible, for sure. We need to talk to everyone else who heard the shots and went to investigate, put as close a time-frame on it as we can. And we need as much background on Roddie as we can get, see if there might another motive, check out all his associates - you know the score.'

Rimmer settled himself in the passenger seat:

'Yeah. I'll get on to all that.'

'Right. I'll drop you at the station, you'd best co-ordinate things from the incident room. I'll take another look at the club, then talk to Faith and Ken when they come on duty tonight. Meanwhile…' he reached for his mobile phone 'I'd better call Tracy, warn her I'll be late for dinner.'

* * *

Three boys emerged from the junior classroom wing of Elwood Priors School and strolled around to the bicycle shelters. Simon Walker, a pace behind his friends, turned and waved a final farewell to Luke - Luke Hanlon had always been his best mate in school, but he was a boarder; outside school, his allegiance switched to his new friends. All three accepted the arrangement without thought - Daniel and Jacko, like Simon, were day pupils, local boys from the villages just outside Grancester, while he lived in the plush suburb of Alderley Park.

As they unlocked their bikes, Jacko turned to Simon:

'Hey, Snow, d'you have to go straight home?' The boy whose white-blond hair gave him his nickname thought for a moment:

'Nah, guess not. Dad'll be down the restaurant - what're you thinking of doing?'

'My folks'll both be at work too - why don't we go down the GPS for a bit?'

'I dunno' put in Daniel 'I'll get it in the ear from my Mum if I'm late.'

'Here…' Jacko delved in his coat pocket, produced his mobile phone 'call her!' Daniel grinned, took the phone from the dark-haired boy, while Simon cautioned:

'Don't let anyone see that, you know we're not supposed to have mobiles in school!'

'It's all right, I don't switch it *on* during school!' Jacko reassured him. Daniel watched the display come to life, dialled his home number - an expression of disgust crossed his face:

'Damn! It's engaged.'

'Tell you what, come down with us, call her again when we get there. If she gives you a hard time, you can go straight home then, can't you?' Jacko suggested. The policeman's son hesitated for a moment before nodding:

'Yeah, why not? Come on, let's go!'

Over the frontage of what had once been a hardware shop in Market Street, the name 'Grancester Play Station' glared down upon the citizens of the town in garish modern colours. Three bicycles skated to a halt in the gathering gloom of the chill afternoon, and three boys dismounted eagerly:

'Got your chain, Snow?'

'Yeah, here.' Jacko threaded the lock chain through the back wheels of all three bikes, fitted the end into the combination lock and spun the dials to a random setting; Daniel gestured to a poster in the window of the amusement hall:

'Hey, look! They've got Captain Cuthroat!' The poster, as lurid as the establishment's own display, proclaimed the arrival of the latest arcade computer game, an unlikely cross between the labours of Hercules and a hunt for pirate treasure.

'Yeah - come *on!*' Jacko led the way inside, the three searching their pockets for the right change for the machines. His mobile telephone lay forgotten, Daniel's good intentions lost in their enthusiasm for the challenge to come.

* * *

Seated in his office once more, David Russell leant back in his chair, feet up on the edge of his desk in his usual relaxed thinking pose. By the time he'd left the club's premises again, the search teams were nearly finished, their trawl through the building and the alley outside revealing nothing new. His Sergeant was downstairs in the incident room, overseeing the detail of the broader investigation; the groups of officers digging into McKeenan's background, going over previous incidents at the club, following any thought or trail that might shed light upon the man's death.

His own thoughts revolved around Lucy Cavendish. Had she murdered her lover? Hers was the only obvious motive, so far - and what of the gloves, apparently hers? Had they been worn by the killer, as Terry Owen had suggested? And if so, whose hands had been inside them? As slender and shapely as the rest of her, Lucy's hands were quite small - so, if not hers, only other hands as slim and delicate could have got them on. Another of the girls? Presumably. But then, what was the motive? Jealousy - was Roddie a womaniser? There was no indication of that, from the statements he'd read. He needed to know more, a lot more, before he could start to make any judgements of what had really happened last night.

A knock sounded at the door.

'Come in!' D.C. Steve Campbell put his head around, stepped inside at Russell's wave: 'What have you got, Steve?' Campbell grinned:

'Pretty much what you'd expect in a bachelor flat, sir. Pictures of the girlfriend, and her daughter, in several places around, so I'd think their relationship was, or at least had been, pretty solid.' His grin broadened: 'And these!' He held out a handful of plastic evidence bags. Russell took them, turned them over in his hands; one held a wad of currency, mostly twenties, one a number of small white tablets, one a quantity of a white powder, another small plugs of what could have been tobacco, but probably wasn't. He looked up at the Constable:

'Well, well! Where did you find these?'

'Hidden in the carcase of a chest of drawers, tucked away behind a drawer.'

'So, our Roddie was dealing drugs.' He held up each bag in turn: 'Cannabis - Ecstasy - Cocaine; or Heroin? And the proceeds! Get these over to the lab, Steve, I need a positive identification of each as quickly as possible. Was McKeenan a known dealer?'

'Not that I've heard, sir. I'll check with my informants, and ask around in the canteen, see if anyone's come across his name at all. Do you think he was selling at Sweeney's?'

'Has to be likely, given that he was in there most nights - but he was chancing Gidding's wrath if he was!'

'Yeah, not half! I'll get these to The Mad Professor for you.' He took the bags back from Russell, turned to go but looked back as the Inspector asked:

'Nothing else in the flat to interest us?' Campbell shook his head:

'I don't think so, sir. We've taken a number of files, papers relating to his business, by the look of them, and I'll have the financial boys go through them. But I'd be surprised if there's anything there, if they're his official records - he'd hardly be declaring illicit earnings to the Inland Revenue, would he?'

'Okay, Steve - and thanks.'

Russell sat back again as the Detective-Constable left. The revelation that Roddie had been involved with drugs opened up a whole new aspect to his murder; he leant forward again, picked up the telephone, dialled the incident room, to be reassured by Rimmer that he already had the information - and McKeenan's files - from Campbell.

So - had drugs been behind Roddie's death? Rivalry over territory - had he been treading on someone else's toes? Or had someone else tried to muscle in on *his* patch? What he needed now was every snippet of information, every rumour, every hint, that might be circulating in the town's underworld. He'd have to brief the entire force, not just his own team but every officer, to keep their ears open, to tap up their various snouts for any word that might have a bearing on his case.

He felt a strange kind of relief as he contemplated this new trend. Lucy Cavendish had left him with an impression of herself which hadn't fitted in his mind with the possibility that she might have shot McKeenan, an impression of an innate, almost ingenuous honesty and truthfulness which would have been at odds with the deviousness of a murderess. He'd found it difficult to imagine her having the cold-bloodedness to shoot Roddie, dump the gun and her gloves in that bin, put on a fresh pair, and then emerge from the ladies ready with an act of surprise and grief.

It was becoming a complex enquiry. He needed, as they'd said earlier, to pin down the sequence of events at the club as closely as possible - he and Doug would have to interview all of Gidding's staff, in detail, clarify the information from their initial statements; and try to get a better impression of the personalities involved, at the same time. He had to find out where the gun had come from, who it belonged to. And, perhaps most important, why had Roddie been heading out into the alley? He'd said to Lucy that he had business to attend to - what business? And with whom? Had someone been waiting out there for him, someone who had been in place before the taxi-driver had arrived, someone who had fallen out with him over his drug dealing?

But then, you came back to the gun, found *inside* the club. And the gloves. He ran his hands through his sandy hair in a gesture of frustration - he could go little further until the forensic lab came back with some answers. Once they knew for certain that they had the murder weapon, and how the gloves fitted into the story, they would be able to push forward from a more solid foundation.

He glanced up at the clock on the wall. Tomorrow would have to do for those interviews; Ken Dixon and Faith Hallam should be in any time, and he wanted to get their thoughts and ideas from the scene as they had found it, and especially the WPC's impression of the Cavendish girl.

CHAPTER NINE

It was nearly seven o'clock before David Russell left his office that night. He made his way down the stairs to the car park and the waiting Jeep, if little further forward with his investigation, at least feeling that the picture was becoming clearer in a slow, step-by-step manner.

The Sergeant and WPC who had been first on the scene had come in a little early for their evening shifts, and knocked on his door to go over their reports with him before setting out into the night once more. The older copper had been able to add little: 'I felt my priority was to contain the scene and the people, sir, rather than try to make any assessments about what had happened.' Russell had nodded his acceptance of the man's judgement, as he had gone on to say that nothing in the situation he had found, and no-one in the crowd he had encountered, had raised his suspicions. Russell knew that, as a career policeman, Dixon's instincts would almost inevitably have been aroused, even if subconsciously, by anything that had been, or appeared to be, out of place.

The imposing female officer, on the other hand, had added to his visualisation of the scene. She had confirmed the details of her report, but then had gone on to give him a more subjective description of what she had observed outside the club, and later at the hospital. She enlarged upon her feeling that the girl had been holding out on her when they talked:

'I was talking to her as much to try to ease her shock, as to learn anything, sir, but I still felt I should try to get an idea of her reactions before she had time to think them through. And I'm certain she was ducking the truth at times.'

'Oh? How, exactly?' Russell prompted.

'When we were talking about the victim, sir. She'd said about him wanting to leave, but when I asked why he would feel that way, I thought she was... avoiding saying something, if you know what I mean? And again, when I asked if she had any idea why anyone might want to hurt him, I felt there was something she didn't want to say.'

'No idea what it might have been?'

'No, sir.'

'Hmm. How would you assess her reaction to his death? Could she have been putting it on?' Faith looked up, surprised by the question:

'I doubt it, sir. She seemed... genuinely distressed, deeply so. And shocked. Are you thinking that she could have had something to do with it, sir?' Russell pursed his lips:

'There are some indications in the evidence so far that suggest she might, yes. That tiff between them is the only possible motive we've identified as yet, for one thing.'

'I see - I'd be surprised if it were true, sir, given her state of mind last night. If it is, she's a better actress than I'd have given her credit for.'

'Okay - thanks, Faith. You too, Ken. I'd better let you two get to work before Mr Armstrong comes looking for you.'

Before leaving, he'd called the scenes of crime section in their basement lair, which also housed the division's limited in-house forensic laboratory. While much of the really high-tech stuff had to be farmed out to HQ, or to contract laboratories, the Mad Professor was often able to perform wonders with the limited resources at his disposal on the spot. He came on the line, sounding as always both slightly bewildered and more than slightly annoyed at being disturbed:

'Oh, it's you, Dave. If you're after the low-down on your body in the alley, I'll have it for you tomorrow, with a bit of luck. The gun's gone off to ballistics, with the two bullets we've got so far, and I think I've got enough traces of blood from those gloves for the DNA laddies to match it to the victim. The other traces are definitely gunshot residues, the kind of powder mix that would fit with the type of gun and bullets - so it looks like we're flying on this one!'

'Okay, Terry - anything else you can tell me at this time?'

'No-o... But: There's something odd about the *pattern* of those residues. I can't see quite what's wrong, but it's as if... hang on - I wonder...?'

'What is it, Terry?' There was a long silence from the other end, then:

'Yes, I'll bet that's it... I'd only just started looking at this, Dave - I'll have to check this out. I'll call you back, right?'

'What's on your mind - come on, Terry, give!'

'No - let me make sure. I'll call you.'

'I'm going home now - call me there. Or in the morning, I guess.'

'Oh... oh, is it that time already? Okay, I'll talk to you tomorrow, Dave. 'Bye.' The phone went down before Russell could say anything more. There were times, he reflected, when the SOCO Sergeant didn't know how close he came to being strangled by one or other of his colleagues.

The drive home took him a matter of minutes only. The new police station had been built by the old Northampton road, which, once out of the town, led through the village of Bevington where he lived, and adjacent to the dual carriageway which bypassed its Southern side. To the relief of many villagers, the new road had had the effect of drawing a firm, enclosing line which seemed to effectively preclude any further expansion of the conurbation in their direction.

At Old Laundry Cottage, he let himself in through the front

door, hung up his coat and went through into the kitchen. Tracy looked around from the dishwasher, where she had been stacking dirty plates inside:

'Hello, Darling - heavy day?' He crossed the room, kissed her on the cheek:

'Could have been worse, Love.'

Their son looked up from the bowl of apple pie he'd been finishing, but instead of greeting his father, he spoke to his mother:

'You don't tell *him* off when he's late for dinner!' She rounded on the boy:

'Oh, *Daniel!* That's different, and you know it! Your father's job keeps him late sometimes and we all have to live with that, as you know very well. Besides, *he* called to let me know he'd be late!'

'I *did* try, too!' Daniel was stung to retort.

'Not very hard! If you'd...' Russell held up his hands to silence them both. *I don't need this,* he thought, *not tonight.* After a brief pause, he spoke to his son:

'Good evening, Daniel.' The boy averted his eyes:

'Hello, Dad.'

'I gather you were late home?' Daniel looked up, opened his mouth to speak, but his father gestured him to silence again:

'I don't want to know, not yet anyway. Have you done your homework?'

'Yes, Dad.'

'Okay. Finish your sweet, then give your mother a hand to clear away, while I get my dinner in peace, all right? Where's Sarah?' he asked his wife.

'She's with Becky, next door, the Ransome's gave her dinner tonight. Just as well, with...' Russell held up his hand again:

'Later, please, Love? Let me eat, and unwind from the day, okay?'

'Of course - sorry, Darling. I've got some casserole in the oven for you, I'll rustle up some chips to go with it, all right?'

Russell nodded his thanks, dropped into a chair at the table. Opposite, Daniel looked at him for a moment before turning his attention back to the apple pie.

Tracy bustled around for a few minutes, and then placed a hot plate before him, laden with beef casserole and chips. Daniel finished his pie, got up from the table and took his plate to the dishwasher and began to help his mother loading it and wiping down the work surfaces. As he ate, Russell glanced up:

'Dan? I thought we might have a look at that glitch in your controller, in a little while.' The boy looked round:

'Er - yeah, that'd be good, Dad.' Last time out, his yacht, 'Lady Emma', had shown an intermittent reluctance to turn right in response to his finger on the controller's joystick. But the boy knew full well that his father's sudden interest in the problem was an excuse to get him alone with him in the study - and the result had to be a lecture about his row with his mother. *Oh well, better get it over with!*

'Right, then - when I've finished eating, and got a mug of coffee to hand, okay?'

'Okay, Dad.'

Several minutes later, Russell pushed the empty plate away.

'Apple pie, love?' Tracy asked.

'Not yet, thanks - I'll have a bit for my supper, later, okay?' She nodded:

'I'd better go and get Sarah, it's high time she was in bed.'

'Let me.' Russell got to his feet, turned to the door but then looked back at his son: 'Daniel - do you want to go into the study, put the cloth over my desk and get out 'Lady Emma' and her controller? Oh, and make sure we've got some fully-charged batteries for them. I'll be there in a minute.'

'Yeah, okay, Dad.'

He walked around to the cottage next door, scorning putting his coat on for such a short trek. It was quickly opened to his knock by Becky Ransome's mother; as he stepped inside, his daughter came hammering down the stairs at the sound of his voice, and launched herself from the third one up, straight into his arms:

'Daddy!'

'Hello, Sprout!' He staggered under the impact, but managed to stay on his feet. Thanking Mrs Ransome for looking after the child as she slung the little girl's coat over his shoulder with a laugh, he carried her back home, depositing her on their own stairs with instructions to go and get ready for bed. Dropping his jacket over a kitchen chair, he headed for the study.

'I'll bring you in a coffee in a while, okay?' Tracy called after him. He let his thanks drift over his shoulder as he closed the door.

Daniel was already seated in front of the big old desk, an old tablecloth spread over its oak and leather surface. In front of him, the sleek shape of 'Lady Emma' lay with the decking removed, exposing the electric servos which operated her steering mechanism; the boy was beginning to remove the covers of the radio controller as well. Russell took his own seat behind the desk:

'Right, Dan - you carry on there, take a look at the contacts on the joystick. I'll check these servos.' The sandy head lifted, nodded, returned to its task. A few moments later, it raised again, a look of triumph in the hazel eyes below its quiff:

'Got it! Look, Dad!' He held out the unit, its internals exposed: 'There's some shi… muck, here on the rheostat!' Russell followed the pointing finger, nodded in agreement:

'Yeah, that's got to be it. You know what to do?'

'Er - clean it?'

'Carefully! Get a bit of fine emery cloth, put a drop of oil on it, and rub it until it's clean and shiny again. Then wipe it off, make sure there's no oil or dust left behind, or it'll soon be just as bad again.' The boy nodded, turned to his task.

Russell himself carried on, checked the servos anyway on the principle that he might as well, now he'd started. He put the decking back in place, wiped the varnished surfaces clean of dust and fingerprints, and laid the model down on the desktop. Daniel was still gently cleaning the contacts in the controller; his eyes flicked up at his father, down again. He was unsettled, waiting for the lecture to come, unsure why it hadn't started already: *Come on, Dad, get it over with!* Russell had caught that glance; he asked, quietly:

'So - what happened today?' Daniel stopped working, looked up: 'I didn't mean…'

'Save the explanations, just tell me what happened.' His father cut across him. Still more off-stroke, Daniel hesitated, then said:

'Well - after school, Snow and Jacko wanted to go down to the GPS for a bit…'

'That's the arcade, in Market Street?'

'Yeah. Well - I *said* I'd get in trouble if I was late home, but… Jacko lent me his mobile, and I *did* ring, but it was engaged. So he said, let's go anyway, you can try again from there. So we did…' He trailed into silence.

'And when you got there?' Daniel looked down at his hands:

'I… I guess I forgot.' The silence dragged out, until he went on: 'I did remember - but that was when we were on our way home, later, and… it was too late by then.'

'So when you got home, you got roasted?' The boy looked up again, grinned self-consciously:

'You'd better believe it!'

'Hmm. And knowing you, you snarled back at your mother, and just made it worse?' The boy's head drooped again as he nodded sheepishly.

'What is it, with you and your Mum lately? You always seem to be snapping at each other.' Daniel raised his eyes, a look of pained innocence in them:

'She's *always* on at me, these days! Telling me off for doing things, or *not* doing them - I can't seem to do anything right!'

'Maybe that's because, in her eyes, you *are* getting things wrong?' Russell saw the self-righteous fire fade from his son's eyes. He looked down again, shrugged his shoulders:

'Maybe - some of the time. I don't mean to... but...'

'So - what should we do, do you think?' He looked up, startled; he'd been expecting another roasting from his father, but here he was, asking his opinion!

'I... I dunno.'

'Okay. I'll tell you what I think. You should go to your mother, as soon as you're finished there, and say you're sorry about today. You should promise her that in future, you're always going to make sure she knows where you are, and what you're doing. And you'd better *mean* it, especially that last bit. Right?'

'Yes, Dad.'

'And - I want you to carry your own mobile phone with you, all the time, right?'

'But - we're not *allowed* to have them in school!'

'I know, Dan. But... there are times, when rules, however well intended, need to be... worked around - you understand?'

'Ye-ah, but...'

'I don't want you getting yourself in trouble, so for Heaven's sake make sure it's switched *off* while you're actually in school. But, the moment you get out in the afternoon, you switch it *on,* understand? That way, you can get in touch, if you and your mates come up with any more hair-brained escapades on the way home. And *we* can get hold of you, in case we need to. And if any of the teachers catch you with it on you, you're to tell them it's *my* rule that you carry it, at all times. If they don't like it, they can talk to *me* - you're not to give it up, even to them. You understand?'

'Yes - sure, Dad!'

'But remember - if you drop yourself in it by *using* it during school time, you're on your own!'

'All right!'

The silence that held for the next few seconds rang with the camaraderie of father and son, until Daniel said tentatively:

'Is that all, Dad?' Russell laughed:

'You were expecting another bollocking, were you?' The boy just nodded.

'What good would it do, Daniel? You know you screwed up today - just learn from that, okay? Oh, and - *please* try to keep the peace with your mother, right? Do the little things she asks you to, and without a great performance of being hard done by, all right?' Daniel's face fell as he looked away. Russell sensed that reminding his son of the tension that had started to develop in the family had been a mistake - in the moment he'd got the boy on his wavelength, he'd put a spoke in his own wheel. Better to have left it at that, and allow things to settle down in their own way, tackle other problems if they continued to arise. *Lord, save us from the sensitivity of adolescents!*

'I'll finish up there, if you like, put the controller back together for you. You go and talk to your Mum.' Daniel nodded, rose to his feet and turned to the door; Russell watched him, quickly stood up before he could leave the room:

'Dan?'

'Yes, Dad?' The boy looked around.

'Come here, son.' He went to meet him, took him by the shoulders, looked into his eyes for a moment before drawing him into an embrace:

'We *do* love you, you know. More than you can possibly understand' he mumbled into his son's hair as he felt the youngster's arms tighten around his waist.

CHAPTER TEN

The next morning David Russell found it impossible to dispel a disturbing feeling of failure as he drove into the town. He still felt that, however well it had appeared to go, his chat with Daniel the previous evening had left matters less than resolved - they'd appeared to deal with the immediate row, but the underlying problem still troubled him. But now, he had to get his mind back on the job, focus on the search for Roddie McKeenan's killer.

He was just locking the Jeep in the station car park when he heard the gruff tones of the Detective-Superintendent behind him:

'Morning, David.' He turned:

'Morning, sir.'

'How's the McKeenan case going?' They walked side-by-side to the rear entrance of the building.

'Oh, fair, sir - it's early days, of course.'

'Mm. Got the press coming today, three o'clock.'

'Ah - I should be getting on with things, there's a lot I need to do today…'

'All right, all right! I *can* handle them on my own, you know!' Wilson's dislike of having to face the press alone was well known, and even something of a standing joke around the local force.

'Of course, sir.'

'So - what can I tell them?' Russell paused, in the act of opening the door:

'Well, you can fill them in on Roddie's background, of course

- but there isn't too much more you can say at the moment, except to reassure them we're following a number of leads.'

'Ha! The usual smoke-screen? What about the drugs you found in his flat?' Russell thought for a moment:

'I think I'd rather we kept quiet about them for now, sir. If there *is* a drugs connection with his murder, it might be best to keep people guessing about how much we know.'

'Mm - okay, if you say so. What do you see as the priority right now?'

'It was my intention to talk to the people who can help me to pin down the exact sequence of events at the club - the barmen, hostesses and so on, and the taxi-driver of course. I need the clearest possible picture of what happened, who was where, who did what. That way, I might begin to see where the gaps are, who could have been in a position to kill Roddie and take cover before the body was found. And, hopefully, I'll get at least some preliminary results from forensic today. If I can build up a clear picture of *what* happened, I might begin to see who and how.'

'Right. Do you need more resources?'

'I could use all the manpower you can spare, for a day or two, sir, while we try to talk to everyone on Mr Armstrong's list of the customers who were in there that night. Once that's done, maybe we could scale back a bit.'

'Okay - I'll ask if Clive can spare you a PC or two, pro tem., as well as the extra bodies you've already got from Wootton Hall Park.'

'Thank you, sir - I wonder, if he's available, could you ask Mr Armstrong if I could have PC Dorman as one of them?'

'I'll ask - you think a lot of that boy, don't you, David?'

'Chance has involved him with my investigations several times, now, sir; and each time, he's acquitted himself very well. So yes, I do.'

'Mm. That'll be why you were prepared to back his application for CID a while ago?'

'Yes, sir.'

'Mm. Well, if he makes a good showing this time, maybe *I'll* back him if he applies again.'

'I'm sure he'd be most grateful if you did, sir.'

'Well, we'll see. Keep me posted, David.'

'Of course, sir.' The two men went on into the station, Wilson to his top-floor office and Russell to look for his Sergeant.

He found him in the first-floor incident room, went over to stand by the desk he was occupying:

'Morning, Doug.' Rimmer looked up:

'Morning, boss.' He gave Russell a second look: 'You look thoughtful?'

'Eh? Oh, problems at home, Doug. No, problems is too strong a word - Daniel upset his mother. He was late getting home, been out with his mates, forgot to let her know. Had to put on my U.N. act, restore the peace.'

'All quiet now?'

'Yeah, I think so.' He kept his reservations to himself, changed the subject: 'Anything in from forensic yet? Or the pathologist?'

'No, not so far. What's the programme for today?'

'You've got teams out chasing down all the people who were in the club Wednesday night?'

'Yeah. We're working our way through Strongarm's list - and no duds yet, either!' Russell laughed:

'It was a good thing the lads on the spot had the presence of mind to check ID's! If they hadn't, you can bet your life we'd have at least a few dozen Mickey Mice among 'em. The PM's going to ask if we can borrow a couple of spare PC's from uniform - put them on that job, too, and maybe we'll get to the end of it before Christmas. I want us to go and see the taxi-driver, and then those of Gidding's staff who were first on the scene after the shots - we need to pin down the time-frame as tight as we can, place people at the exact time of the shooting as far as possible.'

'See if Lucy could've shot him, and got back inside the ladies loo before she was seen?'

'That's one possibility. But who was he going out there to meet? Or was that an excuse to get away from the girl? Why go out there, though, unless...? Oh, hell, Doug, there're just too many unknowns at the moment. Let's try and get some more facts, give ourselves a bit more of a framework to speculate on. Come on.' He turned away; Rimmer got up and followed him out of the room, picking up a list of names and addresses as he did so.

In the car park, Russell threw his keys to the Sergeant:

'You drive, Doug.' Rimmer caught them, grinning - he relished each opportunity to get behind the wheel of his superior's imposing four-wheel-drive. In the car, he asked:

'Where first, boss?'

'Broadbent, the taxi-driver.' He checked down the address list:

'Alan Broadbent, 37 Denbigh Street...' His voice trailed off - there was a faint bell ringing, deep down in his mind, barely audible among the confusion of his other thoughts, but there never-the-less. Unable to get a grip on it, he mentally shrugged his shoulders as Rimmer started the car and drove out into the street, turned toward the town centre.

'Bit early, aren't they?' Russell surfaced from his reverie at the Sergeant's comment:

'What?'

'Christmas lights, already!' In the street as they passed, two council workmen were stringing festoons of coloured bulbs among the streetlamps.

'It is nearly December, Doug!'

'Yeah - I suppose it is, at that.'

There was something familiar about the street of terraced houses, the slightly run-down property they parked in front of, as well. Rimmer rang the doorbell; after a brief pause, the door was opened by a shortish man, with balding grey hair and a pronounced belly protruding between his singlet and the waistband of his grubby trousers.

'Mr Broadbent?'

'Yeah, that's me.'

'Detective-Sergeant Rimmer, sir, Grancester CID. This is Inspector Russell.'

'*Inspector,* eh? This'll be about the other night?'

'That's right, sir. Could we come in?'

'Yeah, sure.' He led the way inside, into a rather dingy sitting-room whose furnishings had seen better days, waved them into the two easy chairs and perched himself on the edge of the settee.

'I give 'em a full statement at the club, when it 'appened.'

'Yes, sir - we've got that, but I wanted to talk to you myself, get a clearer picture in my mind, if you understand?' Russell told him. The man nodded:

'Okay - why not?'

'I wonder if you could run through for us, quickly, just what you saw and heard after you stopped in Butcher's Lane that night?'

'Yeah - well, like I tol' the copper then, I pulled round the corner, just into the lane, to have a quick break. If you're outa sight, you're not so likely to get some bugger interrupt you in the middle of a sandwich, yeh see. I'd 'ad a bite, and a swig from me flask, was just reading a chapter of me book, when I 'eard the shots. I looked up, a'course, saw the flash of the last one, realised what it were and grabbed me phone, dialled 999. That's about all I can tell yer.'

'What time was it you stopped there?'

'Oh, 'bout one-twenny-two I think it was I called in to tell the office I was 'aving me break. The despatch records'll confirm that for yeh.'

With the mention of despatch records, something clicked into place in Russell's memory:

'We've met before, Mr Broadbent!' The man smiled, a little ruefully:

'Yeah - I was wonderin' if you'd remember. Long time ago.' Russell laughed:

'Policemen are like elephants, Mr Broadbent - we never forget!

Sometimes it takes us a while to make the connection, though.'

'Twelve, thirteen years back? That kiddie who was killed, up at the ol' quarry, 'fore they turned it into a country park. You and the other copper were all set to blame me, for a while.'

'Yes, indeed! Until your alibi came through. We got the real killer, in the end, you know?'

'Yeah, I 'eard - last year, wasn' it?' Russell nodded:

'We'd better get back to Wednesday night, Mr Broadbent. How long had you been in the alley before you heard the shots?'

'Oh, ten minutes, mebbe, not much longer.'

'You didn't switch on your headlights, to see what was happening?'

'Not bloody likely! If someone's bangin' away with a gun, I'm not gonna let 'em know I'm there if I can 'elp it, am I?' Russell laughed again:

'No, I suppose not! You didn't actually see Roddie McKeenan's assailant?'

'Nah, couldn't see no-one, it was too dark. Just that flash from the gun.'

'And no-one came past your cab, either before or after the shooting?'

'Nope. They couldn'a got by without me seein' 'em. I backed the car out, just roun' into the 'Igh Street, so the ambulance could get by, but I was still right by the corner. No-one come out of the alley, as I saw.'

'What about as you were reversing the car? You must have been looking away then, if only for a few seconds?' The man thought before replying:

'Yeah, I guess so - but it was just a coupl'a seconds. Mebbe someone *could* 'a sneaked by, then, but I'd 'a seen 'em in the 'Igh Street, wouldn'I?'

'Probably. Okay - I don't think there's anything else, Mr Broadbent. Can we get in touch if we need to talk to you again?' He shrugged:

'Yeah, I guess so. Yeh know where to find me.' He rose with them, showed them to the door. Outside, Russell turned to him:

'Thank you, Mr Broadbent, you've been most helpful.'

'Yeah, no trouble. And - no 'ard feelin's, 'bout before, Mr Russell, right?'

Russell nodded, turned away to the car.

In the Jeep, Rimmer asked:

'Was he talking about the Philip Dorman case?' Russell grinned:

'Yeah! We thought, for a while, that he'd been up by the quarry just about the time the boy was killed. But then we found the girl in the taxi office had screwed up the times on her sheet, he was actually somewhere else - got him off the hook.'

'Just as well, for his sake! Where now, boss?'

'The ones I want to speak to next would be Stevens, the barman, and the other hostess, Elsa Jurgens, the one who saw Lucy come out of the ladies. We'll go on to the others afterwards.'

'Right.' Rimmer consulted the list of addresses, started the engine.

CHAPTER ELEVEN

Some ten minutes later, the Jeep pulled up outside a small block of flats on Adelaide Square in the Greenland Estate. Rimmer glanced up at the building:

'Adelaide *Court!* Bloody developers - how can you call it a court when it's a damned high-rise?' Russell chuckled:

'Builder's licence, I guess! Where's Stevens live?'

'Number 14 - second floor, it says here.'

'Okay, let's go.'

He swung the car door open, but paused as the radio crackled into life:

'Delta 131, Delta control: Mr Russell?' He picked up the microphone:

'131, Russell'

'Sir, we've got Dr Somerfield on the telephone - shall I patch him through to you?'

'Please, Maisie.' A pause, then the pathologist came over the air: 'David? Iain Somerfield.'

'Morning Iain - what have you got for me?'

'McKeenan, your shooting victim - what you expect, probably. Any one of the shots would have killed him, so your gunman was making certain! Two bullets passed straight through, the third - not necessarily in that order, you understand - lodged against a rib in his back, behind the left lung.'

'You've recovered it?'

'And sent it off to ballistics, yes!'

'What else can you tell me about what happened?'

'Well - he was shot from a distance of about eighteen inches, I'd say. Small, relatively low-powered weapon, 9mm. The killer was directly in front of him, and I'd guess that all three shots were fired in quick succession - the line of penetration doesn't vary, so he wasn't falling as he was hit.'

'Right! That fits with what we have from witness statements and the like.'

'That's the bare bones of it, David; I'll send on my full report for you, but I thought you'd like the important bits straight away.'

'Yes, thanks, Iain. Was there any trace of drugs in his system?'

'Samples are off for analysis - I'll know tomorrow, probably. Certain amount of alcohol, for sure; and he'd eaten not long before he died, chicken and chips. But perhaps you knew that?'

'Indeed! Thanks again, Iain.'

'No trouble. Be seeing you.'

Russell replaced the microphone. The Sergeant had been listening to the conversation:

'Backs up what we knew already, doesn't it?' Russell nodded:

'Yeah - doesn't add anything, really, but it confirms Broadbent's story, as far as it goes, and the statements from the people who heard the shots.' He paused: 'You know, he's the only person we can positively place in the alley with Roddie…'

'You're not thinking he could be our killer?'

'Broadbent? It's possible, isn't it? But then, how does he get the gun into the ladies loo, inside the club? And those gloves - if the killer was wearing them - you saw the size of his hands, he'd never get those big paws into them, would he?' Rimmer shook his head:

'No chance.'

The two stepped out of the car and made their way into the apartment block. On the second floor, Rimmer knocked at the door of flat number 14; after a short delay, it was opened by the barman, looking somewhat rumpled:

'Yes?'

'Mr Stevens?'

'Yes?'

'Detective-Sergeant Rimmer, sir, Grancester CID. This is D.I. Russell.'

'Oh - good morning, Gentlemen. This is about the shooting at Sweeney's?'

'Yes, sir - can we come in?'

'Please!' He stepped back, waving them inside, and closed the door behind them. The living-room of the flat was nicely furnished but rather chaotic, with magazines and papers strewn about, and evidence of breakfast still on the table in the corner.

'I'm sorry the place is in a mess - my girlfriend's at work, and I haven't got round to tidying up yet. Take a seat, please.'

'Thank you, sir.' The two policemen sat side-by-side on the settee, the only uncluttered seating they could find; Stevens shifted some papers from one of the chairs, and sat facing them.

'What can I do for you?'

'We'd like to go over your statement regarding what happened the other night, if you don't mind, Mr Stevens?' The man shrugged:

'Of course, if it'll help?'

'You knew Roddie McKeenan, Mr Stevens?' Russell put in a question.

'Sure - I think everyone at Sweeney's knew Roddie!'

'Was he popular?'

'Yeah, everyone liked him. He was a real nice guy, you know? No side to him, he'd chat with anyone - and they all seemed to get on with him, whoever they were.'

'So he was never short of company, at the club?' Stevens laughed:

'Nor anywhere else, I'd imagine!'

'The girls liked him?'

'Sure! But he and Lucy were an item, you understand? The other girls would flirt with him - and he with them, come to that - but it didn't mean anything.'

'He wasn't seeing someone else, that you knew of?'

'Two-timing Lucy? No! He'd have to be crazy - she's a lovely girl. And he wouldn't dare, she's got a bit of a temper - typical red-head!'

'How much of a temper - nasty?'

'Not really - if you upset Lucy, you'd know about it, but the next minute she'd be all smiles again. She's the sort that'll let fly, leave you in no doubt what she thinks, but then forget about it once she's had her say.'

'We've been told that he wanted to finish with her - did you know that?'

Stevens hesitated, then replied:

'I'd heard. He hadn't said anything to me, but Karl told me - he'd probably heard it from Elsa, his sister. She and Lucy are quite close, you see.'

'Did that surprise you?'

'Yeah - yes, it did. I thought - we all thought, I guess - that they were fixed for life. But you never know, do you?'

There was a brief pause before Rimmer took up the questions:

'Were you aware at any time of Roddie being involved in anything illegal?'

A guarded look came into the barman's eyes:

'What have you got in mind?' Rimmer glanced at his superior, received a slight nod of the head. He went on:

'Could he have been selling drugs, either in the club, or elsewhere?'

Stevens didn't reply immediately, and when he did, both policemen had the impression he was picking his words very carefully:

'Roddie was the kind of bloke who would make a buck when he saw the chance, you know? If an opportunity came his way, he'd grab it. He had his own business, the decorating work - but he'd take anything else that came along. I doubt if the taxman got to know about a lot of it - but that was his business. If some of the things he got mixed up in were less than legal, it might not surprise me - but I can't tell you what they might be. Drugs?' he shrugged his shoulders: 'Anything's possible, I suppose - you think he was a pusher?'

'I can't tell you that, Mr Stevens - it's just a possibility we're looking into. I'd appreciate it if you'd keep that under your hat, if you don't mind?' Russell asked.

'Yeah, sure - it's no business of mine, is it?'

Russell took up the questions:

'Mr Stevens - do you know if anyone at Sweeney's, anyone who worked there, owned a gun?' The barman raised his eyebrows, hesitated, and prevaricated:

'What kind of gun?'

'A small hand-gun, the kind of thing that would fit in a pocket, or a hand-bag.' Stevens slowly shook his head, replied hesitantly:

'Not that *I* can tell you, no. Given the... kind of place it is, I wouldn't rule it out, though.'

'Thank you. Now, if we can go over the events of Wednesday night?'

By the time they left the flat, Russell felt he had a better grasp on the exact sequence of events, and their timescale, over the few vital minutes of the shooting. Stevens had gone through it with them, willingly and carefully putting the best estimate he could make on the passage of time from when he'd heard the argument in the corridor outside the toilets to the time he'd heard the shots from the alley, and rushed out to find Roddie slumped against the wall.

In the car, Rimmer went to start the engine, but Russell put out a hand to stop him:

'Hold on a mo, Doug, let's think. Roddie's killer had to be either in the lane waiting for him, or followed him out of Sweeney's, right?'

'Right. And the only accesses are from the High Street...'

'Which means they'd have to get past Broadbent in his taxi...'

'Or through the club.'

'No other way in or out?'

'No. Only through the other premises which back on to Butcher's Lane, and the searches found no trace of anyone in those backyards. No-one in the flats above the shops heard or saw anyone, even the ones who heard the shots and got up to see what was going on. And the lane's a blind alley, so no way out the other end.'

'So we keep coming back to the club. And the gun, and the gloves, in the ladies loo. Is there any other way out of Sweeney's into the lane, apart from the door Roddie used?'

'Yeah - there's a door from the kitchen.'

'And the kitchens were deserted, after about midnight, right?'

'Right.'

'So - someone *could* have gone out that way, to make a pre-arranged rendezvous with him, let's say…'

'Or, someone…'

'Lucy?'

'That's my bet, yes!' Rimmer grinned, carried on: 'went out after him.'

'But if that's the case, the kitchen door would have been locked, so they'd have had to get back in through the door into the corridor.'

'Which ties in with the gun and the gloves.'

'Yes - but suppose someone *had* used the kitchen door, they could have doubled around inside, through the bar, to dump them there, couldn't they?'

'But why bother? Why not drop them in one of the kitchen bins - they'd have probably been there longer before we found them, that way, as well.'

'Ye-es… Let's go and take another quick look at the scene, Doug. We'll go and see the Jurgens girl later.'

'Whatever you say, boss.'

Back at the nightclub, Russell pushed through the front doors into the lobby. As he went on into the ground-floor bar area, the short figure of Frank Duffy hurried across to meet them:

'What can I do for you gentlemen?' The words were polite, but the body language said he was annoyed at the interruption.

'D.I. Russell, and D.S. Rimmer - we're investigating your murder. Mr Duffy?'

'That's right - I'm the bar manager here. We're trying to get ready to reopen tonight.' There was the slightest emphasis on the second word of his statement.

'We don't want to hold you up, Mr Duffy; we'd just like to take a quick look around, if that's all right?'

'I thought you fellows had done here? Oh - go ahead, if you need to. I'll be in one or the other bar, if you need me.' He turned to go, but Rimmer stopped him:

'We'll need to talk to you sometime, Mr Duffy - to go over your statement with you, you understand?'

'Yes, okay - can we do that tomorrow? I'm very busy - we've a lot to do today, after your people have been tramping around in here.'

'Of course - we'll call you, shall we?' The man nodded and walked off. Russell chuckled:

'Strongarm said he was a prickly son of a bitch! Come on, Doug, I want to go over the ground, in the corridor and the kitchens.'

They spent some time, going over the scene, pacing the distances, following the footsteps of the known participants, checking the timings of various movements, known and surmised, of witnesses, victim, and possible killers. When they returned to the Jeep, Russell was looking thoughtful; as he turned the key in the ignition, Rimmer ventured:

'Lucy could have done it, couldn't she? She could have followed him out, shot him, got back before anyone came.' Russell nodded:

'She could. But, if she's telling the truth, and she was in the ladies, so could someone else. And as we've seen, someone could have used the kitchen exit equally well to go and meet Roddie, and get back without being seen.'

'But…'

'Let's save the speculation for now, Doug. I wonder if The Mad Professor's done his thing with those gloves? Let's call back at the station, grab some lunch and talk to him.'

CHAPTER TWELVE

Sandwiches, half-eaten, in one hand, mugs of coffee in the other, the two detectives hurried down the stairs to the basement lair of the scenes of crime team. In the SOCO office, a plain-clothes constable looked up as they entered:

'Hello, sir, sergeant - can I help you?'

'Is the Professor about?' Russell asked; the seated man grinned, nodded to the rear of the building:

'Playing with guns, out the back, sir!' All three shared a chuckle at the forensic officer's infectious enthusiasm.

'Thanks, Tolman.'

'Any time, sir.'

They found Owen in the sound-proofed test chamber, in the act of stripping off a pair of thin but strong fabric gloves. He looked up at the sound of their approach:

'Oh, hi, Dave, Doug. I was going to call you.'

'What have you got for us, Terry?'

'Ah, well...' He laid the gloves carefully down on the bench: 'The Sweeney's shooting?'

'Yes, Terry.' Russell kept his tone patient.

'Right - first, then, the gun you found. Been recently fired...'

'How recently?'

'Oh, say within twelve hours of when it was found. The remaining cartridges are identical with the bullets recovered in the alley - three empties.'

'So it is our murder weapon?' Rimmer asked.

'Ah - can't be *certain,* of course. Not unless the ballistics lab can match what's left of those bullets to it.'

'Oh, come on! It'd be pushing coincidence beyond credibility if it wasn't, wouldn't it?'

'Oh, I expect you're right, Doug - but still...'

'Doctor Somerfield's retrieved the third bullet, Terry.' Russell interrupted before the argument could develop; Owen's eyes lit up:

'He has? Excellent! That should give them a much better chance!'

'Anything else?'

'Fingerprints, of course. All over it.'

'Whose?'

'I don't know! No-one on the files - presumably, whoever owned the thing.'

'And whoever shot Roddie McKeenan?' Owen shook his shaggy head:

'Doubt it - unless they're one and the same, of course. Your killer wore those gloves.'

'So - what else can you tell us about what happened?'

'Mmm - I've examined his clothing, and I'd say from the pattern of powder-burning that the muzzle was about twelve or eighteen inches away. Neat grouping of shots - probably fired in quick succession. The impacts held him against the brick wall behind him, so he didn't fall until it was all over. And...'

'And?'

'You remember that pretty little hand-bag I found in the bin? The gun had been kept in that, and there were traces of oil on the lining, tiny rips where the sharp edges had caught the fabric as well. And fibres of the lining material caught on the gun, as well'

'Anything else in it?'

'Only a part-used pack of tissues, a little powder compact, a lipstick - things you'd expect.'

'And what else, Terry?' Owen grinned at the Inspector, a twinkle in his blue eyes:

'Oh, the gloves, you mean?'

'*Yes,* Terry! You were being all mysterious with me on the phone last night - out with it, man!'

'Ah, yes - well, I wanted to check my idea, you see. That's what I was doing when you came in.'

'And?'

'Ah! Look here…' he laid the gloves he had just taken off out carefully: 'See how the powder has burnt some areas…' he pointed: 'And left others in shadow? I've just fired an identical gun with these on my hands, and the pattern of powder burning is exactly the same as on the ones you found at the club.'

'So what does that tell you?' *I will, I'll strangle him one day!* Russell thought. Owen's face split into a huge grin:

'Your killer was left-handed, Dave! He held the gun in his left hand, so…' he picked up the gun from the bench: 'Braced it with his right, like so, and bang - bang - bang!'

'Really?'

'Absolutely!' Rimmer snorted:

'Well, that rules out about two-thirds of the population, I suppose!' Russell laughed:

'But how many of our likely suspects are left-handed, I wonder? Is there any way of telling who has worn them, Terry?'

'I've swabbed them out, turned them inside-out to get every trace I can, and sent it off for DNA analysis. You said they probably belong to the girl?'

'Lucy Cavendish, that's right.'

'I'd expect to find her DNA, then. Even after cleaning, the chances are that there will be enough skin flakes and so on still adhering to prove that.'

'What if someone else had put them on, just for the time it took to shoot Roddie?'

'Hmmm…' Owen sounded sceptical: 'I'd expect to find a trace

- but it's a bit more of a long shot, maybe. We'll see what the lab comes up with. It'd have to be someone with small hands, mind?' Russell nodded:

'Yeah, I know. But we have to consider it, don't we?'

'Surely. One of the other girls? They'd be about the only people who could have worn them, I imagine. There's no sign of straining in the seams, or anything like that, which might suggest they'd been forced onto hands that were too big for them. Not that I've noticed, anyway - I'll check again to make sure, shall I?'

'Please, Terry. You'll let me know, about that, and the ballistics and DNA?'

''Course.'

'Soon as you can?' Owen gave a devilish chuckle:

'I promise, Dave!'

* * *

Half an hour later, the Jeep drew up outside number 14, The Briars, in the quiet residential district of Oakfield. The neat little semi was tidy enough, but the front garden had an unkempt air about it, somehow depressing in the chill drizzle that had begun to fall from the heavy pewter skies.

The girl who opened the door at Rimmer's knock was petite and full-figured, curly blond hair framing her round face, a look of enquiry in her bright blue eyes:

'Hello?'

'Miss Jurgens? Sergeant Rimmer, Grancester CID - this is Inspector Russell.'

'Oh! Come in, please!' She waved them inside: 'You're looking for Roddie's murderer?'

'We are, miss' Russell confirmed 'and we'd like to go over what happened with you, if you don't mind?'

'No, of course not - but I have to get ready for work, soon. The club's reopening tonight, you know?'

'Yes, we know - but I need to get a clear picture of events on Wednesday, you understand? Is your brother here - we could do with a word with him, too?'

'Karl's out, I'm afraid - he's gone in early to help set the bars up. But how can I help?' She led them into the cosy living-room, indicated the easy chairs as she sat herself on the settee.

'When did you know something had happened?'

'When I saw Aaron dash out of the bar.'

'You didn't hear the shots yourself?' She shook her head:

'No. I guess Aaron and Karl heard them, because they had the windows behind the bar open - but the sound didn't reach me, or any of the customers, as far as I could tell. I just saw him run, and went after him.'

'Where were you, exactly?'

'Sitting at a table, about half-way towards the front of the room, over near the corridor where the toilets are.'

'Near the door by which Mr Stevens left the room?'

'Yes.'

'Alone?'

'No, I was talking to a customer, socialising, you know? It's part of the job, making them feel welcome.'

'The *male* customers?' Rimmer asked. There was a glint of fire in the glance the girl threw him as she replied:

'Mostly, yes, Sergeant! A lot of them come in for that bit of company, a chat with a pretty girl, as much as for the drink or the dancing.'

'You left your customer at the table?' Russell interjected smoothly; she turned back to him:

'Yes. I excused myself, left him there with his drink - I realised it must be something important, because Aaron's usually pretty laid-back, doesn't rush anywhere.'

'You followed him outside?'

'Yes. I found him bending over Roddie, checking his pulse. He looked up at me, and... and, just shook his head...' Her own head bowed forward, tears suddenly squeezing from between her eyelids. Russell reached across, touched her arm in sympathy:

'I'm sorry to distress you, making you go through this again. But you see how important it is to us?' She nodded, raised her eyes to his:

'I'm sorry - but it's just so *horrible!* Who could want to hurt Roddie? He was... He was... so *nice!* He'd always stop and talk, have a laugh with everyone...'

'You liked Roddie?'

'*Everyone* liked him! I never heard anyone say a bad word about him.'

'You knew about his business, how he made his living?' Rimmer took up the questions again. She shrugged:

'A bit - I guess most of us did, he was hardly a secretive man.'

'What about - sidelines, perhaps? Was he inclined to get involved in other enterprises, aside from the decorating?'

'It wouldn't surprise me! I can imagine him dabbling in anything that would make him a buck!'

'Even things that might have been illegal?' She gave him a careful look:

'Maybe...' she said slowly.

'Could he have been selling drugs, for example? On the quiet, in Sweeney's, perhaps, without Mr Gidding getting to know about it?' She gave him a strange look, half puzzled, half amused:

'Oh, I doubt that! Mr Gidding doesn't miss much, Sergeant!' The two policemen exchanged glances at this evasiveness, both aware that she'd answered the second part of the question rather than the first. Russell turned back to her:

'Who else was there, in the alley?' he asked gently. The girl paused, thinking.

'Oh... Fred, Fred Collins - he'd come down from the upstairs bar. I think they must have heard the shots, too. Petra - she followed me, I think, when I left the bar. Di wasn't there - I think she was upstairs somewhere. And there were a few of the customers, the ones who realised something was wrong and came to see if they could help - but I couldn't tell you who they were.'

'Your brother?'

'Karl? He stayed behind the bar, when Aaron left, to keep an eye on things. Mr Duffy'd have a fit if they left it unattended! So, I suppose, did Darren and Pete, upstairs.'

'What happened next?'

'Things were pretty confused! Fred went to call for an ambulance. Aaron and Petra were trying to help Roddie, even though I think they both knew it was too late. I went to find Lucy. Oh, and Fluffy was there by the time the ambulance turned up, but I'm not sure when he arrived, or where he'd been.'

'Fluffy?' The girl suddenly giggled:

'Mr Duffy - it's our nickname for him. His name's Frank, but someone shortened it to Fluffy, and it kind of stuck. No-one would *dare* use it to his face, mind you! He insists on being *Mr Duffy* to everyone.'

'You didn't know where Lucy was, when you went to look for her?'

'No - she'd been in the room, chatting to someone up at the bar. But she wasn't there when I went to find her. She came out of the ladies just as I went back into the corridor - I tried to stop her going outside, but she pushed past me, and ran out to Roddie, and…' The thought of her friend's grief brought the tears back to her eyes; she dashed them away with her fingers.

'How did she seem, when you stopped her?' Rimmer asked; the girl thought for a moment:

'Well, puzzled, at first. She didn't know what was wrong; then, when I told her it was Roddie, she… kind of stared at me, as if I was crazy. Then, like I say, she forced her way past me and ran out to him.'

'You hadn't seen her leave the bar?'

'No. Karl told me later that she'd followed Roddie out when he left, a few minutes before… before he was shot. But I didn't see her go, myself.'

'Okay, thank you, Miss Jurgens.' Russell appeared to wrap the questions up, half-rising from his seat, but then threw out a Columbo-style afterthought:

'Oh - one more thing: Do you know if anyone at the club owned a gun?' The girl looked up at him as he straightened up, a sudden wariness evident in her expression:

'A gun?'

'A small pistol of some kind, maybe?' She stared at him, then shook her head slowly:

'I don't think so, Inspector. I mean, it's hardly the kind of thing you'd tell everybody, is it?'

'Maybe not, at that. All right, thanks again, Miss Jurgens.'

Outside, the two men settled themselves in the car again. But before Rimmer could start the engine, Russell turned to his assistant:

'Why is everyone ducking and diving, Doug? What don't they want us to know?' Rimmer chuckled:

'You've noticed that too? Whenever we ask about Roddie's extra-curricular activities, or about the gun.'

'Right! I'm inclined to assume that they all *knew* he was dealing drugs, but don't want to let on. And they know damn-well whose gun that is.'

'Yeah. I'm sure you're right, boss. It's a shame the fingerprints from the gun didn't come up on the records - they've got to be the owner's, haven't they?'

'If need be, we'll fingerprint the whole damn lot of them, find out whose they are! If they turn out to belong to Lucy Cavendish… But then, her reaction when Elsa told her what had happened hardly fits if she's the killer, does it?

'Good actress, maybe?'

'She'd have to be, to fool someone who knows her that well!

Come on, Doug, let's try to catch up with the rest of Gidding's staff before we pack in today.'

'Okay - who next?' Rimmer started the engine.

'The other barman, Fred What's-his-name, the one she mentioned who'd also been on the scene. And we'll have to come back to talk to her brother, sometime.'

CHAPTER THIRTEEN

As he set off for home again that evening, David Russell once more reflected that his knowledge of events at Sweeney's two nights before was becoming clearer. He was beginning to refine the chaos of those moments into a sequence of actions and movements, involving mostly the club's staff, and in doing so narrowing down those who could have been involved in the murder. Almost all of them could alibi each other for the vital couple of minutes - only Lucy Cavendish was unaccounted for by their assorted testimonies, which would be the case if her claim to have been in the ladies toilet was true.

Or? Had she, in fact, been out in Butcher's Lane, wreaking a terminal vengeance on her lover? Possible, certainly. She would have had time to be back inside, in that loo before Stevens had run out to see what was going on - in their interview, he'd admitted to a slight delay in reacting, an exchange of words with his fellow-barman along the 'what was that?' 'I don't know' 'you go and see, I'll hold the fort' lines. And of course, that was where they'd found the gun and the gloves...

Who else? One of the customers? Had Roddie been going out into the alley to meet someone else to conduct his 'business', someone who had shot him and slipped back into the club, as they were surmising Lucy might have done? But who would have had a sufficiently intimate knowledge of the building to do that? And what of the forensic evidence - the gloves, the gun... Were they

Lucy's? The gloves almost certainly were…

He was relieved to find peace reigning at home that evening. Perhaps his talk with Daniel the previous night had had a broader effect after all - at least, over his dinner and through the evening he was left to mull over his thoughts on the case without having to act the peace-maker. Next day was Saturday - but he'd have to be in the office, with a murder on his hands; but, maybe he'd be able to get a day off on Sunday…

* * *

Paddy Thomas sipped at his pint of Murphy's. Normally a sociable, garrulous fellow, tonight he was perched, alone, on a stool at the bar of the Mailcoach in Victoria Square, the oppressively dark décor, all blackened oak, suiting his mood.

Christened John by his loving but thoughtless parents, he had readily adopted the nickname attached to him by the English when he'd followed his old schoolfriend Roddie over from Northern Ireland. But now, Roddie was gone: He shook his head in remembered disbelief, took another swig at his beer. It was ironic, wasn't it? They'd survived the shooting ground of strife-torn Belfast, only for someone to gun his mate down in a quiet Northamptonshire town.

And that wasn't all that was on Paddy's mind. The police were inevitably swarming around everywhere - the nightclub, Roddie's flat - had they found anything? He'd had a visit himself, a fresh-faced young DC who'd knocked on his door, come in to ask him about Roddie - checking background, he'd said, calling on all of Roddie's known associates. The copper hadn't made any mention of anything illicit, just asked about Roddie himself, enquired into the part-time work he did for him sometimes, when he had a big decorating job on. No trouble - but he still felt uneasy, aware that he might be on pretty thin ice, if they learnt about Roddie's other income: Suppose they decided to look into his own regular trips back home? But then, why should they? It was Roddie they were interested in, not *him!*

He was raising his glass once more when he felt a hand on his shoulder:

'Evenin' Paddy.' He glanced around:

'Mick! What'll you have, mate?'

* * *

Unlike Paddy Thomas, the death of Roddie McKeenan hadn't upset Curtis Roseberry in the least. Quite the contrary, in fact - it had neatly solved a problem for him; he sat in the plush office above his music store in Kettering, a glass of Southern Comfort to hand, a curl of smoke rising from his Cuban cigar, a pleased smile on his dark face.

Roseberry was of Jamaican descent, the son of immigrants who had lived close to the poverty line until his father's death six years before. But old Jonas Roseberry had lived to see his son rise to a level of affluence he himself had only dreamed of - Curtis had started the Black Rose music shops from a poky hole-in-the-wall operation in Wellingborough, where the family had lived, and built it up until he now owned four, much more respectable outlets, one each in Northampton, Kettering and Corby as well.

But Curtis Roseberry's income did not rely solely upon sales of CD's and cassettes. The police forces of each town in which he operated knew him to be the man who controlled the supply of illicit substances in the bulk of the County - but they had so far failed to gather enough evidence to implicate him in anything more shady than the occasional parking fine. They knew he was behind most of the pushers in the area, the source of supply for most of the drugs sold on the streets and in local clubs; but not in Sweeney's! And that was why the death of McKeenan was making him smile. He'd had a man in the Grancester nightclub, for a while, two years before - But Gidding, the owner, had set the man up, tipped off the police; now, he was inside, and likely to remain there for a while yet.

The news that someone else was selling drugs in Sweeney's, apparently with impunity, had not pleased Roseberry. His enquiries had, a few days before, given him the name of the interloper. But now, that impertinent Irishman was dead - leaving the field open, perhaps, for him to insert his own man once again? Especially if he could find out how *he'd* been getting away with it, keeping Gidding off his back - time for the ferrets to get to work, sniff out the detail of what had been going on…

* * *

The following morning, before he could even set in train his planned pursuit of the investigation, David Russell found one, at least, of his questions answered. The two had barely stepped into Russell's office before the internal phone rang, and Rimmer scooped it up:

'Yeah?'

'Oh, really?' He cocked one eyebrow at his superior: 'We'll be right down.'

'Frank Duffy's in reception, boss. Wants to talk to you.' Russell, too, raised his eyebrows:

'Oh? Come on, then!'

In reception, they found the diminutive bar manager waiting for them. Barely five foot four, the ex-jockey still looked lean and fit in his early fifties, despite the peppering of grey in his black hair. Russell strode over to greet him:

'Mr Duffy - what can I do for you?'

'Good Morning, Inspector.' Duffy shook the proffered hand, quickly slipping his own back into the pocket of his coat: 'Nothing special, perhaps, but you did say you would need to talk to me - I thought I would come by early, as I expect to be busy again later, and for the next few days. Get it out of the way, if you see what I mean?'

'Oh - okay, Mr Duffy, I guess we could go over things with you now, if it suits you. Is one of the interview rooms free?' He turned to the desk sergeant, who replied, waving along the corridor behind him:

'Take your pick, Mr Russell!'

'Come on through, then, Mr Duffy.' Russell opened the security door as the sergeant released it from within, handed the other man through. Rimmer led them into the corridor, pushed open the first door, waved them inside. Duffy sat one side of the central table, leaning back in a show of relaxation, his hands still thrust into the pockets of his coat; the two officers took seats facing him.

'Now, Mr Duffy, what can you tell us about the events of Wednesday night?'

'Not a lot, I'm afraid. I missed all the excitement.'

'Oh? How was that?'

'I'd gone down to check the cellars, only realised that something had happened when I came back up into the lower bar. I asked Karl Jurgens where Aaron was - he'd been missing before I went downstairs - and he said that he'd gone to check what they thought had been gunshots from out in the alley behind the club. By then, he and Petra were out there, and Lucy of course - Fred Collins was on the phone, calling the ambulance, I assume.'

'So you were unaware of the shots being fired?'

'That's correct.'

'Where had you been immediately before you went down to the cellar?'

'I'd just come down from my office, on the top floor - checked quickly in the bars, the upper one first, then the lower, and then down to see how the stock levels were. I was there for a few minutes, then came back up to find all hell breaking loose.'

'Mr Uris was still in the office?' Duffy nodded:

'That's right. I'd left him there when I came down - I like to check the bars regularly throughout the night, make sure everything is running as it should. And I needed to stock-check the barrels.'

'Okay, Mr Duffy. We've got your statement, that you gave the officers on the night, of course, but you can understand that we need to double-check everything in a case like this.'

'Oh, certainly, Inspector! I like everything to be spot-on, myself, never leave anything to chance!' Russell smiled at the man, vaguely annoyed by his bumptious manner. He glanced at Rimmer, inviting his Sergeant to take over:

'Mr Duffy - just one or two questions, if I may?'

'Of course, Sergeant!'

'Thank you, sir. Have you had any suspicions, over recent weeks perhaps, that someone might be dealing drugs in the club?'

'Good Lord, No! We don't permit anything like that, as I'm sure you know - Mr Gidding is very strict about any hint of drugs in Sweeney's. If we caught any of our staff doing that kind of thing, they'd be out on their ear straight away!'

'Maybe not staff, perhaps someone from outside, a regular customer?'

'Oh no - again, they'd be barred at the first hint of pushing drugs there.'

'I see. Mr Duffy - Lucy Cavendish, the hostess?'

'Nice girl - very popular with the customers! What about her?'

'She and Roddie McKeenan were very close?'

'Oh, yes! They'd been together some time, years, in fact. But I'd heard that they were finishing - someone told me he wanted to ditch her.'

'Who told you that, Lucy herself?' Duffy shook his head, frowning in apparent concentration:

'No, not Lucy... I'm not sure I can remember - one of the other girls, I think.'

'She always wore gloves when she was at work, is that right?'

'Oh, yes - always very smart, she is, well turned out. The

gloves were a little touch of her own - she always says the customers like that bit of class. She kept several pairs in her locker, you know, so that she could change them if they got soiled.'

'There were extra pairs there on Wednesday night?' The man shrugged:

'I assume so - at least one or two. They're probably there now; she hasn't come back to work yet, you understand? Under the circumstances...'

'Of course.' Rimmer nodded sympathetically. Duffy turned his gaze on the Inspector:

'Talking of Lucy... McKeenan was shot, right?'

'Yes?'

'Well - I don't want to point a finger, you understand, but - you know that Lucy owns a gun?' Russell felt the Sergeant's eyes flick toward him as he replied cautiously:

'Go on, Mr Duffy?'

'Well - yes, she does. She bought it, oh, a year or two ago. She'd had some trouble, a customer who got rough, knocked her about a bit before Joe Haston could deal with him, and she got it just as a sort of insurance. Always carried it in her handbag - if a punter wanted to go upstairs, she'd go and get the bag from her locker, take it with her.'

'Upstairs?'

'On to the dance floor, of course! In the lower bar, she felt safe with the barmen close at hand - but up there, she thought she was vulnerable, after what happened before, you understand.'

'What kind of gun, Mr Duffy? Had you seen it?'

'Yes, once - she showed us all, when she got it. A little thing, fit nicely in her bag, but she said it fired quite a large bullet - nine millimetre, would it be?'

'You wouldn't know where that gun is now?'

'No - unless it's still in her bag, in her locker in the changing room. But surely, your men searched the building right through, didn't they? They would have found it if it was there?'

'That's right, Mr Duffy.' The man looked from one of them to the other, but neither rose to the bait, leaving him uninformed about the results of the search. After a moment's silence, he gave up and asked:

'Is there anything else I can tell you gentlemen?' Rimmer looked at Russell, who shook his head.

'I don't think so, Mr Duffy. We can contact you again, if we need to?'

'I suppose so - if you can make it early in the day, I'd be grateful. Afternoons I like to be at the club, making sure everything is on top line for opening.'

'We wouldn't want to disturb your rest?'

'Don't worry, Sergeant! I'm always up by seven, whatever time I retire; legacy of my riding days. It was nothing, then, to be out on the gallops before five am!'

'Very good, sir. Thank you for coming in today.'

CHAPTER FOURTEEN

After seeing the bar manager out, the two detectives returned to Russell's third-floor office. The Inspector slumped into the chair behind his desk, swinging his feet up onto its edge; the Sergeant took his habitual perch on another corner.

'Well, Doug?'

'Well, boss! It all keeps coming back to Lucy, doesn't it?'

'Yeah. If Duffy's right, and that's her gun.' Rimmer shrugged: 'Those fingerprints'll soon prove that, surely? We've got to bring her in, take her prints, and a DNA sample. Match those, and...'

He let his voice trail off.

'Yeah. I just find it difficult to see her as a cold-blooded killer, that's all.'

'Oh, come on, boss! He was shot with *her* gun, by someone wearing a pair of *her* gloves; she was on the spot, can't account for her time when he *was* shot - and, she has the only viable motive we've come up with!'

'Yes, I know! All the evidence we've got points to that. A lover's tiff, and a killing in a moment of blind anger - but if so, she showed remarkable presence of mind in getting away from the scene and dumping the evidence in the few seconds available to her before someone came running.'

'Instinctive self-preservation? Or blind luck?'

'Bit of both, I imagine.'

The two sat in silence for a minute or two, then Russell looked up at the Sergeant again:

'Who's trailing Roddie's background?'

'Steve Campbell - he's got young Dorman helping him out, and another couple of DC's.'

'Nothing of interest?' Rimmer shook his head:

'Don't think so. No-one of interest to us in his circle of acquaintances, that they've found so far anyway. And nothing in his routine that tells us much we didn't already know.'

'Nothing more on the drugs?'

'Nah. No indication of where he got them, who the supplier is - Steve can't find any connection to Roseberry, who'd have to be the obvious bet. I'd be inclined to assume he was selling at Sweeney's, despite Duffy's opinion, wouldn't you?'

'Yes. Begs the question whether Duffy *did* know, and was turning a blind eye, maybe.'

'Taking a cut, even?'

'Possible. I'd assume, in that case, the two of them would be able to pull the wool over Gidding's eyes, if they kept it all pretty low-key.'

'Yeah - what's the betting? Nice little bit of pocket-money for the both of them, eh?' Russell gave an amused snort:

'But - does it have anything to do with his death?'

'It'd be a good guess usually, but this time you can't get around the fact that everything points at Lucy, whatever else was going on in the place.'

'Hnh! You're right, Doug, we've got no option but to pull her in, have we? Come on, let's get it over with.'

But, at the house in Glebe Farm, they found their intentions frustrated:

'Oh, I'm sorry, Inspector - she's taken Freya out for a while.' Mrs Hepple had met them on the doorstep.

'Do you know when they'll be back?'

'Not exactly - around tea-time. They've gone shopping; and

Lucy was going to take her to the pictures later. She's still so upset, poor little mite!'

'How's Lucy herself?'

'Oh, managing! She's coping, keeping up a bold front when Freya's about - but she's hurting desperately, I know, even if she doesn't let it show.'

'All right, Mrs Hepple - we'll come back later, if that's okay?'

'It's important?'

'It is.'

'Very well, then, Inspector. About tea-time, as I said.'

'Thank you, Mrs Hepple.'

Returning empty-handed to the station, Rimmer went up to the incident room to check over anything new from the wider enquiry, while Russell descended once more to the Mad Professor's lair. He found the bald pate and wild grey tonsure gleaming at him over the desk in the scenes of crime office, where Owen was shuffling documents, engrossed in their content. He looked up as the Inspector entered:

'Morning, Dave! I was just getting the latest results together for you.'

'Oh? What's new, Terry?' The forensic officer sat back, clasping his hands behind his head:

'I've heard from the DNA boyos, for one thing. You remember the traces of blood on those gloves?'

'Sure.'

'Well - not enough to get a very good trace, but what they *have* got matches Roddie's DNA. And the sample from inside the gloves?'

'Yes?'

'A good, clear result. Same wearer for both pairs, the blood-stained ones Lucy gave you, and the ones worn to shoot him. We ought to get a sample of her DNA, to match with them?'

'I'm working on it! No sign of anyone else having worn the ones used to kill him?'

'Not that I can see. No sign of stretching or straining in the gloves themselves, so if anyone else did wear them, it was someone with similar hands to hers. And no sign of foreign DNA.'

'What about ballistics?' Owen leant forward, shuffled through the papers again:

'I've got their report here somewhere, too. As we expected - the gun you found was used to kill him, no doubt of it. That third bullet, from the body, confirms that.'

'It's looking pretty bad for Lucy, then?'

'If it's her DNA in the gloves - and her prints on the gun - yes, I suppose it is.' The round, ruddy face turn up to meet Russell's gaze: 'You're less than happy about that, aren't you, Dave?' Russell sighed, nodded:

'That's right. That's what all the evidence says, but...' he shrugged, laughed at his own doubts: 'I guess I'm being swayed by a pretty face!'

'Well, get me her DNA, and her fingerprints, and let's see if we can tidy up the loose ends!'

'Okay! When we find her, I'll do that!'

'When you find her?'

'We went to pick her up just now, but she's gone out, taken the little girl for a treat. Doug and I are going to bring her in later - you can get your samples then.'

'Right! Call me, I'll be here.'

'Will do, Terry.'

* * *

In the nondescript little house, in a quiet backwater of Oakfield, Karl Jurgens elbowed the door of his sister's room open and pushed his way in, careful to keep the tray level in his hands.

'Hi, Sis!'

Elsa rolled over, raising one arm to brush the hair out of her eyes:

'Hey, baby brother!' She smiled up at him: 'What's this, breakfast in bed?'

'Breakfast? It's almost twelve o'clock!' He put the tray down in front of her as she pushed herself upright in the bed, leant back against the headboard.

'Thanks, Karl.'

'You okay, Else?' His tone was concerned; she nodded:

'Yeah, fine.' She held his eyes for a moment: 'I still can't believe it though, you know?' Her brother sighed:

'Me neither. Poor Luce!'

'Yeah, right! She was going to have a bad enough time of it, if he'd upped and left her - but now…'

'Yeah.' They sat in silence for a moment, as Elsa abstractedly munched on a piece of buttered toast. She raised her eyes again:

'Did those two coppers get hold of you?'

'No?'

'Two detectives - a sergeant and an inspector. They were here yesterday. I think they're the ones in charge, you know? They wanted to go over my statement with me - and they said they'd want to talk to you, too.'

'Oh - well, I guess they'll get in touch, if they want to.'

'Yeah, but… Karl - they know about Roddie's… sideline, they called it.'

'The drugs?'

'Yeah.'

'Oh…' He considered this before going on: 'How much do they actually *know*? I mean, they'll have gone into his background, they'll know what kind of bloke he was - it could be just a lucky guess. Maybe.'

'And maybe not! I think they *know,* Karl.'

'Yeah.' He gave in to her greater wisdom: 'They asked you about it?'

'In so many words! I told them I'd no idea about anything like that going on.'

'Good girl! That's got to be the best line to take.'

Elsa suddenly laughed, her blue eyes twinkling:

'The best thing is, though - they asked me if I thought he'd been doing it on the quiet, *under Gidding's nose!*' Her brother gave a snort of laughter himself:

'Really? They don't know everything, then, do they?'

* * *

Late that afternoon, with the cold Winter night closing in, the Jeep was back in Glebe Farm. Once again, the older woman answered their knock on the door:

'Oh, hello, Inspector, Sergeant. Come in - Lucy and Freya are just back from town.' She led them through into the comfortable living-room. Lucy Cavendish was just helping the little girl out of her heavy coat; she looked around as they entered:

'Hello! I'm sorry if we've kept you waiting - Muriel said you'd called this morning.'

'That's all right, Lucy. There are one or two things we need to clear up.' She studied his expression before turning to her daughter:

'Freya - take your coat and hang it up, there's a good girl. Then, why don't you take Granny Moo up to our room, and show her your new things?' The child looked from her mother to the two policemen, aware of an undercurrent she couldn't understand in the atmosphere. She turned her eyes back to Lucy as Mrs Hepple took her gently by the shoulders and guided her out of the room:

'Come on, darling - what's Mummy bought you while you were out?'

Once they were out of the room, Lucy turned to Russell again:

'What can I do for you, Inspector?' Russell drew a deep breath as he looked into the deep emerald eyes which were regarding him with a concerned curiosity:

'We'd like you to come down to the police station with us, if you would, Lucy. As I said, we have a few things we need to talk to you about, questions surrounding Roddie's death that we have to resolve.'

'Will this take long?'

'I'm afraid it could take a while. We need to check your fingerprints and DNA against certain evidence we have - for elimination, you understand. We'll get you a meal, later, if that becomes necessary, of course.'

'I see… Well, I suppose the sooner we go, the sooner it'll be done with.'

'That's fine, then - shall we go?'

'Let me just tell Freya and Muriel where I'm going?'

'Yes, of course - we'll wait outside.'

With a last, slightly worried glance she turned and hurried from the room. They heard her steps going up the stairs; Russell beckoned the Sergeant to follow him out of the front door. A few moments later, Lucy joined them; Rimmer took her by the arm in a gesture that could have been either chivalrous or restraining, and handed her into the back seat of the car.

Back at the station, they took her through the formality of booking her into custody, and had her fingerprints and a DNA sample taken by one of the Mad Professor's assistants. Throughout, Lucy had begun to realise that her fears were becoming reality - she'd felt from the moment she'd seen the two officers at the house that something was wrong, and now, they seemed to be virtually putting her under arrest, even if the word hadn't been mentioned. 'Helping the Police with their enquiries' - that was how they phrased it, wasn't it? As the custody sergeant went to lead her away, she turned to Russell:

'This is more than just a few simple questions you have, isn't it, Inspector?'

'It's… it *could* be rather more serious, Lucy. We'll tell you more, as soon as we have the results of the tests, I promise - we'll try not to leave you here for too long.'

She nodded, not knowing whether she could trust his assurances, but unable to do other than comply; she let the grey-haired sergeant lead her away, appreciating his sympathetic smile.

Inspector and Sergeant returned to Russell's office. Resuming his seat behind the desk, Russell picked up the phone, dialled the extension for the basement:

'Terry? David Russell. I need a match on those fingerprints as quickly as you can do it. I suppose the DNA will take a while?'

'Right-o! I'll get on them straight away, call you back in half an hour or so, okay? DNA'll have to go off to the lab, won't get an answer before Monday, if we're lucky.'

'Okay - I guess that'll have to do. But chase 'em, will you?'

'Sure, sure - leave it to me, Dave! Call you later, okay?'

'Thanks, Terry.'

Rimmer had perched, as usual, on the edge of the desk. The two men talked over the evidence against Lucy, getting things clear in their minds preparatory to interviewing her, until the telephone rang. Russell grabbed the receiver:

'Russell.'

'Hello, Dave - Terry Owen. It's a match, mate! All the prints on the gun match the ones you sent down a little while ago, no question of it. I'll get you a full analysis in due course, but for now, you can take it as read.'

'Right! Thanks, Terry.' He dropped the phone back on its rest, looked up at Rimmer and nodded:

'Prints on the gun are Lucy's, Doug.'

'Has to be hers, then. Even if she *was* wearing the gloves when she shot Roddie.' Russell nodded slowly:

'Yeah. Come on - let's go and see what she has to say.'

CHAPTER FIFTEEN

Lucy followed the two detectives in silence from the cell to the interview room. She had spent the last hour fretting quietly, wondering just what was really going on, trying to puzzle out what could have brought on the sudden heavy-handedness in their attitude to her. The situation she found herself in was disturbing enough - but the worst thing, she found, was the feeling that the things that were happening were out of her control, the really frightening element being that of not knowing, not understanding, what the police were thinking.

Now, she took the seat indicated at the table, opposite the two plain clothes men. The uniformed WPC - the same one, she realised, who had been with there the night Roddie died - stood at ease by the door, treating her to a quick, encouraging smile; one of the officers, the sergeant, placed a box-file on the table, the kind normally used for storing documents, and rested his hand on the top, as the Inspector snapped two tapes into the recording machine by the wall, and spoke into the microphone in front of him:

'Interview with Miss Lucy Cavendish, concerning the murder of Roderick McKeenan on November 27th. Present, Detective-Inspector Russell, Detective-Sergeant Rimmer, WPC Hallam. Interview commenced at' he glanced at his watch 'eighteen forty-one.' He turned to Lucy:

'Okay, Lucy - as I told you, we need to clarify a few points regarding your statement of the events of last Wednesday night. Or Thursday morning, to be accurate. Would you mind describing what you did for us again, from when you saw Roddie leave the downstairs bar in Sweeney's nightclub?'

She drew a deep breath, giving herself time to get her thoughts in order, and did as he asked, going over her actions once more, from their brief words in the corridor to the time she knelt beside her dead lover in the alleyway outside. She spoke clearly, carefully, trying to be accurate and not allow the anger she could feel rising in her to reach the surface. When she stopped speaking, the Sergeant opened the questioning:

'How long would you say you were in the toilet, before you heard the noises and ventured out?' She thought for a moment:

'A few minutes, three or four, maybe five at the most. No more, I'm sure.' He nodded:

'And no-one else was in there with you, during that time?'

'No - I've told you!' She could feel her temper rising again.

'You see, that's one of our problems, Lucy,' Russell told her: 'No-one can vouch for where you were, what you were doing, at the time Roddie was shot.'

She stared at him, momentarily incredulous: They couldn't be thinking - no, that would be utterly ridiculous! But Rimmer was talking to her again:

'Can we talk about Roddie for a minute?' She turned to him, nodded:

'If you want to?'

'He said to you that he was going outside to do some business?'

'That's right.'

'Have you any idea what that business might have been?'

'No, none.'

'Do you think, maybe, that could have been a ploy, a way of getting away from the argument you were having?' Although annoyed at the implication that he might have been trying to avoid her, she gave the idea some thought:

'No - I don't think so. But - I suppose, I can't be sure.'

'You knew all about Roddie's business?'

'The decorating? Of course!'

'What about any, er, sidelines?'

'Sidelines?' Rimmer glanced at his superior - she wasn't going to give anything away! He turned back to her as Russell took a turn:

'We have reason to think that Roddie had, shall we say, certain other interests, additional ways of making an income. Ways that might not have been entirely legal?'

She drew a breath again: They knew! About... What should she say? Nothing, her instincts told her:

'Not that I knew anything about, Inspector.' He gazed at her for a moment, then nodded:

'All right, Lucy.' She held his gaze, defiant despite the empty feeling in her stomach that told her he knew she was lying. Rimmer took up the questions again:

'Assuming he was going outside for a purpose, do you have any idea who he could have been expecting to meet, for this undefined business?' This time she could be honestly unhelpful:

'No, no idea.' Again, Russell interjected a comment:

'You see, that's another thing, Lucy. We can't find any trace of anyone else out in Butcher's Lane that night, around that time. So, if he was going out there for business, who was he going to do business with?' And again, their eyes met and held until she looked away, confused and worried about where this interview was going.

'You habitually wear gloves, when you're at work in the club?' Rimmer's sudden change of tack caught her off-guard:

'Yes, I do.'

'Why is that?'

'It's - because the customers like it. They like - the touch of class, I suppose you could call it.'

'By customers, you mean the men you accompany, in the bar, or on the dance floor?'

'Of course!' They knew, they had to know, about the other things that went on upstairs, away from prying eyes - but she wasn't going to give them the satisfaction… She expected them to pressure her on that subject, but instead, Rimmer asked:

'You keep spare pairs, at the club?' Again, she felt unsure of her ground:

'Yes - yes, in my locker.'

'That's in the changing room, off the corridor at the front of the building?'

'That's right - next to the ladies.'

'Did you have occasion to change your gloves that particular night?'

'No, I didn't.' She shook her head, more and more puzzled about where these questions were taking them. Rimmer went on:

'The gloves you were wearing that night…'

'I gave them to you!' She cut across him: 'With the rest of my clothes, the other day at the house!' He nodded, raising a hand to calm her outburst.

'Yes, we have that pair. But…' He lifted the lid of the boxfile, took out two clear plastic envelopes, each with a beige leather glove inside, laid them on the table in front of her:

'Do you recognise these gloves, Lucy?' She leant forward, looking closely. 'You can pick them up, if it would help' he went on. He restrained the instinct to give Russell a significant glance when she reached forward to the envelopes - with her left hand.

'They *look* like mine - the same style…' she peered at the label: 'Same brand, same colour.'

'They're yours, you think?' She raised her eyes to his, aware of his choice of words, and corrected him:

'They *could* be mine. But I'm sure I'm not the only person who wears that style and colour, Sergeant.' He smiled, dipped his head briefly in acknowledgement of her insistence on careful accuracy:

'They *could* be yours?' She nodded, smiled back:

110

'That's right, Sergeant.'

Rimmer sat back, allowing the silence to draw out for a moment. This was a very clever woman! She was giving them nothing, fencing with them at every turn, her attitude and self-possession was only serving to convince him more strongly that she was the one who had shot down Roddie McKeenan, and then covered her tracks as best she could on the spur of the moment.

'Where did this pair come from?' She finally broke the silence. Russell tapped the bags:

'These were found in the ladies toilet. In the waste bin.' She looked at him, dumbfounded:

'What were they doing there?'

'That's what we need to know, Lucy.'

'Would *you* know? Had you thrown a pair away, maybe, that evening?' Rimmer asked her. She shook her head:

'No - they're far too expensive to chuck them out just because they're a bit grubby! And...' She turned them over again: 'There's nothing else wrong with these. I didn't throw them away, I can assure you!'

'You're naturally left-handed?' The apparently innocuous question took her by surprise:

'I am. So's Freya - it must run in our family!'

'You own a gun, Lucy.' This time, the Inspector's quiet words threw her completely. She stared at him, her mouth open in surprise, sat slowly back in her seat, her mind in a whirl of confusion. It hadn't been a question, more a statement that he was asking her to confirm; she leant forward, her elbows on the table, aware that anything less than the truth now was going to get her in pretty deep:

'Listen, Mr Russell...' She paused, knowing she was about to wreck her own career, possibly even get herself hauled up in front of a magistrate, or worse:

'You know, you *must* know, I'm sure, that my job at Sweeney's involves... more than just sitting with the clients and chatting to them? You know… the other things we offer. Up on the top floor, right?' He just nodded, unwilling to interrupt her frankness; she went on:

'One night, a couple of years ago, I had a client who… wanted things I wasn't prepared to go along with. He started to get rough when I said no - turned out to be a really sadistic son-of-a-bitch, knocked me about quite a bit before I could knock the telephone off its hook. I knew that would alert the boys down at the desk, if the light came up with no-one on the line. But by the time Joe had got up to the room, he'd… hurt me quite badly. I needed a good few weeks to get over it; and then, Roddie got me a little gun, told me I should carry it with me, to protect myself, if anything like it ever happened again.'

'What sort of gun is it, Lucy?'

'Oh, little pistol kind of thing. A… a Walther, is that it?'

'And what happened to the man who attacked you?'

'Joe and Bruce threw him out, told him not to come back.'

'This incident wasn't reported to us?' She turned to Rimmer at his question; the irony in her voice was unmistakable as she replied:

'No, Sergeant!'

'Where's that gun now, Lucy?' Again, Russell's quiet voice drew her attention:

'In my locker, at the club, I imagine. I didn't feel happy, carrying it around - and it was there, if anywhere, I might need it, so I always kept it there, in a little fancy handbag. I'd generally slip in there, grab it before I went upstairs with clients - at least, the ones I didn't know.'

'*This* bag, Lucy?' Rimmer lifted it, too from the box, placed it down in front of her. She reached out, touched it:

'Yes… yes!' She raised eyes wide with incomprehension, looked from him to the Inspector. Russell nodded, gestured towards the box in front of his Sergeant. Rimmer took out another evidence bag, laid it down on the table in front of the girl. Its solid clunk against the wood seemed to echo in the silence; she gazed down at it, raised her eyes again to Russell's, fear beginning to overlay her uncertainty:

'It is yours, Lucy?'

'It looks like it - but... I wouldn't be certain it is, no.'

'This gun is covered in your fingerprints, Lucy.' She looked into his eyes without speaking as he went on:

'Given that, would you accept that this *is* your gun?'

'I... I suppose so.'

'This was found in the bin, in the ladies toilet. With those gloves. And the hand-bag.' She held his gaze, incredulous, and suddenly, really scared.

'And, Lucy, this gun was used to kill Roddie McKeenan.'

'No... It can't be!' Her eyes flicked from his to Rimmer's, then back to the steady, hazel stare which seemed to accuse her:

'You think... You think *I* shot him?' Suddenly, she was on her feet, shouting down at him:

'You must be crazy! How can you be so bloody stupid? I *loved* him, I wanted him to give up that crazy idea of going away and leaving us, I wanted him *back,* can't you understand that? The last thing I would have done is *kill* him!'

The WPC had come forward, gently but irresistibly urging her back into her seat. Rimmer spoke:

'Perhaps you did want him back - but perhaps he wasn't listening. Perhaps you lost your temper with him?' She stared at him for a moment, then slumped forward, shaking her head as she buried her face in her hands, sobbing with rage and frustration. Then she raised her head again, auburn hair dishevelled, emerald eyes tear-stained:

'Mr Russell - I think I need a lawyer, don't I? I won't talk to you again until I can speak to my solicitor.' He nodded, turned away and spoke for the tape machine:

'Interview terminated at nineteen twenty-nine.'

CHAPTER SIXTEEN

Outside the interview room, Russell turned to Lucy. The expression on the girl's lovely face was one of shock and disbelief, sufficient to give him another twinge of the recurrent doubt he still felt about her guilt:

'You have your own solicitor?' She nodded distractedly, pulling her thoughts together:

'Yes - Alison Greening, of Weaver, Adams and Barrie. In Northampton.'

'You have her number?'

'I think so - yes, in the diary, in my handbag. But it's only the office…'

He turned to the WPC:

'Faith - will you take Lucy to the phone, see if you can track down Miss Greening for her? There may be an out-of-hours number on their answering machine. And let her call Mrs Hepple - she'll want to talk to her daughter, I'm sure.'

There was a gleam of gratitude in the look the distressed girl gave him at this.

Faith took her charge gently by the shoulder, led her off towards the custody office and the telephone. Russell stood and watched them go, lost in his own thoughts until Rimmer spoke:

'She did it, boss. No question.' The Inspector gazed at him distractedly for a moment:

'Get off home to Julie, Doug. I'll see you in the morning, okay?

And give her my apologies for keeping you so late on a Saturday night.'

'Are you going to charge her?'

'Maybe in the morning. I want to talk to the Super first.'

'Okay boss. See you then.'

''Night, Doug.'

* * *

David Russell could feel the tension in the air as soon as he walked into the house that evening: *Oh no - now what?* Sarah was playing contentedly on the carpet in the living-room with her Barbie dolls, but he only needed one look at the way Daniel was slumped in the easy chair, gazing grumpily at a television drama he would normally not have bothered with, to know that something was awry.

'Daddy!' Sarah leapt to her feet, rushed to give him a hug: 'Can you come and play with me? Ken's going to be a p'liceman, jus' like you!' He laughed, gently disengaging her arms from around his legs:

'Maybe in a little while, sweetheart. I'm ever so hungry now - is Mummy getting my dinner ready?' The little girl nodded:

'She's in the kitchen. You promise?'

'I promise! When I've had my dinner, and a bit of a rest, all right?'

'All right, Daddy.' She went back to her game; Russell went across the room, put a hand on his son's shoulder:

'Hi, Daniel.' The boy looked up, his smile half-hearted:

'Hello, Dad.' Russell squatted on the arm of the chair:

'So what's wrong?' The slump of his son's shoulders was infinitesimal, but told Russell he'd been right to expect trouble.

'I lost my phone today.'

'*Lost* it?' Anger and guilt flared together in the boy's eyes:

'Yeah, I know! How could I be so bloody stupid!'

'Mum given you a hard time, has she?' Russell felt his own

annoyance at this revelation tempered by amusement - he could imagine what Tracy's reaction had been! Daniel looked up at his father again, and the hurt and anger in his eyes softened at the sight of Russell's grin:

'You could say that, yeah.' Russell clapped him on the shoulder a couple of times:

'These things happen, Dan. It's a nuisance, if only because we'll have to get you a new one, but we'll get over it.' He nearly laughed out loud at the relief on the boy's face. Daniel returned his grin:

'Thanks, Dad! And - I'm sorry, really.'

'You'd best tell you mother that, hadn't you?' Daniel's grin turned rueful:

'Yeah, perhaps I should. But… she always gets so mad at me, and…'

'I know - instinctive self-defence, right?'

'Something like that, I guess.'

They sat in companionable silence for a minute or so, until the door swung open:

'Davey - I thought I heard you come in.' Russell got to his feet, slipped his arm around his wife's waist and gave her a quick kiss:

'Hello, Darling - sorry I'm so late again.'

'You still on that murder case, Dad?' Daniel asked from the depths of the armchair.

'Yes - you been following it on the news today?' The boy turned in his seat:

'Yeah - they said you'd arrested someone, the girlfriend, yes?'

'Not quite - she's…'

''Helping with your enquiries', right?' Daniel interrupted. Russell laughed:

'Right!'

'Did she do it?' Russell heaved a sigh:

'All the evidence points that way.'

Tracy had been following this exchange with mounting annoyance. Now, she interjected:

'Danny told you about *our* little crime, did he?'

'Crime?' Russell sounded puzzled.

'He had his phone stolen this afternoon.'

'You didn't say it was stolen, Dan?'

'I'm not certain it was, Dad.'

'Oh, come on, Danny! It disappears from your pocket in that damned amusement arcade, and you don't call that theft?' Russell drew a deep breath before asking:

'What happened, then?'

'Daniel?' Tracy prompted when the boy didn't answer immediately.

'We were at a loose end this afternoon, so we went down the GPS...'

'We?'

'Me, Snow and Jacko.' Russell resisted an impulse to correct his son's grammar:

'And?'

'Well - sometime while we were there, I realised my phone was gone. It'd been there before we went, 'cause I'd called Mum to tell her where we were.' Russell raised his eyes questioningly to his wife:

'I was out shopping, with Sarah. The boys were all here, when I left.' He turned back to Daniel:

'Did you tell anyone?'

'Yeah - I told the manager there. He said they'd had it happen once or twice before, they didn't know who was doing it. He said there wasn't much he could do - I suppose he's right, really.'

'Did he call the police?'

'He said they'd reported the other ones, he'd let them know it'd happened again.'

'Okay - I suppose that's about all he could do. I'll ask what's happening about it tomorrow.'

'Tomorrow? You have to go in, Davey?' Tracy sounded disappointed.

'I'm afraid so, love. We've only got until early Monday to question the girl over the murder, so I need to get on with it.' She shrugged, resignedly:

'The perils of being a copper!'

'Yes, love. I'm sorry.' He kissed her cheek again. She smiled into his eyes for a moment, but then returned to the previous subject of discussion:

'This amusement arcade?'

'The Play Station?'

'Yes - I've said to Daniel before, I don't like them going there, love. There's too many nasty characters hang around places like that, aren't there?' He held her at arms length, gazing into her troubled brown eyes, and replied cautiously:

'They do tend to attract undesirable elements, for sure.'

'Will you tell him not to go there? He won't listen to me!' He frowned, feeling an uncharacteristic anger at her words: *Do you have to put me on the spot like that?* Caught between his wife and his son, whatever he said was going to make matters worse rather than better. *Damn it, Tracy!*

He looked down at Daniel, seeing the appeal in his eyes:

'Your mother's right, you know that, don't you, Dan? There are people who hang around there that we'd rather you didn't mix with, you can understand that.' His hope for a voluntary agreement were dashed by the boy's next words:

'But we *don't* mix with them, Dad! We just go to play on the computer games - it's about the only place worth going in town!' Russell couldn't help heaving a deep sigh before replying:

'I don't think you should go there, if your mother doesn't want you to.'

'But, Dad...!'

'Listen to your father, Daniel!' *For Heaven's sake, Tracy!* Russell felt that surge of anger again, wishing his wife would leave him to deal with things.

'Daniel?' The boy looked at him for a moment, then dropped his eyes:

'All *right*, Dad! I'll tell the others we can't go there any more.' Russell felt a sudden urge to apologise to his son, but knew that would only fragment the family's relationships even further. Tracy stretched up to kiss his cheek:

'I've got a couple of pork chops under the grill for you - chips and peas, okay?' He smiled down at her:

'That'll do fine, love.'

He allowed her to lead him from the room into the kitchen, aware of the anger and disappointment in the hazel eyes that followed him.

CHAPTER SEVENTEEN

'What time do you have to go in, love?'

David Russell had been relieved to find the atmosphere over breakfast somewhat less frosty. They were all sitting around the kitchen table, Radio 2's 'Sunday Love Song' programme playing quietly in the background. He replied to Tracy's question:

'I said I'd meet Doug there about ten.'

'Do *you* think his girlfriend killed him, Dad?' Daniel raised his eyes from his bowl of cereal. Russell looked across the table at his son, struck again by the boy's astuteness - he'd noticed, even with his other worries, his father's choice of phrase the previous evening.

'I'm not sure, Dan. The evidence all points to her, but I'm not completely happy about it.' He sat in thought for a moment, aware that something else had been affecting his thoughts about the case before Tracy had spoken. His mind ran back; and then he had it:

'Did you notice the song they were playing just now? There was a line there...' He tried to recall the words: 'Something like 'why should anyone take notice of another love that failed'?' Daniel nodded, puzzled; Russell went on:

'Well, that kind of sums up how I feel about this case. I can't help the idea that that's what I'm *supposed* to think, that she shot him a jealous rage. You understand?' The boy nodded again:

'Like it's too easy?'

'Not exactly, but that's getting close.' He glanced at his watch, drained off the last of his coffee and got to his feet: 'I'd better go - I'll see you all later.'

''Bye, Dad.'

''Bye, son. 'Bye-bye, Sarah.' He bent to kiss his daughter; she gave him a quick hug:

'Bye-bye, Daddy.'

He gave Tracy a quick peck on the cheek:

'Can you take Daniel into town, get him a new phone? I think that place in Midland Road is open Sundays.' He sensed another pointed remark coming as she opened her mouth; but she caught the look in his eyes, smiled as she held it back:

'Yes, okay, love. We'll go down as soon as I've washed up, all right, Daniel?'

'Okay - thanks, Mum.' Russell treated them all to a last wave and went out to the car.

On the way into town, he mulled over his feelings about Lucy. Everything he could prove said unequivocally that she *had* killed Roddie, but still, he was not content. Instinct? Intuition? Or, as he'd said jokingly to the Mad Professor, was he really being swayed by the girl's undeniable beauty, taken in by her skilful dissembling? Today, he had to make up his mind, charge her, or release her. In the face of the evidence they held, there wasn't a choice...

As he turned into the station car park, his thoughts returned to last night's tension in his family. He felt again the annoyance with Tracy, that she'd forced him into being the heavy-handed father; but then, she'd been right, he too would be easier in his mind if their son wasn't hanging around a place where people of doubtful character were to be found - like pick-pockets! He couldn't really blame her; if only Daniel had been a bit more careful, kept his phone out of sight... Things had seemed to be back to normal this morning; But, he thought with a sinking heart, for how long? What would be the next thing to cause a row between his wife and his son?

Doug Rimmer entered his superior's office a bit after ten o'clock, to find him sitting morosely behind his desk. Russell looked up at his Sergeant's cheerful greeting:

'Hi, Doug.'

'You all right, boss?' Russell grinned:

'Yeah - sorry! Tracy and Daniel had another bust-up yesterday - he went to the Play Station, you know, the amusement arcade in Market Street? Someone lifted his phone from his pocket.'

'No kidding? Poor kid - I bet he was pissed off!'

'Yeah - and then, of course, his mother had a go at him. You can guess the rest!' Rimmer nodded sympathetically:

'There're times I'm glad Julie and I decided not to have kids, not yet, at least.'

'More trouble than they're worth!' Rimmer gave him a canny look:

'You don't mean that!' Russell laughed, shook his head:

'Of course not! I love them both to bits - but I could do without this frosty atmosphere in the house when I get home from here, sometimes.'

'Sure, I understand. What's the programme for today?' Rimmer changed the subject.

'I'd like you to interview Lucy again, Doug. Grab a WPC from somewhere - did they get hold of her lawyer, do you know?'

'Not sure - I'll go and find out, set up an interview for what ever time the woman can get here, shall I?'

'Okay. If they didn't get hold of her, call in the duty brief, right? We need to get on with this.'

'Are we going to charge her?' Russell drew a deep breath, let it out through his teeth:

'I can't see any option there. See what else you can get out of her, let her see how strong the case against her is, maybe she'll give in and admit it. I'm going to talk to Mr Wilson.'

'He's in?'

'I called him from home, said I needed to see him. He should be on his way.'

'Right - I'll get started, then.'

'Okay, Doug - call me if anything develops.'

'I will, don't worry!'

* * *

Detective-Superintendent Harry Wilson stepped out of the lift, walked across the corridor and tapped on Russell's office door. He pushed it open, caught the swing of his senior Inspector's ankles from the corner of his desk down to the floor:

'Morning, David - you wanted to see me?'

'Good morning, sir. I'm sorry to bother you on a Sunday, but I wanted to talk to you about the McKeenan case.'

'You've brought the girlfriend in, I understand?'

'Yes, sir. Last night.'

'Got enough to charge her?'

'More than enough, on the face of it.'

'So where's your problem?' Russell chose his words carefully:

'I'm not happy that I know enough about the background to the case, sir. We've never explained the drugs in Roddie's flat, for one thing. And he's led a pretty mixed life, before coming here - I'd like to know more about his background, too.'

'But if she shot him, how important is all that?'

'I'm… not sure, sir. I think we might be missing something, there could be more to his death than we're seeing.'

'You think she might *not* have done it?' Wilson sounded almost incredulous.

'I just want to be certain, sir.'

'Not falling for a pretty face, are you? She's quite a cracker, if the picture in today's Grancester on Sunday's anything to go by!'

'She's all of that, sir!' Russell couldn't help the amusement in

123

his eyes, that the staid senior officer would read the local tabloid. Wilson caught his expression:

'Don't take it, you understand - gets stuffed through our door whether we want it or not, like all these freebies.'

'Yes, sir, of course. But no, as I said, I'm just not entirely happy; I have a feeling that it's possible we're being manipulated, somehow. Given an easy answer, when the truth's far more complex.'

'Hmm. So - what do you want to do?'

'I think we'll have to charge her, the evidence is too strong to do anything else - and if there *is* any more behind it, that'll maybe make people relax, get careless. But I want your permission to go on digging, at least for a while.'

'Hmm. Does Sweeney's figure in your doubts, David?'

'To a degree, yes. It's my belief that Roddie was passing drugs there, in a quiet way so as not to arouse Gidding's suspicions. Possibly in collusion with someone who worked there. He was there three, four nights, most weeks, so it's the obvious conclusion.'

'Which someone - Lucy?'

'That has to be a possibility. Doug and I had wondered about Duffy, the bar manager - he would be in the best position, maybe, to keep things quiet.'

'You could be right.' Wilson considered for a few seconds: 'All right, David. Keep digging, if you want to - but try not to drag it out too long, right? We've got plenty more on our plates, as always!'

'Thank you, sir. I'll try to bring it to a conclusion as soon as I can.'

'Mm. Okay - I'll see you tomorrow. Supposed to be playing golf with some damned bigwig from local industry this afternoon.'

Russell smiled at the CID chief's pretended grumpiness as he stood up to open the door for him - Wilson's love of his golf was well known throughout the station.

'Goodbye, sir - thank you for coming in.'

* * *

In the ground floor interview room, Rimmer was just beginning the second session with Lucy Cavendish. The girl had spent a disturbed night in the cell, sleeping in short snatches, when her sheer exhaustion overcame the turmoil in her mind. The policewoman had helped her to get in touch with Miss Greening, after a number of calls; the solicitor had been calmly reassuring over the telephone, had promised to contact the police and attend any further interviews. She had spoken to Muriel Hepple, and listened to the woman's outrage that they could even think she might have killed Roddie; she had tried her best to calm Freya's fear, telling her daughter that she would be home soon, in spite of her own doubts, in spite of the pain and sadness that swelled in her heart at the sound of the little girl's tears.

Now, she sat at the table once more, facing the Sergeant. A different WPC stood by the door; but now, she had the reassuring presence of Alison Greening at her side. The solicitor was a large, buxom woman in her thirties, smart as always in a dark grey business suit and pale green silk blouse; now, she somehow managed to radiate a sort of calm solidity, helping Lucy to hang on to her temper as well as easing her horror as the plain clothes officer made point after point, bringing out just how much evidence they had against her. She found herself giving in to a kind of helpless frustration - how could this be happening? With each point he made, she could feel her control gradually slipping; there was a kind of horrible inevitability about it, each separate piece of evidence he brought out adding to the monstrously impossible conclusion that she had to have murdered Roddie, until she began to question her own sanity, to wonder if, indeed, she had killed him, and somehow obliterated the memory...

Suddenly, she was weeping, her hands over her face, on the

verge of a total breakdown. Rimmer stopped mid-sentence, as she felt Alison's reassuring hand on her arm:

'Interview halted at eleven fourteen, to allow Miss Cavendish to recover herself.' She heard the sympathy behind the hard edge of his voice. Alison spoke:

'Could I have a few moments with my client, Sergeant?'

'Of course. We'll wait outside.' He gestured the WPC to precede him, and closed the door on them.

'Lucy?' She took the proffered handkerchief, dried her eyes:

'I'm sorry - but…' she shook her head in helpless disbelief, unable to put her feelings into words. She felt her anger rising again, but held it in check as the other woman put an arm about her shoulder, asked calmly:

'There is only one important question here, Lucy. I have to ask, you understand?' She nodded, not needing the words to be spoken, looked around at the solicitor, more tears running down her cheeks:

'I didn't kill him! I don't understand how they can have so much that… But I *didn't!* You've got to believe me!' Alison nodded:

'I believe you. You have to trust me, Lucy? If you're innocent, there will be a way we can prove it, whatever evidence they have. There is another solution which will explain all that - all we have to do is find it, all right?' She nodded, dabbing at her eyes again:

'Right. But…'

'No buts, Lucy! We can do it. If a bunch of Mr Plods can come to a wrong conclusion, then us clever ones can come to the right one, can't we?' She was rewarded with a brief smile, a nod:

'Sure we can!'

'Are you all right to go on now?' Another nod; the solicitor got to her feet, put her head out of the door:

'Sergeant? We're ready now.'

CHAPTER EIGHTEEN

It was nearly half past twelve when Rimmer returned to his superior's office, kicking the door open with his foot so as not to spill the mug of coffee he held in each hand. Russell looked up from the stack of reports on his desk:

'How'd it go, Doug?' Rimmer shrugged as he took his habitual perch on a corner of the desk:

'She didn't give me anything, boss.'

'You laid it on the line?'

'Yeah. You know, I almost feel sorry for the girl - she broke down at one point, we had to take a break, let her get over it. If she'd just give in, admit she killed him - they could go for diminished responsibility, couldn't they?'

'Mmm - maybe. But she held out, admitted nothing?'

'Not a thing.'

Russell sat in thought for a minute or so, while Rimmer sipped his too-hot coffee. He tapped the reports in front of him:

'I've just been going through these. All the statements and interviews with the people who were there, from Strongarm's list of the customers.'

'What've you got, anything useful?'

'Well, there are five - no, six - who admit having gone out either into Butcher's Lane or the corridor when they realised something had happened. All from the lower bar; one of them's the guy the other hostess, Elsa, was sitting with just before. They all confirm the same sequence of events, and of course he effectively alibi's her. And this one' he waved a sheet of typescript 'is the man who was in the loo with Stevens.'

'He tells the same story?'

'Yeah, pretty much. He noticed the voices outside the door, but obviously didn't know who they were. The only slightly odd thing…' he paused, thoughtfully: 'He says he *thought* the sound of the door slamming, which Stevens told us about, came from the ladies, next door. Stevens himself, if you recall, said it was the outside door, the one into the alley.'

'Stevens would know the place better - his reaction has to be more likely to be right, surely?'

'You'd think so - but if this guy's right, it might tend to support Lucy's story - suppose he heard *her* slam the door of the ladies behind her?' Rimmer stared down at the Inspector in disbelief:

'Come off it, boss! We've got a solid case against her, there's no way she didn't do it - you can't be trying to tell me we've got it wrong!'

Russell didn't reply immediately. He sat back in his chair, his chin in his hand, elbow propped on the arm. The Sergeant was still staring at him in amazement when he raised his eyes again. He grinned, shook his head:

'I'm just… not entirely happy, Doug. Mr Wilson's given me permission to keep on digging, for a while at least. I'd like to know more about Roddie, his past, his background; and I want to know about those drugs in his flat. *Was* he selling at Sweeney's? Did Duffy - or anyone else, come to that - know about it? Are they all acting cagey because they *knew* he was pushing under Gidding's nose?'

'Is it important?'

'*I* think so, Doug.' Rimmer's dismissiveness had annoyed him: 'It's… all *background,* to the crime.'

It was Rimmer's turn to think before opening his mouth. He could not conceive why, given the weight of evidence, the Inspector might remotely doubt the girl's guilt, and he found his own annoyance growing - he didn't want to spend hours or days on a wild-goose-chase which would only prove to be wasted effort in the end, when she was convicted. But - Russell's habit of keeping all the options open was well known, and he didn't want to risk falling out with a man he held, otherwise, in considerable respect. The angry retort which had been rising to his lips gave way to diplomacy and logic:

'Yeah, I can see that, boss. But - is it remotely *possible* that anyone else could have killed him?'

'I don't know, Doug. We have to rule out the idea of someone escaping from the scene other than through the club, because of the gun and the gloves. And both the bouncers, and the hat-check girl, say that no-one left by the front entrance during the relevant times.'

'So our killer had to be among the people inside, when our boys arrived?'

'Seems so. And there are only three out of all the list that have proved to be completely false, untraceable. All the others, we've got statements from over the last few days.'

'One of those three, then?' Russell shook his head:

'No. I've checked the descriptions - all male, none of them could have worn Lucy's gloves.'

'It had to be a girl, because of the size of those gloves, didn't it?'

'I'd assume so.'

'So - did any of the girls interviewed have the opportunity to have shot him - leaving aside motive and the like?' Russell shook his head again:

'Not that I can see, Doug. The other hostesses were all talking with various people at the times we're interested in, they're all alibi'd by someone, and in full view. Among the customers, the girls all seem to have been in groups...'

'No surprise, in a place like that!' Rimmer interjected.

'...and not a one of them is unaccounted for.'

'So?' Russell shrugged:

'Yeah, I know! We come back to Lucy, every time. But… It doesn't *feel* right, Doug. If what people have said about her character, about how her temper works… If she killed him, she had to have gone, after their row in the corridor, got the bag with the gun from her locker, and a spare pair of gloves, then followed him outside. That suggests a kind of cold, calculated act, which doesn't fit. A planned act, a formulated cover-up - it's not how I can see her reacting.'

Rimmer thought for a moment:

'Hold on - by her own admission, she'd been 'upstairs' with a client, shortly beforehand, right?'

'Right…'

'Suppose - we can assume, I think, that she wasn't on the dance floor, but in one of the top floor rooms getting laid, yeah?'

'Right! I see what you're thinking, Doug: She would have had her bag, with the gun inside, with her…'

'And, she seems like the kind of girl who goes prepared - did she carry a spare pair of gloves in the same bag, do you think?'

'Likely, I'd say. So, if she hadn't returned the bag to her locker…'

'She had the gun, and spare gloves, with her. *Now,* it fits, doesn't it? They row, she follows him in a blind fury, shoots him in a temper when he won't talk to her any more - and then, runs back inside, dumps the gun and gloves in the bin, pulls on the clean pair, emerges with her act of innocent grief!'

Russell sat back, ran both hands through his sandy hair. He looked up at the Sergeant, perched triumphally on the edge of the desk:

'You're quite right, Doug. If we look at things that way, it adds up. Even her disposal of the evidence fits with the way people say her temper cools as quickly as it rises. She comes down to reality, sees what she's done, covers her tracks the best way she can on the spur of the moment.'

'I reckon so, boss.' Russell nodded:

'I should have seen it that way, thought of the possibility she had the bag with her.' He grinned, went on: 'I'm not at my best, Doug! This business at home is niggling at me, stopping me focussing the way I ought to. But, I'd still like to know more about Roddie, and his shadier activities. You never know, we might be close to uncovering something interesting - it would be good if we could pin down his source, maybe put a supplier or two behind bars on the back of this investigation, wouldn't it?'

'Sure would! Do you want me to call the drugs team at HQ, tomorrow?'

'No, let's follow this along on our own, for now. We've already asked them if they know of anyone who might have been the source, I take it?'

'Yeah - couple of names, but they don't seem likely. And nothing from any of our lads informants, which is unusual. Almost as if he was getting his supply from outside the area, somehow.'

'That's possible, isn't it? But he didn't travel much, did he?'

'Only locally, around his customers - the legitimate ones, that is!'

'We can try another look at his associates, see if any of them might have been acting as a courier, perhaps.'

'Right. Steve Campbell's still on the trail of his background, I'll get him on this line in the morning, tell him to focus on the drugs angle.'

'Okay. How far has he gone back, do you know?'

'How do you mean?'

'I'm wondering about Roddie's time before he came over to England.'

'Doubt if Steve's gone that far back. Do you want him to call the Ulster police, see if they know him?'

'Yes, you never know, maybe he had form over there. Although, I suppose he was only a teenager then?'

'He's been over here about ten years, so yes, that would make him nineteen, twenty maybe, when he left. Old enough to have a record, though.'

'Especially in Northern Ireland, if he'd had anything to do with the troubles! Was he partisan about all that, do we know?'

'I'm not sure - I'll ask Steve, tomorrow.'

'That's fine, Doug. Right now, let's go and charge Lucy - is Miss Greening still on the premises, do you know?'

'Probably - she was still with her in the interview room when I came up here.'

'Come on, then. Let's go and get it over with.'

CHAPTER NINETEEN

Little more than half an hour later, David Russell climbed into the Jeep to go home. The greyness of the morning had finally broken; a clear, ice-blue sky was flecked with an occasional cloud, allowing the chill sparkle of the Winter sun to brighten the skyline. With a bit of luck, he'd just about make it for Sunday dinner!

But at the exit from the Police Station car park, he hesitated, and then turned the other way, towards the town and away from the village where Tracy and the children would be waiting for him. Twenty minutes later, he was in Glebe Farm.

'Inspector Russell - come in.' Muriel Hepple opened the door at his knock; her tone was less than welcoming, but he followed her into the lounge, remained standing as she turned to face him:

'Mrs Hepple - I mustn't stop, but I wanted to talk to you.'

'What is it, Inspector?' But before he could reply, the hall door burst open again and the little girl dashed in, stopped, looking up at him:

'Where's my Mummy - is she coming home?' The light of hope in her eyes belied the redness of sorrow around them; Russell's heart went out to the child as he shook his head, squatted down to bring himself to her level:

'I'm sorry, Freya - not just yet, I'm afraid.'

'What is it, Inspector?' The woman's tone was guarded as she repeated her question; he looked up to her from where he faced Lucy's daughter:

'I wanted to tell you myself - I didn't want you both to see it on the news, or somewhere. We've charged Lucy with Roddie's murder.'

'*What?* You must be *insane!* You can't possibly imagine that girl could kill the man she loved!' Freya just gazed at him, eyes wide, mouth open, as Muriel Hepple's outburst poured down upon his head. He spoke to the child:

'Freya - I want you to know, I haven't stopped trying to find out all about what happened to Roddie. There are things I still don't know - and it's my job, as a policeman, to find out the *truth,* do you understand?' The blonde head nodded uncertainly; he went on: 'But, you have to understand, as well, that sometimes people do things, when they're angry, or upset, that they wouldn't do normally, that they'd be very sorry for, later...' She was shaking her head, a reflection of her mother's temper growing in her eyes until she interrupted him:

'Not my Mummy! She wouldn't... She'd never hurt anyone! You're wrong! You're stupid!'

'Freya...' He reached out, to try to comfort her.

'Don't touch me! I hate you!' She turned and ran from the room; they heard her feet clatter up the stairs, into the room she shared with her mother, the muffled thump as she threw herself onto the bed. Russell got to his feet, to find Muriel holding him in a hard stare. He shook his head, reluctant to meet her gaze:

'I'm so sorry, especially for her' he gestured to the room above 'but I have to do my job, whatever the consequences.'

There was an uncomfortable silence, until the woman gave a sigh:

'I know - but she's right, you know? Lucy didn't kill him. I don't know what happened, what makes you think she did, but you *are* wrong.'

'As I told Freya - I am still investigating Roddie's death, and the circumstances around it. And it wouldn't worry me to admit a mistake, if we were to show that someone else killed him; but you have to understand, we have a lot of evidence, both scientific and circumstantial, which points to Lucy having done it. I can't tell you what that is - but I *can* tell you that we haven't been able to identify *anyone* else who could have shot him.' Muriel pursed her lips, shook her head:

'But, *someone else did!* I know Lucy better than anyone, I would think - and I'm telling you, she didn't kill him! Now, I'd better go and see to Freya, make sure she's all right. If you'll excuse me?'

'Mrs Hepple - a quick question, I won't keep you: You knew Roddie pretty well, too?'

'I think I did, yes.'

'Did you know he was selling drugs?' This brought her up short; she drew a deep breath before replying thoughtfully:

'No, I didn't. You're *telling* me he was?'

'There's no doubt of it. Probably at the nightclub, although we can't be certain of that, yet.'

'Well! I suppose, it was the sort of thing he wouldn't want us to know about - me, or Freya, anyway. Did Lucy know?'

'We think it's likely, although we haven't questioned her about it yet.'

'I see. But, surely - *that* would be why someone killed him - some kind of fight over that?'

'Possibly - if we could find someone else who had the *opportunity* to have shot him, when and where it happened.' She held his eyes for a moment:

'Trust me, Inspector - *someone else* did just that! Now, I must go to Freya.'

'One more thing, quickly, if I may?'

'Quickly, please!'

'Roddie was Catholic, wasn't he?'

'That's correct.'

'Did he ever express any opinions about the conflict in Northern Ireland - was he partisan about all that?' She laughed:

'No, not at all! He always said that that was why he came to England, to get away from what he called all that sectarian nonsense. If it was mentioned on the news, he'd just mutter about 'bloody idiots, all of them'!'

'I see, thank you. I'll let myself out, Mrs Hepple.'

She turned at the bottom of the stairs, as he went to the front door:

'I appreciate you coming to tell us, about Lucy, Inspector.' He nodded, stepped out into the cold, bright afternoon as she went up in the direction of the little girl's quiet sobbing.

* * *

'Davey! Just in time to carve!' Tracy Russell looked up from the dining table as her husband stepped into the room from the hallway of Old Laundry Cottage. He raised his eyes at the five places set; she laughed:

'Becky's up with Sarah, playing - I said we'd give her dinner.'

'Where's Daniel?'

'He's in his own room, finding out how to work his new phone.'

'You got him one all right, then?'

'Yes - that shop you said about *was* open. He's over the moon; we got the latest model with all kinds of fancy gadgets on it. I wouldn't know what to do with most of them!' Russell laughed:

'Nor me - I can just about make phone calls with mine!'

He followed her into the kitchen, set about carving the joint of beef while she dished up the vegetables. Carrying the plates through, he called up the stairs:

'Dan! Sarah! Becky! Dinner's on the table!'

The thunder which followed would have done justice to a herd of wildebeest on the plains, as one teenager, one four-year-old and one almost-five-year-old tumbled into the room.

* * *

That evening, with the dark of the Winter night shrouding the village, David Russell and his son sat, as they often did of a Sunday night, on opposite sides of the old desk in the study. The two little girls had returned to Sarah's room, going back to their game; Tracy sat watching the Antiques Roadshow in the lounge.

The old desk, an antique itself, was covered with an old sheet. On one side, Daniel was stripping out the radio control unit from the 'Flying Dragon', preparatory to fitting it with the latest, fastest-responding version he could afford; on the other, his father was sanding down the hull of the 'Saint Valentine' ready for a fresh coat of varnish. As he worked, Russell spoke, without looking up:

'Dan?'

'Mm?'

'Pleased with your new phone?'

'Yeah! It's brilliant!'

'Can you make it do all things it's supposed to?'

'Yeah, just about!'

'That's good.'

A pause, then:

'Dad?'

'Yeah?'

'I feel... really rotten, you know?'

'Why's that?' He looked up, into the boy's troubled gaze.

'Well... I had such a row with Mum, when the other one got pinched - but now, she's gone and spent all this money, got me the best one in the shop. I... thought she'd just buy me a kind of basic one, you know? But...' He shrugged. Russell nodded, smiled at his son:

'I know. However it seems sometimes, she *does* love you, you know? We both do. And... maybe, she's just as upset about your row as you are, had you thought of that? Perhaps, if you said to her what you've just told me, it might help make things better, mightn't it?'

'Yeah - p'raps you're right. I'll try it!'

The silence felt rather easier, for the next little while. Russell spoke again:

'Dan?'

'Mm?'

'You ever thought about trying sailing - properly, I mean?'

'What? In a *real* yacht, you mean?' The boy looked up, surprised; Russell grinned at him:

'Well, not a yacht, perhaps - a little dinghy, or something.'

'No - I'd never thought of it.'

'Would you like to try it? I mean, you do well with our radio-controlled boats, don't you?'

'It'd be… pretty different, wouldn't it?'

'Probably!' There was a lull in the conversation while the boy considered the idea; then:

'Yeah - might be fun, mightn't it? Have you ever done anything like that?'

'Not me! Even if my Dad *was* in the Navy! I've been on warships, even submarines, but never actually *sailed* anything.'

'So - we'd have to teach ourselves, would we?'

'Well - I thought, maybe we could get you a course, or something. At one of the sailing clubs round here, perhaps. There's the one at Linford Lakes; or even, the little one on the lake up here, in the old quarry.'

'The Country Park? Yeah, there is, isn't there? But - wouldn't *you* come too?'

'Mmm - probably not. We could send you - then you can teach me, if you want to. Or, it might be something you'd like to do on your own, with Jack and Simon, perhaps?'

The boy considered this for a while; then said:

'Yeah - that would be great, wouldn't it? I mean, I love doing things with you, Dad - but it's good to do *other* things, as well… you know?' Russell smiled at his son's skilful diplomacy:

'I'll see what I can find out then, shall I?'

'Yeah - thanks, Dad!'

CHAPTER TWENTY

By lunchtime on Monday, routine had pretty much re-established itself in Grancester Police Station. Enquiries surrounding Roddie McKeenan's death were continuing, as sanctioned by the chief of CID, despite the fact that Lucy Cavendish had made a first appearance in front of the local magistrates. As the investigating officer, Russell had requested that she be remanded into police custody, in order to be on hand for further interviews as required - a request with which the magistrates, aware of the County's prevailing lack of available accommodation for female prisoners on remand, were only too pleased to comply.

David Russell's attention had been diverted, to some degree, by the impending trial of a man he had been instrumental in arresting the previous Summer. Luca Giuliani was charged with complicity in the distribution of forged bank-notes, as well as conspiracy to murder both a local businessman and the ten-year-old son of another; now, the complex case was about to come before the Central Criminal Court, and Russell's presence as a witness would be required at some point. Nevertheless, over his cheese and pickle sandwich, and mug of canteen coffee, he was again going over all that the investigation had revealed about McKeenan's background in the hope of finding something which would support, or erase, his doubts about the case against Lucy.

In the incident room, on the floor below, Doug Rimmer was overseeing the further enquiry. Darren Trent, one of the D.C.'s answering to Russell's team, had the task of tracking Roddie back to his roots in Northern Ireland; the other, Steve Campbell, was focussing rather upon the drugs connection. At that moment, he was going through the interviews with the nightclub's customers, from the night of the murder, to see if there was anything which might suggest that drugs were obtainable in the premises where, ostensibly, they were firmly forbidden.

He leafed through the reports, his expression saying that he didn't expect to find anything at all. But then, his eyebrows went up, and he sat back in his chair with a smile of surprise:

'Well, what do you know?'

'What've you found, Steve?' Trent looked up from his own labours.

'Oh, just a useful contact. Maybe.' The friendly rivalry between the two meant that they would often keep each other guessing about their progress, allowing for the possibility of a moment of triumph when, or if, things panned out. Trent's own eyebrows raised in question; Campbell just tapped the side of his nose in a knowing gesture.

* * *

Joe Denham, by chance, was the same age as Roddie McKeenan had been when he died. Not one of life's natural winners, he made an adequate living working five nights a week as a kitchen auxiliary in Martelli's, the town's high-class Italian restaurant, spending his time cleaning, fetching, chopping, washing, rushing from task to task as directed by Toni Giacomelli, the head chef. He'd worked the weekend; this week, he wouldn't have a free night until Thursday, his days off varying from week to week.

Just before five that evening, he wheeled into the little delivery yard behind the restaurant on his ageing pushbike. Switching off the headlamp, he stepped off and leant it against the back wall of the building, fumbling for the lock and chain in his coat pocket. He was just snapping the lock to, when a voice from behind made him jump:

'Hello, Joe!' He jerked his head round, looked up at the figure wreathed in shadow above him, caught the flash of a smile:

'Oh, Mr Campbell - it's you!' He stood up.

'Did I startle you, Joe?'

'Yeah, not bloody 'alf! You shouldn't creep up on folk like that - you might 'ave given me a 'eart attack!'

'Sorry, Joe.' The D.C.'s voice didn't sound in the least apologetic. He went on: 'You were in Sweeney's, the night Roddie McKeenan got shot.'

'Yeah - so what? It was me night off, last week, Wednesday 'n Thursday - I c'n do what I like on me night off, cen't I?'

'Of course you can, Joe! It just made me wonder, that's all.'

'Wonder what, Mr Campbell?' The man's tone was guarded.

'Whether you might have been picking up a little of what does you good, Joe.'

'What? I'd 'ardly be gettin' any grass there, would I? You know old Gidding's attitude to drugs!'

'Well now - my information says that might not be the case, Joe. Did you know Roddie?'

'No - well, yeah, maybe. Jus' to say 'ello to, you know?'

'He wasn't selling you any cannabis, then?'

'What? No, 'course not!'

'Oh, come off it, Joe! You're still smoking regularly, and you're getting it somewhere - where else would you go on your night off, than where you could get restocked?'

'Listen - we've got an agreement, 'aven't we? I tell you all I hear about other stuff, 'n you leave me alone wi' my little bit o' fun, right?'

'Sure, Joe - but now, your little bit of fun might help us with a murder. So, I need to know, Joe - was Roddie selling you marijuana?'

'I thought you'd got 'is girlfriend for that? Why's my little habit important, all of a sudden?'

'That's for me to know, and you to wonder about, Joe. Come on, give, before I insist on searching your pockets!'

In a defensively instinctive move, the skinny kitchen assistant thrust his hands into his coat pockets. He thought hard for a moment, before looking up into the policeman's eyes:

'Is there the usual, you know, cash incentive, 'ere?'

'Could be, Joe - depends what you can tell me.' Denham hesitated briefly, then capitulated:

'Oh, al'right! Yeah, Roddie was keepin' me supplied. I'd meet 'im, usually in the club, on me nights off. He'd slip me a bit, on the quiet like, tell me not to let on where I was gettin' it. 'E was always cautious, like, watching to see 'oo was about - I suppose 'e'd 'a bin banned, if they caught 'im.'

'Do you know if he was supplying other people, too? Different things, maybe, as well?'

'I dunno, Mr Campbell. I 'spect so; but I don't *know.*'

'Where was he getting the stuff, do you know that?' Denham shook his head:

'No. I did ask 'im - in case it might 'elp you, o' course - but 'e wouldn't say.'

'He didn't tell you anything?'

'No. Well - 'e *did* say as 'ow 'e didn't get his supply locally; 'e 'ad 'is own courier, 'e said, brought it over for 'im.'

'Brought it *over?* Where from?'

'I dunno!'

'Who is this courier, Joe?'

'I dunno that, either. One of 'is mates, I suppose.'

'A fellow Irishman, you mean?'

'Maybe - I dunno, I tell you!'

'Okay, Joe. Thanks - that's confirmed what we thought, at least.'

'So - what's in it for me, Mr Campbell?'

'All right, here you go, Joe!' Campbell pulled out his wallet, peeled out a couple of notes, handed them to his informant: 'Don't spend it all at once!'

He turned to go, then looked back over a shoulder with a last question:

'Joe - one last thing: Roddie was still being careful, even when Gidding wasn't in the place, was he?'

'Oh, yeah! One time, 'e stuffed everything in 'is pocket, sharp-like, when Duffy walked in.'

'Frank Duffy, the bar manager?'

'Yeah, tha's right.'

'Okay, thanks Joe. You'd better get in to work, before they miss you!'

'I 'ad 'n all! 'Night, Mr Campbell.'

''Night, Joe.'

Denham disappeared into the kitchens; once he was out of sight, Campbell reached for his radio:

'Delta Control, Delta 392.'

'Go ahead, 392.'

'392 - is Mr Russell still there?'

'I think so, Steve - you want to talk to him?'

'Please.'

'Hold on.' After a pause, the Inspector's voice crackled from the speaker:

'Russell - what is it, Steve?'

'I've just spoken to Joe Denham, sir - you remember, my informant, works at Martelli's? He was in Sweeney's the night McKeenan died.'

'Yes, of course! I saw the name on the list of customers, didn't twig it was your man. What have you got from him?'

'He confirms that McKeenan was selling at the club, but says he was keeping it very quiet; seems he was particularly afraid of Duffy finding out about it.'

'Duffy? You sure, Steve?'

'That's what Joe says, sir. I asked about his supply line, as well, and Joe said something about him having his own courier, bringing the stuff over for him.'

'Oh? Any indication of who - or from where?'

'No, sir, claims he doesn't know any more. I think he's on the level, he doesn't usually hold out on me.'

'Okay, thanks, Steve. You off duty now?' Campbell laughed: 'Quarter of an hour ago, sir! I'm off home, if that's okay?'

'Of course, Steve. See you tomorrow - and thanks again.'

'Good night, sir. 392 out.'

Russell sat back in his chair, lifted his feet to the corner of the desk. Duffy? If Roddie was concerned about him, it sounded as if they had not been in collusion on the drugs business. Perhaps Duffy was as opposed as he made out, acted as Gidding's lookout. Or perhaps Roddie's show of fear was just skilful dissembling, an act designed to throw any possible suspicion of their conspiracy aside!

This case showed no sign of becoming any easier to unravel, the more they learnt about it. But, he felt confident, in time it would. There were more facts, more details, to be discovered, and sooner or later they would begin to see the full picture of Roddie's secondary business, how, or if, it impinged upon his death. If they could trace the supply… It sounded, from what Campbell had said, as if the drugs were being shipped in from somewhere abroad. By one of Roddie's associates? Tomorrow, he'd take another look through the list of the Irishman's cronies, see if any of them fitted that particular bill - but now, home, dinner, and a quiet evening!

CHAPTER TWENTY-ONE

Tuesday morning, and David Russell called the nucleus of his team together for a quick case conference. The extra hands he'd had on loan had all returned to their normal duties, with the arrest and charging of Lucy Cavendish, some to Northampton, the local uniform men to their regular shifts.

He brought Rimmer and Darren Trent up to speed with Steve Campbell's discovery of the previous evening, and set out their tasks for the next little while:

'Steve - keep your nose to the drugs trail, will you? Get us anything at all from the grapevine, even the least hint of anything that might relate to Roddie and his dealings. Do you think Joe Denham could give you anything more?'

'I don't know, sir. He's usually pretty good, if he tells me anything he's normally up front, gives me what he's got. But I can have another go at him, if you like? He might have other information that he's holding back, about the local drugs scene, to make a buck out of later - things that might not seem related to him, but which could help us, maybe.'

'Yes - won't hurt to keep him on his toes, will it? And you're in touch with HQ's drugs team, anyway, I take it?'

'Yes. They know that I want anything which might be connected.'

'Okay. Darren - what have you got on Roddie, so far?'

'We've been over all his known acquaintances, sir. He doesn't

145

seem to have had a lot of real friends, just buddies he'd meet up with for a drink every now and then, some of them ex-pat Irishmen like himself. His daily routine was pretty regular; he'd attend to his painting and decorating business during the daytime, either go to Lucy's house in Buckingham Street for his evening meal, or else eat out - he doesn't seem to have been fond of cooking for himself! Then, either at home with Lucy, or down to Sweeney's for the evening. Pretty unremarkable, really.'

'Except that *we* know he was dealing drugs along the way. Sweeney's has to have been his only outlet, doesn't it?'

'Yeah - unless he was meeting punters while he was out at jobs in the day. He'd often breakfast in Jack's Café, in Midland Road, especially if he'd been at his own flat overnight, and Mrs Jack says he sometimes met another man there, have what looked like serious talks while he ate - the other guy'd just have a cup of tea.'

'Do we know who that was, Darren?'

'Not yet, sir. She describes him as a big fellow, tall, heavily built - but she never got a decent look at him. Roddie would always order his tea, collect it from the counter.'

'That might be his courier, do you think?'

'Possibly, yeah.'

'Right - keep on that fellow, find out who he is, if you can. And go through what you know about all of Roddie's other mates, see if any of them fit with what Joe told Steve last night, any of them who travel regularly, especially anywhere abroad. Did you talk to Karl Jurgens, the barman, yet?'

'Yes - caught up with him at home yesterday, sir. He could only tell me what we knew already, confirm what everyone else has said about the sequence of events on Wednesday night.'

'You asked him about Roddie and drugs?'

'Yeah - like the others, he says he didn't know about anything like that going on. And he claims that he didn't know Lucy had a gun, either.'

'Okay, guys - get to it. Doug - can you grab a WPC and go talk to Lucy again? Try and get her to open up about the drugs - she has to have known what Roddie was up to, surely? Try and convince her to help us - it's got to be her best chance of proving her innocence, to tell us all she knows.'

'Okay, sir. But - to be fair, she'll have a job to convince *me* that she's innocent!'

'I know - but give her the chance, Doug? She hasn't been convicted yet - and if she can give us a lead on Roddie's supplier, or anything else useful, it's not going to harm her cause even if she is.'

'Of course, sir. We should have her lawyer in on this?'

'We'd better - give her a call, see when she's free to attend.'

'Right, I'll get on to her now.'

When his subordinates had dispersed, Russell took himself down to the basement, to the subterranean lair of the Mad Professor and his forensic team. He found D.S. Owen in the office, grumbling his way through the paperwork which he hated; the SOCO Sergeant looked up with a smile as he entered, glad of an excuse to put it aside, if only temporarily:

'Morning, Dave! How's detection today?'

'Frustrating as ever, Terry. Any coffee going?'

'Yeah - help yourself.' He gestured at a percolator, bubbling quietly in the corner; Russell poured himself a mug, added sugar, sat down opposite the lab-coated forensic officer.

'What can I do for you, Dave?'

'Any more results on the McKeenan case, Terry?'

'Now, what was it we were waiting for? Oh, yes - DNA...' he scrabbled through the disarray on his desk, extracted a document: 'Here we are. The DNA sample you gave me Saturday night matches what I found inside the two pairs of gloves. Your arrestee is the one who'd worn them. Preliminary result, but it isn't going to change.'

'What we expected, then.'

'Yeah.' Russell sat in silence, thinking. Owen asked:

'How's the case against Lucy looking?'

'Solid, too solid.'

'You're still not happy, are you, Dave?'

'Oh, I should be, I suppose! We can explain everything, fit it all together - the sequence of events, even how her temper fits with her surmised actions - we've got motive, means, opportunity, the lot. But - call me obstinate, Terry, but I'm still not entirely happy, no. I've got this niggling feeling that I'm *supposed* to write this off as a lover's tiff, when there's really far more to it. Is there any way that the evidence *you've* seen could fit with someone else having killed him?'

It was Owen's turn to sit in silent thought, until he shook his head:

'I can't see how, Dave. But then, interpreting this is your job, not mine - I can only give you the science, the facts as the evidence tells them. I can prove that things *are* so - it's a lot more difficult to prove that they *aren't,* if you see what I mean.'

'I'm not sure I do?'

'Well, boy; if there is physical evidence, it tends to show that something *did* happen. It's difficult to find evidence that something *didn't;* something that *didn't* happen *doesn't* leave evidence, you see what I mean? If you want to prove that Lucy didn't kill her boyfriend, the only way to do that is to prove that someone else *did!'*

Russell laughed:

'That's just what Muriel Hepple challenged me to do!'

'Who?'

'Oh - Mrs Hepple is - I suppose the easiest thing is to call her Lucy's mother-in-law, even though she wasn't married.'

'Er - yeah, okay, Dave.'

'Anyway, Terry - the *scientific* evidence we have is that he was killed with her gun, by someone wearing her gloves, right?'

'Yeah - that's what we have which connects her to the murder, pretty well. Plus your other circumstantial stuff, of course.'

'Let's leave that aside for now - is there any way that what we have, scientifically, could fit in if someone else did it?'

'Oh, boy! Well, you can't get around the gun. That gun killed McKeenan, that's beyond question. We can't prove ownership, as the number's not registered, but it's covered in her fingerprints, albeit smeared and smudged for the most part, which is what I'd expect if it had been in her possession for a good time and kicked about in her handbag. And I hear she's admitted it could be hers?'

'That's right.'

'So, okay - the gloves: Whoever killed him was wearing them, the pattern of powder residue, the specks of blood, prove that beyond any question. And that person was left-handed.'

'Could a right-handed person have held the gun that way, fired it?'

'I doubt it. Not impossible, but they'd find it difficult, very awkward - and why do it? Not many people would realise how much we can learn from things like the residues, know to cover their tracks that way.'

'Yeah, I guess so. What about the DNA, from inside them? Could that be faked?'

'I don't see how. The action of putting gloves on, peeling them off again, abrades the skin, picks up traces on the fabric, traces which will usually survive cleaning, bearing in mind that people tend to concentrate on getting the *outside* clean. Which makes me conclude that both pairs belonged to Lucy, that no-one else had worn them.'

'No-one could have just slipped them on to shoot Roddie, got rid of them straight away, without leaving traces?'

'I wasn't sure about that, so I checked with the experts at HQ. They reckon, the same as I do, that even that brief time would leave traces we couldn't miss - like I said, it's the action of putting them on, taking them off, which leaves the traces, so how long they were worn is not important.'

'There's no way anyone else wore them?' Owen gave the Inspector a grin:

'Not unless they wore a *second* pair of gloves, inside those!' But Russell took his intended jest seriously:

'You mean, it would be possible, if they had a pair of thin gloves on inside the leather ones? A pair of latex gloves, like they use for surgery or something?'

'Well - yes, it's *conceivable,* I suppose...'

'And those gloves would themselves have traces of DNA on them? From the wearer, and from the inside of Lucy's?'

'Well - yes, they should do. Maybe not so much on the outside, because they'd only be able to pick up from the minute traces on the inside of hers - wouldn't give you much to work on, probably.'

'If I found you those gloves, could you prove that that's what happened?'

'Oh, I don't know, Dave! I could give you any DNA from the wearer, tell you who that was, I expect - but as to proving the rest: I could try, but no promises, mind?'

Russell got to his feet, a smile on his face:

'Thanks, Terry - it might be a long shot, but at least you've given me something to try! I'll see you later.'

'Yeah - see you, mate!' Owen watched him go, a slightly bemused expression on his round face.

Upstairs once more, Russell walked into the incident room:

'Where's Doug Rimmer?' D.C. Trent, the sole occupant of the room, looked up from his studies:

'Interviewing Lucy again, sir.'

'Oh - right. What have we done with the contents of the waste-bins from Sweeney's, do you know?'

'I guess they'll still be in storage, sir.'

'Can you go and check in the evidence store? I want them gone through, again, especially the ones from the kitchens.' Trent scrambled to his feet:

'Yes, sir! What are we looking for, anything specific?'

'A pair of thin latex gloves, probably looking quite clean and fresh, from the top of one of the bins. If you find them, handle with care, right? We're looking for DNA evidence.'

'Right - you want me to deal with this straight away?'

'Please, Darren. The work on Roddie's mates can wait for a little while, I doubt if they're going to go away.'

'Okay, I'll get right on it, sir.' Trent's tone, and his expression, said that he didn't know what was going on - but, like any good soldier, he'd follow orders even so. In the ground-floor storeroom, he ran into Constable Tolman, one of Owen's assistants:

'Teddy - the waste bins, from Sweeney's - have you still got the contents?'

'Which ones, mate?'

'The kitchen ones - Doc Russell wants another look through them.' Tolman laughed:

'He'll be disappointed, then. We didn't collect the kitchen bins, didn't seem to be any reason to.'

'Oh, hell! You can laugh, it's my arse that's going to get chewed when I tell him that!'

CHAPTER TWENTY-TWO

Trent was back within minutes, a look of trepidation on his face. Russell looked up from the reports he had been leafing through as he approached:

'You look worried, Darren.' Trent nodded:

'I don't how you're going to take this, sir - the SOCO boys didn't keep the bin contents after the search of Sweeney's premises, they didn't think they'd be relevant. And, as Teddy Tolman says, they're so pushed for storage space down there…'

'*Damn!* Oh, I suppose we can't blame them - but as it turns out, that rubbish just might have been critical. We could trace where it went, follow it… But I imagine it'll be in some land-fill site by now. It was just a long shot - I don't suppose it's worth that kind of effort, really. Not to worry, Darren; get back to your researches into Roddie's mates, I'll leave you in peace.'

He returned to his own office, annoyed at the failure of his idea, but accepting that it had been unlikely to bear fruit, anyway. Minutes later, he was joined by Rimmer, fresh from his latest interview with their prisoner; the Sergeant perched on the corner of the desk as his superior looked up, his eyebrows raised in query:

'What luck, Doug?'

'Some, boss. She's admitted to knowing about Roddie's drug trade, but says she doesn't really know much about it. She agrees he was selling in the nightclub, but denies knowing where he was getting the stuff, or any more about it.'

'Well, at least that confirms what Steve's informant told him, and our own assumptions. She doesn't know if he was selling anywhere else?'

'Says not. But then, I don't suppose she would, necessarily.'

'What about the other staff at Sweeney's - did they know?'

'She wasn't keen to say much about that, but her solicitor prodded her to open up a bit - she does admit that most of the barmen, and the other hostesses, *probably* knew, but she won't say categorically that they did.'

'They had to, didn't they, Doug? He couldn't have been selling regularly, right in front of them, without they knew what was going on.'

'I reckon so. Perhaps she's not keen to say, because some of them were among his customers? Reluctant to get them into trouble, maybe.'

'That would make sense. Did she say anything about Duffy - *did* he know? Was he in collusion with Roddie?'

'Doubt it. She says that he was always careful not to let him, or Ike Uris for that matter, see anything. Or Gidding, of course, although he usually isn't there much of the time.'

'Okay - perhaps we were wrong there. That backs up Steve's man again; sounds like Duffy was on the level when he said they wouldn't tolerate drug dealing. Even though it was happening, right under his nose!'

'Yeah. Anything else new?'

'Not really. I had a chat with Terry Owen, earlier - he says there might have been a way someone else could have killed Roddie, despite the forensic: If they wore a pair of thin gloves *inside* Lucy's - that would have kept them clean of any foreign DNA.' Rimmer snorted his derision:

'Bit bloody unlikely, though, isn't it? In that case, this other killer had to be cute enough to know about leaving DNA inside there; and, have small enough hands to fit them. And be in the right place at the right time - and we *know* nobody else was!'

'And be left-handed. Yeah, I know, Doug.'

'Sir? Why, if I can ask, are you so unhappy about the case against Lucy? I mean, we can explain the whole thing, even down to the way her mentality fits with the sequence of events. Forensic, witnesses, motive, means, opportunity, we've got the lot!'

'Yes, I know! But - it still leaves me with a nagging feeling that we're being manipulated. I can't be any more specific than that - but I think there's more to Roddie's murder than we're supposed to see. And it *has* to be connected with the drugs angle.' Rimmer shrugged:

'I can't say that I agree. But, as you said before, the drugs are worth following up, if only because we could end up with something worth having in its own right. And, you're the boss!' Russell smiled at his assistant:

'Thanks, Doug. I might well be completely off target; but let's stick with it a bit longer.'

'Right. I'll keep things going downstairs.'

'Thanks. I should spend some time going over the files on the Giuliani case; he comes up for trial right after Lucy's next appearance.'

* * *

Joe Denham hopped off his bike in the gloom of Martelli's back yard, to find himself face to face with D.C. Steve Campbell for the second night in a row:

'Not a-bloody-gen! I told you all I can 'bout Roddie las' night!'

'You sure of that, Joe?'

''Course I'm bloody sure - I don't 'old out on you, Mr Campbell, you know that!'

'No, I don't think you do, Joe. But - this is getting bigger, my friend. I want *all* the tales, every bit of gossip in the drugs trade round here, and I want it now, comprende?'

'There... there ain't much, Mr Campbell, it's pretty quiet right now. Word is that Roseberry's got most things sewn up - no-one'd want to fool with *'im,* would they?'

'Our old friend Curtis, eh? He must be doing pretty well for himself. But he didn't have Sweeney's sewn up, did he?' Joe glanced over his shoulder, as if afraid of being overheard:

'No, 'e didn't. But…' He stopped. Campbell leant close, peered into his eyes:

'Come on, Joe, what are you holding back from me?'

'Well - it's just a rumour, like - nothing more. But - I *did* 'ear that 'e wasn't too 'appy about someone selling there. 'E'd wanted the place for 'imself, ever since it opened, five year ago. But *'is* man got caught, put inside, didn' 'e? Couple, three years back - your guys and Gidding set a trap for 'im, I 'eard. Now, 'e's found out about someone else selling there, 'n getting away with it, 'n 'e ain't too pleased.'

'Was Roseberry gunning for Roddie, then?'

'Oh, I wouldn' say that! I don' think 'e knows *'oo* it is, just that someone is, you know?'

'He wasn't supplying Roddie, then?'

'No - no way! 'E wouldn''a worried about it if 'e 'ad been, would 'e?'

'I suppose not. You haven't heard any more about where Roddie was getting his stuff, then?'

'No, Mr Campbell, I 'aven't. If I do, I'll let you know, shall I?'

'You'd better, Joe! And - I want everything else you hear, even if it's got nothing to do with Roddie, right? Straight away.'

'Yeah, o'course, Mr Campbell. I'll get in touch 'f I 'ear anything, okay?'

'Good man, Joe! Bye for now, then.' He turned to go, but Denham grabbed his sleeve:

'What about - me retirement fund, Mr Campbell?' The DC laughed:

'Oh, okay Joe, here you go!' He pushed a note at the informant. 'Is that all?'

'More, when you find out more for me, Joe, all right?'

'Yeah, a'right. I'll be in touch, then.'

Denham made his disgruntled way to the back door of the restaurant as Campbell walked out to his waiting car.

* * *

As Steve Campbell climbed into the Ford Focus, glancing at his watch to check if he was officially off duty yet, his opposite number was knocking on the door of the Inspector's office.

'Come in! Darren - take a seat.'

'Thank you sir. I've been going over Roddie's associates, as you said, and I think I might have the one we're looking for.'

'Oh?' Russell's voice betrayed his interest.

'Yes - a John Thomas.'

'You're kidding me! Is anyone really called John Thomas?'

'This guy is, sir - what's so odd about that?'

'You must have heard that expression, surely?' Trent shook his head, puzzled; Russell laughed:

'It's a term some kids use to refer to their…you know! Or at least, they did when I was younger. Hadn't you heard that before?'

'No, sir - bit careless, calling your son that, then, wasn't it? Perhaps that's why he likes to be known as Paddy!'

'Probably! What about this man, Darren?'

'He's a friend of Roddie's, came over from Belfast a year or so after he did. Apparently, they knew each other there, before. He does casual work for Roddie - or did, I should say - in his decorating business. And - he goes back to Belfast regularly, about once every six or eight weeks. Could he be bringing the stuff back with him from there, do you think?'

'Possibly - it's part of the UK, so customs checks aren't that strict, are they? And, such as they are, I expect they're more likely to be looking for explosives and the like.'

'That's what I thought, sir. I've called the police in Belfast, asked them to check into both men, and let us have anything they might have on record, and whatever they can find in terms of background on them.'

'Good thinking! If you're right, I wonder how the drugs are getting into Northern Ireland? From the Republic, maybe? The Ulster police might know - when you hear from them, ask the question, will you?'

'Yes, sir. I'm going off duty now, if that's okay?'

'Sure - see you tomorrow.'

'Goodnight, sir.'

* * *

Russell himself left the office shortly afterwards. At the cottage, he let himself in, and felt his heart sink as he saw the expression in his wife's eyes as she met him in the hallway. She quickly smiled, and reached up to kiss him on the cheek:

'Hello, Darling. Good day?'

'Not too bad. What's wrong?' She feigned innocence:

'Nothing, Dear. I was just going to give Danny a call - he's doing his homework in his room.' He took her shoulders in his hands:

'Come on, Tracy - I saw the look in your eyes. What's he done now?'

'It's nothing - really, David!' He held her, gazing into her eyes, until she looked away: 'Well - he's got himself into a detention, for Thursday night. I didn't want to tell you - I'm afraid I already had a go at him, and I didn't want to get him into trouble with you as well; he's in a bad enough mood as it is.' He nodded:

'I'll go and get him. Dinner's ready?'

'Five minutes.'

He made his way up the stairs, knocked on the half-open door of his son's room, put his head round the edge:

'Hello, Daniel!' The boy looked around from his desk:

'Hi, Dad - come in.' Russell stepped inside, sat down on the

157

edge of the bed:

'Everything all right?' Daniel gave him a wary look:

'What's Mum told you?'

'Not a lot. Why don't you tell me?' The teenager's shoulders slumped as an angry fire came into his hazel eyes:

'It's not *fair!* Georgie - Mr Handford - he's put me in *detention!*'

'Why?' The boy's face suddenly relaxed into a sheepish grin:

'He caught me with my phone, in the lunch break. I was only showing Snow and Jacko, and Luke, what it could do! I wasn't actually *using* it! He wanted to confiscate it, but I told him what you said - he let me keep it, but he gave me a detention anyway! It *isn't* fair!' The pained look was back. Remembering his words to the boy the previous week, Russell kept his amusement in check as he asked:

'Your Mum had a go at you, I suppose, when you told her about it?' Daniel nodded:

'Yeah. I *had* to tell her, 'cause I'll be late home Thursday - she wasn't really angry, just kind of... disappointed, I guess. It made me feel so *shitty!* I...'

Russell gave his son a sympathetic smile, which slipped out of control into a wide grin:

'I told you you were on your own if you got caught with it switched on during school hours! It's not that bad, Dan - if all you get is a detention once in a while, you're not doing badly. And if it's any consolation, Mum didn't want to tell me about it, she knows how upset you are.'

'Really? And... you're not angry?'

'No!' Russell laughed: 'I warned you - it's your own stupid fault, you should have waited until after school, shouldn't you? Do your detention, with good grace, and that's the end of it, right?' Daniel relaxed, grinned across at his father:

'Right!' Russell got up from the bed:

'Come on now - dinner's ready.'

CHAPTER TWENTY-THREE

'Curtis Roseberry, eh?' Steve Campbell had just acquainted the Inspector with his latest snippet of tattle from Joe Denham.

'That adds another slant to things, doesn't it, boss?' Rimmer commented.

'Yes…' Russell sounded thoughtful: 'You say Joe didn't think he was after Roddie specifically, Steve?'

'No, sir - he thought it was just that Roseberry had heard about *someone* selling in Sweeney's, and didn't like it.'

'I wonder? Suppose Roseberry knew more than Joe thinks he did? Could he have been behind his murder, somehow?'

'Eliminating the opposition?'

'It would make sense as a motive, wouldn't it?'

'That's not really Roseberry's style, sir' Campbell interjected: 'He'd more likely try to scare him off, he likes to rely on his reputation as a hard case. Murder would be too risky for our Curtis, I'd have thought. But I wouldn't put it past him, if it came to it.'

'Perhaps he *was* trying to scare Roddie off - perhaps that's why he was talking about leaving Lucy, moving on?'

'Could be, Doug. But Steve's quite right, if Roddie was looking like going away, I can't see Roseberry having him killed - he'd just wait, see if he really did go.'

'Yeah, that'd be more like him. Low profile!'

'Right! Keep your ear to the ground, Steve, see if Joe or anyone else comes up with any more. Do the drugs lads in Northampton know anything about Roseberry being after anyone around here?'

'They've not said, sir - I'll check with them.'

'Okay, thanks, Steve. Keep me posted.'

'Will do.'

Campbell left the office; Russell glanced up at the Sergeant, perched on the desk, a speculative look in his eyes, but Rimmer said:

'I can't see it having anything to do with his murder, can you?'

'Not very likely, I suppose. As we've said, out of character. And it wouldn't get us around the evidence against Lucy, anyway, unless we could show that he sent a girl to kill him.'

'A left-handed one who knew her way around Sweeney's, knew about Lucy's gun, and her gloves... No, not on, is it, boss?'

'Still - let's see what else we can find out. It might give us a lead on Roseberry, somehow - it would be good to nail him, wouldn't it?'

'Yeah - can't see him leaving himself open, though.'

'Unlikely. Look how many years the drugs team in Northampton have had him in their sights, to no avail - he's too damn clever by half! To change tack, Doug - Darren Trent thinks he might have found Roddie's supply line. One of his mates, an old friend from Belfast, is in the habit of going back there regularly, it seems. He could possibly be carrying the stuff back with him - it would fit in with what Joe told Steve before, wouldn't it?'

'It would. He's following it up?'

'Yeah, talking to the Belfast police, to see what they can tell us.'

'Did we ought to talk to this guy - or do you want to wait, see what Darren comes up with first?'

'I think we'll hold fire for now, Doug...'

A knock at the office door interrupted him; it opened, to admit the local head of CID. Rimmer rose from his perch on the desk:

'Good morning, sir!'

'Morning, Sergeant. Morning, David. Any progress on the McKeenan case?'

'Morning, sir. Nothing new, really - we might have a line on where he was getting the drugs, but it's too early to be sure of anything.'

'Hmm. No other murderer come to light, then?'

'Not so far, sir.'

'Have you got anyone, anyone at all, that you would categorise as a suspect? Apart from Lucy Cavendish?'

'To be fair, sir, no. No-one else has come to light who had a reasonable opportunity to have killed him, nor anyone else with any motive - unless the drugs angle will throw up someone, in time.'

'Hmm. What do you think, Sergeant?' Rimmer glanced at his Inspector before replying, cautiously:

'Well, sir, I have to say I think Lucy is our murderer. All the evidence points to her; and as Inspector Russell has said, we don't have another viable suspect. I don't believe that further investigation will change that conclusion - but, having said that, I do think we should follow through on the drugs angle, in the hope that it will lead us somewhere useful.'

'I have to agree with Sergeant Rimmer, David - I think your murderer is downstairs right now. Following the drugs back is fine, as long as it gets us somewhere worth going; I don't want my best team chasing their own tails for ever over some penny-ante drug dealer, who's dead anyway. How long do you expect to be tied up with this?'

'Lucy comes up in court again on the fifteenth; I'd hope to have something to show for our efforts by then, sir.'

'I bloody-well hope so! All right, David, carry on - but don't let other things slip in the meantime, okay?'

'Thank you, sir - and don't worry, we can keep on top of things all right.'

'Very good. Keep me informed.'

'I will, sir.'

* * *

It was after lunch that day when D.C. Trent tapped on Russell's door and put his head into the office:

'Got a moment, sir?'

'Of course, Darren, come in.' Trent sat in one of the chairs facing the desk:

'I've had some information back from Belfast, sir.'

'Oh?'

'Yes - apparently, around ten to fifteen years back, both McKeenan and Thomas were known to what was then the R.U.C. They were still in school then; but both were known sectarian activists. They lived in one of the solidly Catholic areas, and got involved with the local Republican groups, joined a militant bunch calling themselves the U.L.A.'

'The who?'

'Stands for Ulster Liberation Army. Or Association, now we're in the days of the Good Friday Agreement. But they were at that time a pretty rough lot, although not much heard of outside Belfast itself; the R.U.C. had them down for a number of minor bombings, and at least three shootings. Roddie and his mate were never implicated in any violence directly, but they were certainly suspected on more than one occasion.'

'Really? That's bloody odd! Since he's been here, Roddie's disavowed any interest in all that. Do we know what Thomas's views are, nowadays?'

'No, sir - I'll see if I can find out. The Belfast Police are aware that he goes back regularly - they don't regard him as a real problem, but they do keep an eye on him when he's there, just in case. The U.L.A. are one group that has never declared an official ceasefire.'

'What does he do when he goes back, who does he meet?'

'Goes back over a weekend, as a rule - does the rounds of his old mates, spends a lot of time in the bars, stays with his family, then heads back here again. They're not aware of him acting as any kind of courier, but then, my contact said that they're not looking out for that kind of thing, just watching him in case of any trouble. He did promise that they'd do some digging for us, try and find out if it's a possibility that he might be collecting drugs somewhere, bringing them here on his way back.'

'Okay - thanks, Darren. Did you ever find out who Roddie's breakfast companion is? The big guy, that Mrs Hill told you about?'

'No, sir. Not much to go on, really. She couldn't give me much of a description, as I told you - and no-one else remembers seeing him. Might have been a customer, mightn't he?'

'Yes - be it for drugs or decorating! Never mind - but keep your ears open, in case he pops up again. Let me know if you hear any more, about him or Thomas.'

'Straight away, sir.'

Trent got up and left the office. Russell sat musing for a minute or two, then got up himself and made his way down to the CID room on the first floor, where he found the Sergeant typing furiously on a computer keyboard. Rimmer looked up as he approached:

'How goes it, boss?'

'Okay, Doug. Listen - as far as we know, Roddie's shown no interest in the Irish troubles, has he?'

'Not that I'm aware of. None of his associates have said that he was at all bothered about it - in fact, quite the opposite, as I remember. We've spoken to quite a number of the local Irish community, and some of them said that he wouldn't even discuss it, claimed he wasn't interested.'

'That's what I thought; and Mrs Hepple said the same to me. But, it seems he *was* deeply involved, before he left Belfast, belonged to a local group of Republican hot-heads. They even suspected him of involvement in violence 'for the cause'.'

'That's strange - you'd hardly change your views to *that* extent, overnight, surely?'

'I wouldn't think so. Darren Trent is trying to find out more from Belfast, and more about his mate, Thomas; it seems they were both in this paramilitary outfit, before moving to England.

And the Belfast force are going to investigate Thomas's trips home for us, see if he could be Roddie's courier.'

'It's a complicated way of going about things, isn't it? I mean, Roddie can only have been a pretty small-time pusher, and to be bringing in his own supply, even from Northern Ireland, just seems a bit... unnecessary, somehow?'

'Yeah, I know what you mean. If he was just into making a fast buck, you'd think he'd have been better off buying the stuff locally, from Roseberry, even. That way, he'd have avoided any aggro, and cut his hassle to a minimum. Having Thomas carry it all that way, if that's what was happening, was just adding enormously to his risks, surely?'

'That's what I mean.' Rimmer laughed: 'I'm almost beginning to agree with you - there are things about this case that don't make a lot of sense! But - I still think Lucy killed him, even so!'

'We'll see, Doug! You're probably right about that, despite my misgivings. But every way we turn, we seem to come up with anomalies, things that don't fit the way you'd expect. Oh well - we'll get there, if we keep chasing our tails, eh?'

'Let's hope so! And before the PM gives us both the sack!'

* * *

The wreckage of a lunch of beans on toast littered the kitchen table in the little house in Oakfield. Elsa and Karl Jurgens sat facing each other; neither was speaking, both gazing at their plates, wrapped in their own thoughts.

For days now, the house had been unusually quiet. Since the news of Lucy's arrest and subsequent charging, life had rolled brother and sister along in its inevitable, steamroller fashion, without either of them paying it a great deal of notice. The subject had been discussed, if desultorily, leaving the both of them puzzled and uneasy, both certain that a great injustice was looming, but neither sure of what to do about it.

Now, Elsa looked up at her brother:

'Karl?'

'Yeah?'

'I think we should go to the police.'

'What good would that do?' She hesitated:

'Well - how much do they *know?*'

'About what?'

'The drugs, of course!' It was his turn to pause, thinking:

'I don't know, Sis. Not all of it, for sure.'

'Okay, listen - *we* know Lucy didn't kill him, right?'

'Well…'

'Oh, *come on!* You know how devoted she was to Roddie - and how can you even *think* she could have done it, after all she's done for us?'

'Yeah, you're right. There's no way she'd shoot anyone, let alone him.'

'So? If she didn't, someone else did - and that has got have something to do with him selling drugs, hasn't it?' Karl shrugged his shoulders:

'Probably, I guess.'

'What *else* could it be about?'

'Yeah, all right.'

'So - I think we should go and talk to that Inspector, tell him everything, tell him to go after whoever *did* kill Roddie instead of assuming that Lucy did it!'

'They must have pretty good evidence, to have charged her, though?'

'*Karl!* They're still *wrong,* and you know it!'

'Yeah, but… If we tell him all about things, we'll both be out of a job, won't we?'

'I don't know - maybe Ike and Fluffy'll keep things going, whatever.'

'I can't see that! There's no great love lost between any of 'em, is there? They only stay because Gidding pays them over the odds; without him, they'd both cut and run, trust me!'

'Yeah, maybe. But… we can't just sit back and let Lucy go to gaol, can we?' Karl sat gazing into his sister's blue eyes, his expression betraying his indecision, the tension in his mind:

'They'll find out, in time… won't they? Without us having to tell them.'

'Can we *chance* that? And anyway, the end result'll be the same - we'll still be on the dole!' Her brother's eyes, the same blue as her own, slowly cleared; he smiled at her across the scattered plates:

'Yeah, it will, won't it?'

CHAPTER TWENTY-FOUR

The next morning, after a night of family harmony, David Russell stuck his head into the CID room:

'Doug? Fancy a decent cup of coffee?' Rimmer looked up, surprised:

'Not getting it from the canteen, then, are we?' Russell laughed:

'No chance! I thought we'd try Jack's Café for a change.'

'Okay.' The Sergeant stood up and followed his superior down the stairs and out into the car park, where Russell threw him the Jeep's keys:

'You drive, I want to think.'

In the car, as they drove out into the Old Northampton Road, Rimmer asked:

'I assume there's more to this than a cup of coffee?'

'Mmm. I thought we might have a chat with Mrs Hill, about Roddie's mysterious companion.'

'You think he could be important?'

'I'm not sure - I think I just might know who he is.'

'Oh?' Russell laughed:

'I'll tell you later! I could just as easily be making an even bigger idiot of myself!' Rimmer glanced at him, shrugged.

Ten minutes later, he parked the Jeep in Midland Road, just along from their destination. They got out, sauntered into the little café which had once served the railwaymen from the nearby station and now provided sustenance for truck-drivers and local workers alike. At the counter, Russell ordered two mugs of coffee; Rimmer added a bacon sandwich, explaining apologetically that he'd missed breakfast because his wife had left early for work. They sat at a table in the window - had they know it, in Roddie McKeenan's usual spot.

When the Sergeant's sandwich was brought over to them, Russell asked the waitress if Mrs Hill could spare him a moment. Several minutes later, the round, jolly looking woman in a white overall appeared from the kitchen and came over:

'Can I help you gentlemen?'

'Mrs Hill?'

'Enid, please. No-one calls me Mrs Hill! Mrs Jack, sometimes, if they knew my husband.'

'Would you join us for a moment? I appreciate you're busy, but it is important - I'm Inspector Russell, from the local CID, and this is Sergeant Rimmer.'

'I mustn't be long, you understand - can't have the customers kept waiting for their breakfasts!' She took a seat next to the Sergeant: 'Now - what is it, Inspector?'

'It's about Roddie McKeenan, Mrs... Enid!' She shook her head, tut-tutting:

'That poor boy! Such a nice lad, always pleasant and polite, ready with a joke and a laugh. His girlfriend did it, is that right?'

'We're still investigating, Enid - but it does look that way.'

'That's terrible - just shows you what love can do, doesn't it? She's a lovely girl, you'd never think she could do such a thing, would you?'

'You know her, Enid?'

'Oh, well, I've met her a few times. She's been in here with him, sometimes; and that little girl of hers. She's a little treasure, too - so polite and well-behaved. And pretty as a picture.'

'Yes, indeed she is. Enid - you told my Constable that you'd seen another man with Roddie occasionally, for breakfast?'

'That's right, Inspector. I don't know who he is, mind, nor did

I ever get much of a look at him - he never came to the counter himself, Roddie would always collect his tea for him, and pay for it.'

'What *can* you tell us about him, Enid?'

'Oh - now, let me think. He's a big chap, over six foot, and heavily built, like a boxer or something. Very smart, expensive clothes - always wore a hat, one of those flat-rimmed ones, like an Australian, you know?'

'Could you see his hair? Or his face, at all?'

'O-oh... Blond hair, I'm sure. Not like yours Inspector, much paler. As to his face, I never really saw it. But I have the feeling he was sort of heavy-featured, if you know what I mean?'

'That's all you can remember, Enid?'

'I'm afraid so. If I think of anything else, shall I call you?'

'Please do!' Russell dug a card out of his wallet: 'My numbers are on there. And thank you for your help - I'm sorry if we've kept you from your cooking!'

'Oh, that's all right, I'm glad to help if I can.' She went to stand up, then sat down again:

'There is one thing I've just remembered - there was another fellow, with Roddie, just once, maybe twice. A smaller chap, quite thin, narrow face, curly, dark brown hair and blue eyes - he had an Irish accent, just like Roddie, as well. I don't know who he might have been either, I'm afraid.'

'Right - was this other man with him at the same time as the big fellow?'

'Yes - I believe he was... but I couldn't be *quite* certain, now. It was quite a while ago I saw him.'

'You remember him quite clearly, though?' She laughed:

'Oh, yes! I've a good memory for a face. Often can't put the name to it, even when I knew it, but I don't often forget a face!'

'Thank you again, Enid. You'll call, if you remember anything more?'

'Most certainly I will, Inspector! And come by for a mug of our coffee any time, won't you?'

'We will - it's much better than what we get in the station canteen!' She laughed as she rose, and returned to her kitchen.

The Sergeant munched his way through the sandwich, relishing the generous layering of bacon between the thick, crusty bread, his eyes on the Inspector's face. Russell, for his part, was deep in thought. The previous night, while idly watching a documentary on the television, it had struck him who the Irishman's unknown companion might have been. The sketchy description he'd had then only seemed to fit one man that he knew to be involved in the case - but if his guess was right, it was one more thing that didn't make any sense. But as he sat slowly sipping the deep mug of hot, strong coffee, the rather better description Enid Hill had just given them going around in his head, a possible connection began to evolve in his imagination; if he was right, it meant a complete rethink of the circumstances surrounding the murder...

Rimmer finished his coffee:

'Ready, sir?' Russell came out of his reverie, nodded; quickly draining his own mug, he got to his feet:

'Yes - let's go, Doug.' They left the café, strolled back to the car, climbed in. As Rimmer went to start the engine, Russell laid a hand on his arm:

'Wait a mo, Doug. Let me throw an idea at you: Let's suppose, just for the sake of argument, that the situation at Sweeney's is not what we've all accepted. Let's suppose that we, and the rest of the local population, have been taken in by a clever double-bluff?'

'What are you getting at, boss?'

'Well - Gidding is violently opposed to the sale of drugs in the club, right?'

'Right?'

'To the point that he's even co-operated with our drugs team in trapping pushers, right?'

'Yes?'

'But suppose for a moment that he's done that in order to draw attention away from another pusher operating there!'

'What?'

'Think about it, Doug: he runs organised prostitution there, lets the local underage kids in, sells them alcohol and who knows what else, probably runs other scams that even Strongarm's boys don't know about - why would he draw the line at drugs? Especially if he was able to take a cut of the profits!'

'If you put it like that - he's not afraid of making money from other illegal activities, so it does seem a bit strange, doesn't it?'

'Exactly! *Now,* who does Enid's description remind you of?'

'Bugger me! Gidding himself!'

'Six foot plus, heavy-built, blond hair, expensive clothes - only the hat doesn't fit. But if he's trying not to be recognised, how better to hide his face?'

'Yeah - worked, too, didn't it?'

'Nearly!'

'So - how are you putting all this together, boss?'

'I'm not sure how it fits with Roddie's murder - but if he was selling there *with Gidding's backing,* it changes our perspective on things a bit, doesn't it?'

'Doesn't explain the complicated supply line, though. I mean, a man with Gidding's contacts could easily have acquired drugs locally, couldn't he? Why the long-distance connection?'

'I don't know. There has to *be* a reason, but I can't see it at the moment.'

'If Roddie and Gidding were in collusion about the drug business, where does Duffy fit in? He must have known, surely?'

'You'd think so. But everyone seems adamant that Roddie didn't want him to see anything going on - maybe he genuinely *was* against it, and would have given him grief about it. Maybe they actually *had* managed to hide it from him - after all, he spent much of his time in the upstairs office, from what he told us.'

'Yeah, maybe.'

'Oh, come on, let's get back to the station, see if there's anything else new to complicate our lives even more!'

CHAPTER TWENTY-FIVE

When the two returned to the Police Station, they were met by D.C. Trent in the stairwell:

'Sir! I've been looking for you.'

'Doug and I have been out for a coffee.' If the Constable's face registered his surprise, he refrained from comment:

'I've had a call from Belfast, sir. From a D.C.I. in their drugs squad - he says he thinks there is a connection, with Paddy Thomas, that he could well have been supplying McKeenan - but he asked if we can tread carefully, for the moment at least, not let on to Thomas or anyone else what we suspect.'

'Oh? What have we stumbled on to, did he tell you?'

'No, sir - I think it's rather that it could be related to an investigation of theirs, and they don't want any chance of the alarm being raised over there until they can check things out. He did say that our enquiry had given them a different slant on what they were doing, but he didn't want to open up. Not to a lowly DC, anyway - you might find out more if you call him yourself, sir!'

'Okay, thanks. You've got his number?'

'I left a note on your desk, sir.'

'Right.'

In his office, Russell picked up the message pad, read through what Trent had written. Rimmer watched his thoughtful expression:

'You going to call him?'

'No-o… not yet. I want to have a word with Lucy, I think, first.'

'Okay - shall I call her brief?'

'No - I just want to have an informal chat with her. Stay here, Doug, I won't be long.'

He left the Sergeant, looking slightly puzzled, and made his way down to the basement cells. The duty custody sergeant let him into Lucy's cell; she got to her feet as he entered:

'Good morning, Lucy - are they looking after you all right?' She gave him a rueful smile:

'If being locked up in here can be described as all right, yes, I suppose they are.' He echoed her smile:

'I'm glad you're keeping your spirits up - I know how difficult this must be for you.' Her eyebrows went up:

'I doubt if you really have the slightest idea! But thank you for your sympathy, anyway. Inspector?'

'Yes?'

'You're convinced that *I* killed Roddie, aren't you?' He paused, not wanting to further upset the girl, but unwilling to give her any false hopes, either:

'We have a great deal of evidence that says you did, Lucy.'

'I know - your Sergeant has been at pains to point that out! But…' she raised her hands in a gesture of futility 'all I can tell you is that I *didn't!* I was in the toilet, trying to pull myself together… Oh, what's the *use!*' She slumped back onto the bunk, her shoulders sagging, close to tears. Russell hesitated, then sat beside her:

'Lucy?' She raised he eyes to his as he went on: 'We are still investigating what happened last week. You're right when you say that Sergeant Rimmer thinks you killed him - I'm… not *quite* so certain. That's why I want you to help me - I need to know *everything* you can tell me about the drugs Roddie was selling, everything you can remember, however insignificant it might seem. Will you do that?'

The look in her emerald eyes was one of hopelessness as she replied:

'I *have* told the Sergeant all I could! I don't know very much about it - he never said a lot, kept it to himself. I know that was why he came to Sweeney's in the first place, why he was there so often - but he never told me where the stuff came from, and I didn't ask. I suppose I didn't really want to know - it wasn't something he was proud of, just another job, he said; and I didn't want Freya, or Muriel, to find out, they'd have been upset, scared perhaps.'

'I see. The other staff at Sweeney's knew about him selling there?'

'Of course! They could hardly *not* know, could they? Look, Inspector, I don't want to land any of them in trouble, you understand? They probably won't admit to knowing anything… and, some of them were *buying* from him, as well. Oh, nothing really nasty, just cannabis, a few E's perhaps. But, I don't want to be the one to get them arrested; they aren't doing anyone any harm.'

'I understand - I promise I won't harass them about it; but their confirmation of your story would be a help. What about Uris and Duffy - did they know?'

'Ye-es… Ike knew, I'm sure, although I imagine he'd regard it as nothing to do with him. Mr Duffy must have known - but I think he preferred to ignore it, I think he kind of disapproved. Roddie always kept his head down while he was about the bars.'

'He didn't give Roddie any trouble?'

'No…' She paused, then went on thoughtfully: 'Fluffy's a funny bastard at times, he can be really awkward when he wants to. We did have a kind of bad patch - about a year ago, it was, he turned really funny, with me as well as Roddie, gave us all kinds of grief. But then it seemed to blow over, and he was all right again. Perhaps I should tell you - before Roddie came along, Frank had a bit of a soft spot for me. He fancied his chances with me, for a while, but then I met Roddie… He seemed to take it in good part, just backed off and left me alone. Then, a couple of years later, he turns all starchy for a month or two, for no reason!'

Russell nodded:

'How about Mr Gidding?' The girl sat gazing at him, chewing at her lower lip as if unsure what to say; slowly, she nodded:

'Yes. He was… I can't *prove* anything, you understand, but it was common knowledge that he was taking a cut. Roddie was giving him a percentage, in return for leaving him a clear field, getting rid of any other pushers who tried to get in there. Roddie told me that, once, himself - but as I say, everyone *knew,* anyway.'

'So Gidding's big anti-drug stance was all a sham?' She laughed:

'Yes - from start to finish! And he took everyone in, didn't he? Except us who worked there, and we weren't going to let on, or we'd be out of a job, wouldn't we?' Russell chuckled with her:

'I suppose you would! Do you know a Paddy Thomas?' He changed tack; a look of disapproval crossed the girl's face:

'Yes. I don't like him, I'm afraid - he and Roddie had been mates way back, in Belfast. He'd come around to see him sometimes, at the house - but I didn't get along with him. I told Roddie, and he told him to keep away - they would meet sometimes for a drink in the evening, in one of the pubs, or he'd call on Roddie at his flat.'

'Any reason for your dislike of him?' She hesitated, then replied:

'He came to the house once, while Roddie was out. I expect he knew… what I do at the club; anyway, he tried it on. But I smacked him in the teeth, threw him out! He's not very strong, he didn't give me any real trouble, but as I say, Roddie told him to stay away after that.'

'Can you describe him?'

'Oh, he's a skinny fellow, maybe five foot nine or ten, thin face with a rather big nose, blue eyes and bushy, curly brown hair. Talks with a Belfast accent, as you'd expect; I've never seen him looking smart, he always seems to be scruffy and down-at-heel.'

'Right - thank you. Could he have had anything to do with the drugs business, do you think?' She shrugged:

'Possibly. Roddie never said - I assumed they just met to have a drink and a chat about old times.'

'All right. You've been a great help, Lucy - is there anything else you can tell me?' She shook her head:

'Not that I can remember.'

'Okay, and thank you.' He stood up to call for the sergeant, but she grabbed his sleeve:

'Inspector Russell?' He looked down at her: 'Is it possible… could I see my daughter?' He smiled sympathetically:

'We're not supposed to allow visitors in police cells - but I'll see what I can do, see if we can bend the rules a bit, under the circumstances. But I can't promise anything, you understand?'

'All right - thank you. I miss her so much…' Tears glistened in her eyes; he reached out, took her hand in his own:

'I'll do what I can, I promise.' She nodded, smiling through her sorrow:

'Thank you.' Her voice was a husky whisper.

* * *

After a quick canteen lunch, Inspector and Sergeant were again closeted in Russell's third floor office. From his perch on the corner of the desk, Rimmer said:

'So you were right - Gidding himself was behind Roddie's dealings?'

'Or at least colluding in them, yes.'

'Doesn't let Lucy off the hook though, does it?'

'No - but it does make the whole damned situation that much more complicated. We've got one Ulsterman, selling drugs in an English nightclub with the support of the owner, apparently being supplied direct from Belfast by another Ulsterman acting as courier. The whole thing just doesn't add up to a logical operation, however you look at it! The only reason for such a long supply line would be if... Oh, Holy *Shit!*' Rimmer looked startled:

'What is it, boss?' But Russell was scrabbling through papers, looking for the message pad. He found it, stared for a moment, then grabbed up the telephone and began dialling.

CHAPTER TWENTY-SIX

As he waited for the connection to be made, Russell put his hand over the phone's mouthpiece:

'The only sensible reason for the drugs coming from Belfast is if the whole thing is being driven from that end - we've been looking at it from our perspective, Doug, not...' He broke off, spoke into the telephone: 'D.C.I. Callow, please. D.I. Russell, from Grancester, in England.' Turning back to the Sergeant, he went on: 'If that's right, then we're looking at a picture that's a whole lot bigger than we bargained for.'

'I'm not sure I...' But Russell gestured him to silence:

'Chief Inspector? D.I. Russell, Grancester CID. You spoke to one of my Constables this morning.' The voice which crackled from the earpiece had the unmistakable harsh twang of the Ulsterman:

'Yes indaid, Inspector. What can I do for yew?'

'You told D.C. Trent that you are investigating something there which might be related to our enquiry - would I be right in thinking that it has to do with a connection between paramilitary groups and organised crime?'

'That's not what I told yur man, Mr Russell - but yu're quite right. He asked about a John Thomas, who travels betwin here and yur town reg'larly; now, we know this fellow from hus daiys with the U.L.A., befur he left fur England. I don't want ta say too much, in caise we've got thus all wrong - but we've got a sityation where several of these oald Republican outfuts have joined forces, and are heavily inta the drugs trade. Partly ta guv themselves something ta do, I expect, but also ta raise funds fur what they see as the eventyal resumption of the armed struggle. But we've not been able ta traice where all the stuff has been going - uf some of it is being taiken on ta England, it would answer our question; and ut would fit their purposes as well, by causing a spot of mayhem on the mainland.'

'That was my guess, Chief Inspector. You don't want us to rock the boat, I gather?'

'I'd rather yu dudn't, fur a while at least!'

'I see, sir. My problem is that this Thomas is involved with a murder enquiry here - I may need to interview him in that connection. And I think the drugs traffic is part and parcel of our case, so I can't avoid the subject - what do you suggest?'

'Well now - can yu hoald off as long as possible, tackle him oanly when yu have tu; and maybe not let on that yu know anythung aboat any wider enquiry? Just let him think you're on ta him aloane?'

'I don't see a problem with that, sir. I'm sure we can keep him in the dark about anything you're doing at that end, as long as our talking to him isn't going to spook the organisation over there?'

'I doan't see why ut should, necessarily. They must lose the occasional pusher or courier anyway - natural attrition, I guess they'd call ut! As long as yu're happy with that, Inspector?'

'I am, sir. I'll call you before we pick Thomas up, so that you can be ready if there are any repercussions.'

'Okay, thank yeh, Mr Russell. Ah'll be hearing from yew.'

'You will, sir. Thank you; goodbye for now.'

Russell's eyes met his Sergeant's as they both replaced the handsets. Rimmer had been listening in on the second line; his eyes held a question:

'Why would organised crime in Northern Ireland be interested in one little pusher in a tin-pot Northamptonshire town?' Russell laughed:

'Don't let my Tracy hear you talk like that - she loves this place! Look at it from the other end, Doug - start in Belfast, not here. They must have a supply line set up, through the Republic, I expect, and a shedful of drugs to get rid of - what better, from their point of view, to use some of them to sow trouble on the mainland at the same time as raising funds for their cause? I'd bet there are lots of little Roddies, all over England, each trafficking in their own little way, all supplied by little, inconspicuous couriers like Thomas. This could be part of a really big operation we've tripped over by accident.'

'Bugger! Yes, I see what you mean. Each set-up small enough, individually, not to attract too much notice, but adding up to big business!'

'Exactly.'

'But does this have any bearing on McKeenan's murder?'

'I don't know, Doug. I can't see any immediate connection; this has taken my eyes off that target a bit. We'd best leave any enquiry into the Belfast supply to Callow and his team - I think we should go over the last three years, since Roddie arrived here, look again for anything pertinent, in his movements and associates; and at the club, look at anything which has happened there that could even remotely be related to the drugs trade, now we know what was behind it. Can you look after that, Doug? I'd better go and tell the PM what we've found out this morning.'

'Sure, boss, leave it to me. Good luck with the Big White Wilson!'

Russell departed with a grin; Rimmer picked up the phone and dialled the number of the CID room below.

In the Superintendent's plush, top-floor office, Russell went over with his superior what they had learnt from the Ulster D.C.I., and what they had deduced about the scale of the operation. Wilson gazed up at the Inspector, idly polishing his spectacles on his handkerchief, taking it all in; he replaced the glasses on his nose, and sat in thought for a moment before asking:

'How do you rate our chances of prosecuting Gidding?'

'It's difficult to say, sir. Knowing that his involvement was common knowledge around the club and being able to prove anything are poles apart, as you'll appreciate. Even if we got other statements in support of Lucy, unless they give us something stronger than hearsay it gets us nowhere. Enid Hill might be able to identify him - but that proves nothing, either.'

'No - Gidding is too good at covering his own arse. See what you can get on him, all the same - I don't like being made a fool of!'

'Nor me, sir. I'll tackle his staff again; and we'll have to pull this Thomas at some point, whatever D.C.I. Callow thinks about it. Maybe he knows enough to give us a case.'

'If he'll talk!'

'He might, if it'll help save his own skin?'

'Hmm - all right, deal with him, if it'll put Gidding behind bars, David. I want that man - he's been getting away with too much for too long, so if we've got a chance at him as a result of this... Give it all you've got, right?' Wilson paused, then asked the same question that Rimmer had posed:

'Does all this have anything to do with McKeenan's death?' Russell considered, replied cautiously:

'There are two possibilities, sir. Either Lucy Cavendish killed him in a rage at his intention of leaving her, in which case all this is totally irrelevant, or she didn't. If she didn't, then his death is most probably related to his drug dealing in some way.'

'I've been looking over the evidence against her, David. It still seems to me that there is little if any possibility of her innocence - you're still not convinced?'

'Not a hundred percent, sir. I'm still worried that there might have been a guiding hand behind the evidence - we found the gun and the gloves almost too quickly. I mean, they were just dropped into the top of that bin - you'd expect she would have at least

pushed them down to the bottom, tried to hide them from sight...'
He shrugged, unsure of quite what he was trying to express.

'Panic, spur of the moment, David? Are the CPS looking at
the case against her?'

'They are, sir. With a view to reporting before her next court
appearance. Unless we come across anything to change the
situation, I expect them to go for a committal for trial on the
fifteenth.'

'Hmm. Well, if you want to prove any differently, you'd better
get on with it. And don't forget you've got to be at the Old Bailey
soon, for the Giuliani trial - when does that start?'

'Two days after Lucy's appearance here, sir.'

'Hmm. Assuming anyone could have got their hands on the
gun, your biggest sticking point is the gloves, I assume?'

'It's all difficult, sir. The circumstantial and eye-witness
evidence puts her at the right place at the right time, where as far
as we can see no-one else was, and having a row with the victim.
But yes, those gloves rule out most of the people who might have
been on the spot anyway - Lucy has very slim hands, so no-one
except another girl with equally small hands could possibly have
worn them. And Terry Owen is adamant that the killer *was* wearing
them when he was shot.'

'I think you're on a hiding to nothing trying to get her off,
David!'

'As I've said to Doug Rimmer, I could be completely wrong to
doubt her guilt - but I still can't help being uneasy about it.'

'All right, David - keep poking at it, see what you can find. But
don't let it take over your life, okay? There are other balls to be
kept aloft, as you well know.'

'Don't worry, sir. I'll get back to it.'

'Right. Thank you for the update.'

With the charging of their prisoner, the case no longer merited
space in the incident room. Russell found his Sergeant with the

two DC's in the CID office on the first floor, going over all the statements and reports from the enquiry:

'Anything?' Rimmer looked up, shook his head:

'Not that I can see. Nothing we've spotted in Roddie's activities which takes on any different significance now we know what he was up to. And there were only two incidents of interest to do with Sweeney's: The pusher that Gidding helped set up, just over two years ago…'

'The drugs squad thought he was one of Roseberry's men, didn't they?'

'That's right. Might mean that he had a down on Roddie, if he had found out about his set-up there - but then, Joe said he didn't think Roseberry knew who was selling there, didn't he, Steve?'

'Right.' Campbell confirmed: 'Roseberry would have been pretty pissed off to find out about anyone selling where he couldn't; and, as we said earlier sir, it could well have been pressure from him that was making Roddie threaten to cut and run, which suggests that he *did* know. But also, as we said before, it's not his style to kill the opposition - he'd have tried to scare him off, and wait for results.'

'So we're guessing that he'd got Roddie's name somehow, put the frighteners on him?'

'It would make sense, sir. But then, he'd hardly have him shot, if he was in the process of going of his own accord - doesn't add up.'

'No. You said two incidents, Doug?'

'Yeah. The other was the girl who took an overdose, just over a year ago - She'd been a hostess at Sweeney's up to a few weeks previously.'

'Oh? How long for?' Rimmer riffled through the papers on the desk, studied one:

'She'd been there nearly two years. Started as a waitress, then became a hostess after about six months, according to reports at the time of her death.'

'So she almost had to have been a customer of Roddie's, I'd assume?'

'Presumably. And equally presumably was involved in the top-floor activities, as well.'

'Ye-es. So she must have known Lucy, and the other girls. Are there any relatives locally?' Rimmer consulted his papers again:

'Seems not. She was from Newmarket - there's a mother listed here, still lives over there, I imagine.'

'Can you find out, Doug? It's hardly likely to have anything to do with anything, but it might be an idea to look her up sometime. No father?'

'Nothing here about one.'

'What was her name?'

'Emma. Emma Verdon - she was only twenty, poor kid!'

'She'd have been barely eighteen when she started there, then?'

'Guess so, yes.'

'What about her background?'

'Not a lot here - she'd gone to St Bride's School, over near Kettering, the big girl's boarding school - started work at the club soon after leaving there.'

'Wait a minute - didn't Lucy go there?'

'Yeah, I think she did. I wonder if they knew each other then?'

'Oh, I doubt it, Doug - they were, what, five years apart? And you know how kids are about fraternising with other years at school!'

'Might have known *of* each other, even so?'

'Maybe... Perhaps we will look at her a bit more closely, when we've got a minute. For now, I need a coffee - anyone else?'

He made a note of their orders, headed off to the canteen.

CHAPTER TWENTY-SEVEN

That night, David Russell surprised his family by announcing that he was going out. They would have been even more startled to know where he was going - he'd glossed over that information by saying it was to do with his investigation, which was true enough, in all fairness.

His motive, in truth, wasn't all professional. Daniel had come home after his detention in a really furious mood, and upset his mother by being grumpy with both her and his little sister, so the home atmosphere hadn't been all it might be. Dinner had been a silent affair, the boy's anger communicating itself in his lack of conversation as well as his black expression, so Russell wasn't sorry to leave them to it for a while.

* * *

The doorman, Joe Haston, waved him in with a grin when he showed his warrant card. He bought a pint of London Pride at the downstairs bar, restraining himself from flinching at the price demanded by a smiling Aaron Stevens.

He had been sitting quietly at a small table near the door to the side corridor for a few minutes when he became aware of someone approaching him:

'Good evening, Mr Russell - may I join you?' He glanced up, smiled at the girl:

'Good evening, Elsa - please do!' She smiled back and took a seat facing him:

'Forgive my informality - I thought I'd better not use your title in here.'

'Quite - I don't want to cause a stir!' They both laughed.

'What brings you here? It's hardly normal territory for off-duty policemen!'

'No, indeed! I just wanted to try and - I don't know - get a feel for the place when it's working, if you know what I mean.' She nodded, uncertain how to broach the subject she wanted to raise:

'You've charged Lucy with shooting Roddie?' He looked at her, aware of her nervousness, nodded slowly:

'You don't think she did it?'

'I *know* she didn't! I've been her best friend, ever since we were at school together, and I *know* how much she loved Roddie - she could never have killed him, whatever he'd done to her, it just isn't in her!' He held her eyes, seeing the distress in them, and the certainty:

'But do you have any *evidence* that would convince me? Or a judge and jury?' She shook her head, hopelessly:

'No, I suppose not. But - there's a lot goes on here you don't know about, Mr Russell. Whoever killed Roddie must have had something to do with his drug dealing - you do know about that, I remember you asking me about it!' He replied cautiously, not wanting to prompt her in case she could give him something useful:

'We do, yes?' She leant forward across the table, an earnest light in her blue eyes:

'But you *don't* know *everything* about it, do you? You don't know...' She broke off, looked around: 'This isn't the place to talk about it - can we come and see you, in your office?'

'We?'

'My brother and I. We want to do anything we can to help stop Lucy going to prison for something she didn't *do!* Can we?'

'Of course - tomorrow?'

'Okay - when?'

'Let's say - eleven o'clock? You know where to come?'

'Sure! We'll see you then - thank you, Mr Russell.' She went to get up and leave the table, but he asked as she rose:

'Did you know Emma Verdon?'

'Of course!' Her face betrayed surprise and sorrow: 'She was a good kid - we - Lucy and I - kind of looked after her, as much as we could. She - let the drugs get too much of a hold on her, and we couldn't do anything about it, after a while. But - it must be a year ago, since she died?' He nodded sympathetically:

'It was - do you mind telling me more about her as well, tomorrow?'

'If you think it'll help, of course.' Her puzzlement sounded in her tone: 'We'll see you at eleven, then?'

'I'll look forward to it - thank you, Elsa.'

She nodded, strolled casually away. Russell watched her go, a thoughtful look on his face - could she really add anything to his knowledge of the case? It wouldn't hurt to let her and her brother have their say - perhaps they *did* have useful information about the goings-on in the club, even something positive to implicate Gidding with the drug dealing...

* * *

The next morning, he again gathered his forces for a briefing. In his office, with his Sergeant perched on the desk as always, and the two DC's seated facing him, he apportioned the jobs for the day:

'Doug - you and Darren arrange a formal interview with Lucy, with her solicitor on hand, and get a formal statement from her of everything she told me yesterday. Push her for any evidence against Gidding, anything she can remember that might be useable in court. And push her on the subject of Thomas, as well - did she overhear anything that might confirm that he was Roddie's courier?

Steve, I want you to do the rounds of the Sweeney's staff again, while they're at home, tell them we know all about Gidding's involvement with Roddie's drug dealing, see if they can support that with anything useful. All except the Jurgens', they're supposedly coming here at eleven to see me.'

'Do we want to talk to Thomas yet?' Rimmer asked.

'We'll have to, before long. I think he's probably the best chance we've got of nailing Gidding, he's most likely to know some of the detail of Roddie's set-up; but I'd like to know as much as we can before we pick him up. We'll leave him to think we know nothing for now; when we're ready, we'll bring him in, pin him in a corner before he has time to think about it.'

When the three had departed, Russell sat in thought for a while, trying to focus upon the subject of McKeenan's murder. Breakfast at home had been little better than dinner the previous night, Daniel still fuming about whatever had happened in his detention, his mood upsetting Sarah and getting his mother more and more annoyed with him, if only because he wouldn't talk about it. Now, his father shook his head as if to dislodge the distraction from his mind.

Both Rimmer and Wilson had been correct - what they were slowly uncovering about the drugs business did nothing to change the evidence against Lucy, gave him no support for his doubts about her guilt. Perhaps they were right; perhaps she had shot her lover in a fit of jealousy, perhaps it had nothing to do with drugs, and he was barking up a barren tree. But even if that were true, pursuing the drugs angle had proved useful in itself; especially if they were able, as a result, to prove the nightclub owner's complicity, to put him away for conspiracy to supply...

He sighed, forcibly turned his mind to other pressing matters - like the impending Old Bailey trial.

* * *

Just on eleven, the telephone on his desk rang. Returning to the present, he picked it up:

'Russell.'

'Sir? There's a Miss Jurgens downstairs, asking for you.'

'Thanks - I'll be right down.'

He took the lift to the ground floor, collected his visitors and led them back up to his office. There, he seated them and grabbed a passing constable, sending him for coffee; leaning back in his own chair, he opened the conversation:

'Elsa; Karl - thank you for coming to see me. I understand you want to talk to me about Sweeney's?' The girl took up his invitation:

'Yes, Mr Russell. The thing is, as I told you last night, we both know that Lucy can't have shot Roddie. Oh, we can't give her an alibi, prove she was somewhere else, or anything like that; but *we know her,* and we know she *couldn't* have killed him.'

'I see. But, the problem is, all the evidence we've been able to find tends to prove that she *did.* ' Elsa looked despairingly at her brother; he asked:

'I suppose you can't tell us what that evidence is, can you?' Russell shook his head:

'No, I can't, I'm afraid. What I *can* tell you is that we've not been able to identify *anyone else* who could possibly have killed him. Everyone else who was there that night, who could fit the other evidence we have, is accounted for at the time he was shot. So you see my difficulty?' The girl looked at him, puzzled:

'But - you told me last night, that you weren't *entirely* convinced of her guilt?'

'I like to keep an open mind, Elsa. And I have to say, I'm not totally happy about it - I have a nagging feeling that there was more to Roddie's death than meets the eye, that something is being hidden from me. But that doesn't alter the weight of evidence against Lucy, the fact that I can't see how anyone else can have been there at that precise moment.'

'What about whoever it was he was supposed to meet in the lane outside?'

'We've found no evidence that anyone was there - it's our view that he said that just to get away from her, from the argument they were having.'

Neither of his two protagonists replied; they looked at each other, considering this possibility, wondering what they could say that might deflect his arguments. Elsa gave a deep sigh, turned her gaze back on the Inspector:

'Can I tell you a bit about us, Mr Russell?'

'If you wish, Elsa.' She glanced at her brother before going on:

'We're from Zimbabwe, Mr Russell. Our father was South African, from a white farming family, but he moved North to marry a Rhodesian girl, in the days of Ian Smith. They had a big farm, in the South of the country. Dad wanted us, Karl and I, to be educated in England - he always said that you had the finest schools in the world. I came to St Bride's when I was eleven, stayed as a boarder and went home for the holidays; Karl followed me, three years later - he went to Elwood Priors, here in Grancester. And then, when I was sixteen, and he was only thirteen, our parents were killed; beaten to death in their own living room. This was before the world began to hear about Mugabe's atrocities, but it was his thugs behind it, without a doubt.' As she spoke, Russell's brow had furrowed in shocked disbelief:

'I'm so sorry, Elsa, I had no idea!' She smiled sadly:

'There's no reason you should, Mr Russell. Anyway, we were stuck here - with our home gone, there was no point in going back to Zimbabwe. Our schools were terrific, both of them - they kept us on, Professor Galton, my headmistress, and Dr Frankham at The Priors managed to arrange funding to see us through to our A-levels, and in the holidays we would go to stay with relatives in South Africa. When I finished school, I stayed here to be with Karl - before then, Lucy had left. You know all about Freya?' Russell nodded:

'Of course - she's a lovely child, even if I'm not exactly flavour of the month with her!' Elsa snorted with amusement:

'That's hardly surprising! But you know about Lucy getting pregnant while she was still at St Bride's?'

'I do.'

'She had to leave, as you can imagine. She was only just seventeen when Freya was born - the council had put her in a bedsit, near the station, but she took a job at the club, waitressing, to make ends meet. Muriel - you've met her?' Russell just nodded.

'She would look after the baby while Lucy was working. By the time I left school, she'd managed to get a bigger flat - she took me in, helped to get me a job there too. This was before it was Sweeney's, of course - when Mr Gidding had the old place down by the station. She'd become what Mr Gidding calls a hostess, sitting with the customers, chatting them up, getting them to buy more drinks - and providing other services, if they wanted. You understand?'

'I do. We've known all about the top floor activities at Sweeney's for a long time! Our uniformed branch would have liked to put a stop to it, jail Gidding for his part in that kind of thing, but they've never been able to amass enough evidence against him. It was going on back then, too?' The girl grinned:

'Oh yes! Just as well they didn't stop him, they'd have done us all out of a job - and I suppose we'd have ended up in prison too?'

'Possibly. They were always more interested in him; that's why they never bothered you girls. That, and the fact that there was never any trouble at the club, which would have forced their hand.'

'I see! And we all thought the poor old plods had no idea!' She laughed; Russell joined in. Karl looked surprised, but then his merriment formed a third harmony with theirs. After a moment, Elsa went on:

'Things have remained pretty much the same ever since. Karl

got a job as barman, and we all moved with the job when he took the lease on your old police station - we got our own house, eventually, about the same time Lucy bought the house in Buckingham Street. We - Lucy and I - have always planned to get out of the sex business eventually, start our own hairdressing salon, doing manicure, make-overs, all that kind of thing. We've just about got enough capital together now - and Karl is going to be our manager and admin department, aren't you, little brother?'

'That's the plan, Mr Russell.' He confirmed. Elsa added:

'So you see, we owe Lucy nearly everything. You can understand why we can't imagine anyone who could be so selfless with us, could possibly take a gun and shoot the man she wanted to marry.'

Russell sat back in his chair, thinking. What the girl had said was all very well, but it didn't give him any more reason to doubt Lucy's guilt than he had already. He sighed:

'I can sympathise with your feelings - but it doesn't *prove* she didn't kill him. People can do incredible things, things totally out of character, in the stress of the moment. She had quite a temper, and it has to be possible that that took over, long enough for the deed to be done, surely?'

'Oh, I suppose it seems that way - but you don't *know* her! She could flare up, for sure - but not like that!'

CHAPTER TWENTY-EIGHT

The ensuing silence was broken by a knock at the door. Russell got up, opened it and took a tray from the officer waiting outside:

'Thanks, Ron.' He smiled down at his guests: 'Coffee!'

Placing the tray on the desk, on top of a pile of papers, he gestured for them to help themselves.

'Tell me about Emma.' He prompted. Elsa glanced up:

'Why are you so interested in her, after all this time?'

'I'm not, especially - but we're going back, in detail, over the last three years, since Roddie came to Grancester, looking at anything which was connected with the club, or with him. She worked there - and, as we said last night, she was a customer of his.' The girl nodded:

'Okay - but I can't see how she has anything to do with his murder. She started as a waitress, like the rest of us, but Gidding soon spotted her. She'd come straight from school, just like me - because she lived in Newmarket, she needed somewhere to stay, and Lucy took her in, let her have the spare bedroom. She lived there for, oh, over a year, before she got the flat in Northampton.'

'That was where she died?'

'Yeah. Like I say, Gidding spotted her, chatted her up, persuaded her she could make a lot of money as a 'hostess', and she went for it. But - poor kid - she found what she was expected to do - top floor, you know? - was too much for her. She started taking drugs. Not just the occasional E, like the rest of us, serious stuff.

As I told you, it got the better of her. She started missing days at work; then she disappeared altogether for a few weeks - next thing we heard, she'd been found dead of an overdose, in the flat.'

'You say Gidding talked her into it - he didn't do that openly, surely?' She laughed:

'Oh no! Because she was staying with Lucy, he could talk to her in private, there. She told me he worked on her over a few weeks, when he called to collect his cut from Lucy, until he persuaded her. Just like Lucy, and me, the idea of earning a lot of money appealed to her - at first, she would talk about building up a nest egg, like us, then getting out and doing something she wanted - but…' She shrugged.

'He was really keen to get her involved?' Elsa laughed:

'You'd better believe it! He knew she could make a mint, on her back - she was small, and slim, and pretty, didn't look more than about fourteen. Some of the punters really go for that, you understand? It gives them a real kick, thinking they're having it away with an underage kid. She used to play on it - if she thought that was what the guy wanted, she'd pretend, make out she'd slipped into the club somehow, lead them on until they were gasping for it. She used to laugh about it, told us how she'd sometimes squeeze them for more than she was supposed to, slip the extra away without telling Gidding.'

'He didn't realise?'

'He may have done, he isn't stupid! But if he did, he was happy to turn a blind eye - he'd just collect his cut when he went round there, let her get on with it. As it was, she took as much if not more than any of the rest of us. And he was taking his fringe benefits regularly there, as well.'

'Fringe benefits?' Russell knew what she was getting at, but he needed her to spell it out. The girl laughed again:

'That was another reason he was so keen to get her involved - he wanted to get in there himself! He's a randy bastard, takes it wherever he can. Not at the club, of course, that would be too obvious; when he fancies a bit, he stops over for a while when he comes to collect the cash.'

'With you? And Lucy?'

'All of us! He had to be a bit more careful with Lucy, because of Freya - but when she was at school, he had a free hand, if you'll pardon the expression!'

Russell nodded, disturbed but hardly surprised by her revelations. These kind of bullying tactics fitted his assessment of the man - but he needed to get the conversation round to something which might help him. Filing away in his mind the thought that, if the girl would co-operate, he might be able to jail Gidding for his involvement in prostitution, he asked:

'She was getting her supply from Roddie?'

'To begin with, yes. When Lucy and I realised she was getting in far too deep, we got him to stop, cut her off, in the hope it would bring her up short, bring her to her senses. But we'd left it too late, I think. She just went out and found a new source, carried on as before - that was only a few months before she died.'

'Had she been taking drugs before, or did she only start after Gidding got her into the prostitution?'

'She said she'd been experimenting a bit before, in the sixth form at school - just the odd joint, I'd imagine. Once she was into the top floor tricks, it became a way of switching off, avoiding having to face her conscience, I think.'

'Until it took over and killed her?'

'Yeah.' The solitary word came out as a long sigh. Russell let the silence run for a minute or two before asking:

'How much do you know about Roddie's drug dealing?'

'At the club?'

'At the club.' She paused, drawing a deep breath before replying, her face eager with her anticipated revelation:

'You know how Mr Gidding makes a thing about keeping drug dealers out of Sweeney's? That's all a front - *he's* the one behind what Roddie was doing there! He was backing him, taking a cut of the proceeds, just like he did with us - and keeping other pushers out, to leave the field free for him!' Russell nodded calmly, aware that he was taking the wind out of the girl's sails. She gazed at him, uncomprehending, until the penny dropped:

'You *know?* You know about… You're a bastard, Inspector!' He nodded again, smiling at her as she burst out laughing:

'You let us come here, and… you *bastard!*' she repeated. He raised a hand in acknowledgement of her accusation, grinning:

'Contrary to popular belief, my parents *were* married, Elsa. What I need from you is this - can you give me any *proof* of Gidding's complicity in what Roddie was doing? Anything which would stand as evidence in court?'

There was a lull in the conversation, as the girl and her brother absorbed the idea that their news had been no news at all.

'I think maybe that's where *I* come…' It was Karl who broke the silence, until his sister put a hand on his arm to stop him:

'Mr Russell - we seem to be getting a long way away from the reason that Karl and I came here today. We want to help Lucy, make you understand that she didn't kill Roddie; even if we can give you evidence against Chuck Gidding, how does that help her?'

'I don't know,' he answered honestly 'all I can say is that if I know *all* the truth, I may be able to see how and why someone else might have done it.' The girl considered this before trying a new tack:

'Can we assume for a minute that Lucy *is* innocent?' Russell nodded, allowed her to continue: 'In that case - I take it the evidence you have against her is pretty strong, not just, what do they call it, circumstantial?'

'That's right. There's forensic evidence as well as the witnesses who place her there at the time, and so on.'

'Okay, in that case - I know it sounds silly and melodramatic, but would it be sensible to think that whoever *did* shoot Roddie is deliberately *framing* her?'

'Rather than simply trying to escape justice themselves?'

'That's what I mean, yes.' She had put into words the idea which had been in the back of his mind, without his ever expressing it so categorically:

'I think you're right. *If* someone else killed him, we would have to assume that the evidence against Lucy was planted; it's too clear, and specific, to have arisen by chance.' The girl nodded, sighed:

'We'd thought' she glanced at her brother 'that it had to be something to do with the drugs, with Gidding; that they'd fallen out, maybe, or... That if we told you about that, you'd have a different idea of what had happened. But if you knew already... I take it you've gone into all that, investigated the drugs thing, and Gidding, and...' She trailed off, a hopeless look in her eyes. He nodded gently:

'We are still investigating all of that side of the enquiry, Elsa. I *don't* know everything about it, which is why I say that if you and Karl can tell me all you know, it may help, even now. And, in my view it's about time Gidding was brought to book. You know that a lot of what he's done is wrong - coercing young girls into prostitution, the way he's treated you and the others, colluding in supplying drugs to youngsters in his club - it's about time that justice caught up with him, don't you think?'

'Maybe. Tell me the truth, Mr Russell - if we help you, what are the chances of showing that Lucy's innocent?'

'I honestly can't answer you, Elsa. And you must remember, it's not my job to provide her with a defence - but I want to know the truth; I don't want anyone wrongfully convicted, just to clear up my case. I suppose I *can* tell you that some at least of my evidence *could* be explained if someone else held the gun, especially if their intention was to frame Lucy - but the biggest problem is that everyone else who was there that night can account for where they were, what they were doing, when he was shot. There's no-one who cannot prove they weren't out in the lane at that moment…' He paused, suddenly realising that that wasn't *strictly* true: There was someone, who couldn't actually prove where he was - but that was preposterous, he couldn't have killed McKeenan! And yet, there was something else niggling in the recesses of his mind, as elusive as a curl of smoke from a distant chimney, on the fringe of consciousness… Unable to grasp it, he brought himself back to the conversation at hand:

'All I can ask is for you two to give me what you can, let me and my team work on all the circumstances surrounding Roddie's death, and see where it takes us. If Lucy *is* innocent, I would hope and expect that to become clear at some stage in the process.'

The girl turned to her brother; he squeezed her arm where his hand rested upon it, gave her a gentle smile. She looked back at the waiting Inspector, and nodded:

'Okay, Mr Russell. We'll tell you what we can. I can testify about the way the prostitution business is run, how Mr Gidding talked us into it, collected his cut from us, all that. I've kept a little notebook, written down the amount I've taken each time, and how much he's taken when he's come to collect - that should be useful, shouldn't it?'

'It will, Elsa. Would the other girls back up your story, do you think?' She grinned:

'You'll have to ask them! I expect Lucy will, if you tell her it might help prove she didn't shoot Roddie - or I could talk to her, if you like?'

'I'm sure she'll co-operate, if I can tell her that you're helping us already. How about the others?'

'Petra probably would - she hates his guts! I know she only sticks it because of the money, she's threatened to walk out lots of times. Diana might be more difficult - strange as it seems, she's quite sweet on him. No accounting for taste, is there?'

Russell echoed her grin, turned to her brother:

'How about you, Karl?' The young man nodded:

'I don't like Gidding, never have. I could put up with working for him only because we didn't see that much of him! He's a fat, arrogant pig, who's made his money by exploiting other people - not only Elsa and the other girls, but the customers as well. He's always kept the drugs thing really close to his chest, never had anything to do with Roddie at the club. But a couple of weeks ago, I overheard them having a row early in the evening, in the ground-floor storeroom. Roddie didn't usually come in so early - I had the impression he was worried when I saw him, and then, when I went to get something from the store, I heard the two of them having a pretty heated conversation in there, where they were out of sight. Roddie was saying that he had to pack it in, leave the area, and Gidding was getting really angry, telling him he couldn't, threatening to shop him if he didn't agree to carry on.'

'How much detail can you remember, of what was actually said?' Russell asked. Jurgens thought for a moment:

'Most of it, I think. I've got a pretty good memory, generally. Roddie was trying to explain that he'd been visited by a couple of thugs who'd told him he ought to move away for the sake of his health - they'd been sent by a guy called... Roseman? Something like that.'

'Roseberry?'

'Yeah, that's it! Anyway, he was saying that his orders from his commander were that he was not to make any waves, to get out quick if he had the locals on his tail, move on and set up again somewhere else, not to risk anything getting out about their supply route in case it jeopardised the whole operation. It didn't make much sense to me, but that was the gist of if, as I remember.' Russell was nodding slowly:

'It makes sense to me, Karl. And Gidding's reaction was to try to dissuade him?'

'Yeah. He was saying that he'd put a lot of effort into setting things up for Roddie, kept other pushers off his back in the past. He could buy the stuff locally, if Roddie's source dried up, or cut him off - in the end, he gave up, told him to bugger off if he didn't have the guts to stick it out, he'd find someone else to take over.'

'That was the end of the conversation?'

'Yeah. I got back into the bar before they came out, so they didn't know I'd overheard anything. Roddie came over, had a beer - Mr Gidding stalked out the front door, into the lobby. I don't know if he went up to his office, or straight home - he usually leaves about that time, anyway.'

'Okay. Thank you, Karl - and you, Elsa. I'll get you both to give us a formal statement - and if you can let me have that notebook, Elsa?'

'Of course, Inspector.'

Russell picked up the telephone, dialled the CID room:

'Doug - what's happening down there?'

'Sir - Lucy's solicitor can't get here until this afternoon, so we're going to interview her again then. What did the other two want to tell you?' Russell laughed:

'They're still with me, Doug! Can you and Darren take one each, take down a statement? They can give us the start of a case against Gidding, for conspiracy to supply *and* living off immoral earnings.'

'They can? That's great! We'll be right there, take them down to the interview rooms. What about corroboration?'

'We'll have to do what we can, talk to the other girls, the other staff. You can start with Lucy, later - tell her that Elsa's spilling the beans' he grinned across the desk at the girl 'that her confirmation will go in her favour, whatever else happens.'

'Right, boss! It'll be good to put that bastard away, won't it? We'll be up in a couple of minutes.'

Russell replaced the receiver, looked up at the two facing him:

'Thank you again, both of you. My Sergeant and a Constable will be here right away - they'll take a statement from each of you, if that's okay?'

'That'll be fine, Mr Russell' The girl confirmed, glancing at her brother who nodded his agreement: 'I imagine, if you arrest Mr Gidding, it'll meant the club will be finished.'

'I'd assume so, Elsa. I'm sorry if you two are doing yourselves out of your jobs!' She laughed:

'Not to worry! As I said, we were pretty well ready to quit and do our own thing anyway. We can start to look for somewhere to set up, ready for when all the fuss has died down, can't we?'

CHAPTER TWENTY-NINE

After his two witnesses had been ushered out by Rimmer and the DC, Russell sat back in his chair, feeling quietly satisfied. They didn't represent a cast-iron case, by any means, but if the corroboration was forthcoming, Gidding could be facing the end of his unsavoury career in the very near future. That would please the PM! He reached for the telephone again, dialled the Superintendent's office.

A few minutes later, smiling from the CID chief's congratulatory remarks, he rose to go and find some lunch in the canteen. But as he opened the door, the phone on his desk rang; he turned and grabbed it up:

'Russell.'

'Sir? I've got a Doctor Frankham on the phone for you.'

'Frankham?'

'Yes, sir.' Momentarily disoriented, he struggled for the significance of the name; but then the penny dropped:

'Oh, yes - put him through, Maisie.' There was a pause, a click on the line:

'Mr Russell? Colin Frankham, Elwood Priors.'

'Yes, Dr Frankham - what can I do for you?' Russell's heart was in his boots - why would Daniel's Headmaster be calling him at work? What had the boy done now?

'Well, I know how busy you are, Mr Russell - but I was hoping you might be able to spare me a little time today? Is there any possibility you could stop by my office, later on?'

'What is it, Dr Frankham - is Daniel in trouble?'

'Not exactly - I intend to have a word with him, after school, and I would like you to be there, if it's at all possible.'

'I'll be there, Headmaster - what time?'

'Around three?'

'Very good - I'll see you then.' He put the phone down, his feeling of elation dissipated - *Oh no, now what?* - and set off once more for the canteen.

He was finishing his egg and chips when Rimmer entered the room, came over and joined him at the table:

'Not eating, Doug?'

'I'll get something in minute, boss. That girl's quite a character, isn't she?'

'Mmm.' Russell nodded, his mouth full.

'Darren and I've got their statements down in full; I sent him to follow them back to the house, pick up Elsa's notebook and diaries, anything else that might be of use to us. We're on the way, aren't we?' His enthusiasm sounded in his voice.

'I think we are, Doug. We'll need all the corroboration we can get, mind you.'

'Yeah, sure - but this is a great start! What do you want to do now?'

'Well...' His meal finished, Russell lay down his knife and fork, sat back: 'I hope Lucy will agree to back up what Elsa's told us - she has to be able to corroborate all the details of the prostitution racket. And she might well know more about the drugs than she's told us already, especially about Gidding's part in it - if she can implicate him there, it will support Karl's testimony.'

'Yeah, but - she's no great reason to help us really, has she? I mean, if we're going to put her away for murder, why should she co-operate?'

'I want you to get a word with her solicitor before you speak to her, Doug. Tell her that we can pin the drugs and the prostitution charges on Gidding anyway, but that her client's testimony would go a long way towards substantiating the case against him - and we'll let them go for manslaughter on the grounds of diminished responsibility, if Lucy co-operates.'

'Going out on a limb a bit, aren't you? Will the C.P.S. go along with that?'

'Look at the facts, Doug - we're suggesting ourselves that she shot him in a moment of blind rage. That's diminished responsibility straight away, isn't it?'

Rimmer grinned: 'I guess it is! But if they're still insisting she's innocent?'

'It's all we can offer, at the moment. That, and the hope, if you like, that further investigation into Gidding's affairs might offer us another suspect in the fullness of time.'

'Okay - I'll see what I can do. Aren't you going to be in on it?'

'I'll leave her to you, Doug - I've got to be elsewhere, a bit later on. Have you heard from Steve Campbell at all?'

'Not so far.'

'Give him a call, will you, tell him what we've got from the Jurgens', and to try to get the others to come on board as he talks to them. Elsa reckons that one of the girls, Petra whatever-her-name-was, will probably back their story up; and I'm hoping that the other barmen might be able to give us more relating to the drugs trade, once they know we're going for Gidding anyway. I mean, if we nail him, their jobs are down the tubes in any case, aren't they? So they've no more to lose by helping us out.'

'Yeah, right. You want me to see if Mrs Hill can identify Gidding as the man in the café?'

'Do that, Doug. And we'll have to pull that Thomas character in, whatever DCI Callow thinks about it - he must have a pretty good idea of the set-up between Roddie and Gidding, surely? Mr Wilson's already told me we can strike a deal with him if he can give us useful evidence - we'd probably have a job proving anything against him, on what we know so far, so I'd be inclined to let him go if he'll give testimony against Gidding. We've got an address for him?'

'Yeah. A flat - more like a bedsit, really, I understand - down Midland Road somewhere.'

'Neighbour of Roddie's, then, as well as his mate?'

'Close. About six doors down, I think. You want to call Belfast before we pick him up?'

'I will - I promised Mr Callow I would. In fact, I'll go up and do it now.'

'Okay, boss. I'll grab a quick bite, then get on myself.'

'All right, Doug.'

Back in his office, Russell dialled Northern Ireland, asked for DCI Callow. The Ulsterman came on the line:

'Inspector Russell - Tony Callow.'

'Good afternoon, sir. I called to tell you that I need to interview Paddy Thomas, the courier we were talking about before?'

'Oh, yes, Inspector. Yu're going ta arrest him?'

'Bring him in for questioning, rather. My aim is to prosecute the man who runs the nightclub here, where Roddie McKeenan was selling, and I'm hopeful that Thomas can give me useful corroborating evidence to implicate the man.'

'I see. Can yu get what yu want withouat blowing the lud off oar little operation here?'

'I don't see why not, sir. We won't need to discuss your end of the supply line - I can let Thomas think we don't know where he's been picking the stuff up, just that we know he's been carrying for Roddie. I'll aim to scare the pants off him, persuade him to testify against our man in return for turning him loose without charge - that way, your people there shouldn't take fright.'

'I think we can luve wuth that, Mr Russell. As I said befur, these people must expect to lose the odd man noaw and again - ut's un the naiture of their business. And they'll know that yew are going ta push hard, with a murder ta solve at yur end. Keep me informed, will you?'

'Of course, sir - I'll send you copies of anything we get from Thomas, in case it's of help to you.'

'I'd appreciaite that, Mr Russell, thank yew. And thank yu for yur call. I'll let yu get on wuth yur chaise - and the best of luck to yu!'

'Thank you, sir. Goodbye for now.'

'Goodbye, Mr Russell.'

Russell leant back in the chair, looked up at the clock on the wall - nearly two o'clock. He'd need to head over to the school shortly - what the hell did the Headmaster want him there for? Surely his son's infractions couldn't be *that* serious? He wouldn't have time to go and pick up Thomas beforehand - by the time he got back, perhaps Doug would be done with interviewing Lucy, and the two of them could go and find the man. Oh, well - he picked up the typewritten copies of Elsa and Karl Jurgens' statements, read through them to confirm that they matched his recollection of their stories. That done, he got reluctantly to his feet, slipped on his coat and headed down to the car park.

* * *

'Mr Russell - I'm sorry to trouble you like this. Won't you come with me?' Dr Colin Frankham was his usual courteous self when he came to meet Russell in the school's reception hall. He led the way through the oak-lined corridors towards his office, making casual conversation about the inclement weather - outside, a chill grey drizzle was once again falling. In the office, he waved Russell to one of the deep leather armchairs facing his desk, seated himself behind its carved bulk:

'You'll be wondering why I asked you to come here, Mr Russell?'

'I am indeed, Dr Frankham.' The academic leant forward, steepling his hands, fingertip to fingertip, his elbows on the desk-top:

'You will be aware that your son was in detention last night?' Russell nodded.

'I will go into the rights or wrongs of that in a moment. What I wanted to say to you is that the circumstances under which Mr Handford gave Daniel that detention have made me realise that we have a potential problem. You will know that we have a blanket ban on mobile telephones in the school?' Russell nodded again.

'Well, that is fine for our boarders. They can always be contacted through the school switchboard, of course; and most of them do have their own mobile phones, which they keep in their dormitories during school hours. But Daniel's... discussion, shall we call it? - with Mr Handford, the other day, has brought to my attention that the ruling could cause difficulties for our day pupils, such as your son and his friends, in that, while they too can be reached while they are here in school, once they leave the premises, they become incommunicado, so to speak. And I appreciate that they may need to get in touch with parents, or vice versa, at such times. So I am going to propose to the next staff meeting that we amend that rule to allow day pupils to *carry* mobile telephones in school, as long as they are not *used* during school hours. Much as you have yourself instructed Daniel to do.'

'I think that is a very sensible move, Dr Frankham - you have obviously realised my concerns, in my son's case. And, as you say, similar considerations apply to other boys. But - did you need to ask me here to tell me this?'

'Ah - there is another matter, Mr Russell. Your son should be joining us any moment - I left instructions for him to come here after his last class. Discipline must be maintained, Mr Russell, even in the face of such ingenuity as... ah, that'll be Daniel now!' A knock sounded at the door, and Martha Pimblott, the Headmaster's secretary, ushered the thirteen-year-old in:

'You wanted to see me, sir?' The boys eyes glanced fearfully at his father as he spoke. Frankham's face had taken on a stern expression:

'I did, Russell. You were in detention with Mr Handford last night?'

'Yes, sir.'

'You felt that that detention was not entirely justified?'

'That's right, sir.'

'Why, may I ask?'

'Sir - I tried to explain to Mr Handford - I was only doing as my father had told me, by having my phone with me in school.'

'But your father had told you also that you were not to use it during school time, had he not?' The boy gazed at the carpet:

'Yes, sir. But - I only switched it on to show my friends, in the lunch break. I wasn't actually *using* it.'

'That's a rather fine distinction, don't you think?'

'Yes, sir.'

'So - perhaps, given that Mr Handford did not insist upon confiscating the telephone, which the existing school rule requires, perhaps the detention was, after all, a reasonable punishment, if only for disobeying your father's instructions?'

'Yes, sir.'

'So - let us come to last night, shall we?'

'Yes, sir.' Frankham caught Russell senior's curious expression, raised a hand to still his question as he explained:

'We have a system here where boys in detention are set a task, Mr Russell. Usually an essay to write; when their task is completed, they are allowed to go.' He turned to the boy again, whose head remained bowed, his eyes averted:

'What was last night's essay about, Russell?'

'Sir - what would we do if we had a puncture on our bikes, sir.'

'Now - I suspect that Mr Handford intended for you all to write, in some detail, about the procedure for repairing such a puncture. Wouldn't you agree?'

'Yes, sir.' Frankham looked up at the boy's father - now, there was a devilish twinkle in his eye. He picked up a sheet of paper from the desk, on which Russell could see a few lines in what he recognised as his son's neat, rounded script:

'This was Daniel's response, Mr Russell.' Russell took it, quickly read it through, handed it back, keeping his face impassive even though it took quite an effort. The text had read:

'If I had a puncture on my bicycle, I would wheel it carefully to the Cycle Shop in Market Street. There I would have them repair the puncture. Once that was done, I would pay for the repair, and continue my journey.'

His eyes met the Headmaster's. Neither spoke, until Frankham turned back to the boy standing in front of him:

'Mr Handford was not content with this, was he, Russell?'

'No, sir.'

'He made you stay a further hour *after* handing this in, I believe?'

'Yes, sir.'

'Do you blame him, Russell?'

'No, sir.' Frankham grinned sideways at the boy's father, turned back to him, reducing his expression to a gentle smile:

'Look at me, Daniel.' The hazel eyes lifted from the carpet to meet the amusement in the Headmaster's:

'It has been my burden, and my privilege, in many years of teaching, to come up against a great number of boys whose intelligence, ingenuity and resourcefulness when it comes to trying to bend rules, and escape due retribution, beggars belief. This' he waved the offending script 'makes me tempted to rate you near the top of that league. If you choose to apply your quick and agile mind to your *lessons,* Daniel, you could end up leaving this school carrying with you most if not all of the top honours we have to bestow. If not…' He left the remainder unsaid, then went on: 'If you were expecting a further punishment from me, your expectations will remain unfulfilled. Now get out of here before I change my mind!' Daniel gaped at him for a moment before responding:

'Yes, sir - thank you, sir!' He did as he was bid, turning to the door to make his escape, as his father called after him:

'Wait outside, Dan - I'll give you a lift home!' A quick nod over his shoulder, and the boy was gone.

Headmaster and father looked at each other, their shared amusement growing.

'Cheeky little Devil! No wonder he was in a bad mood at home last night!' Frankham just nodded - then his mirth took over, and he burst out laughing. Unable to contain himself, Russell followed suit.

'Cheeky little beggar, as you say! If your son follows you into the police force, Mr Russell, I fear for the future of the criminal fraternity!'

CHAPTER THIRTY

As David Russell was departing from the police station, headed for his son's school, Detective-Constable Steve Campbell stepped out of the lift on the ground floor of Adelaide Court. He'd found number 14, Aaron Stevens' apartment, unoccupied, and was on his way to another of the addresses on his list of Gidding's employees. The message from Sergeant Rimmer had reached him on his way there; the news that they now had sworn statements implicating the nightclub owner in drugs and prostitution had fired his enthusiasm - but his hopes of obtaining corroboration from Stevens had been dashed, at least temporarily. Oh well; he'd try the next name on the list...

But in the lobby downstairs, he met a young couple entering the building. A tall, dark-haired young man, laughingly arm-in-arm with a pretty girl, both wrapped up against the chill, encumbered with bags and boxes. He stopped them:

'Mr Stevens?' The man turned sparkling brown eyes on him: 'That's me!'

'I wonder if you could spare me a few minutes, sir? DC Campbell, Grancester CID.' The girl giggled:

'They've come for you at last, Stevie - I told you they would one day!' He grinned down at her:

'Hush, Katie - don't tell him where we hide the balaclavas!' He looked up again, his expression turning serious: 'I take it this is about Roddie McKeenan again?'

'Indirectly, yes, sir.'

'Okay, come on up. You'll bear with me while we dump the shopping - but we can offer you a hot cup of coffee?'

'That sounds wonderful!' Stevens grinned at the policeman, led the way back into the empty lift.

As he let them into the flat, he explained:

'We've been Christmas shopping, Constable. Katie took the day off, and we've been scouring the town for presents since ten this morning!' Campbell laughed, taking a liking to the easy-going barman and his pretty girl:

'I'll get around to doing mine, one day!'

Stevens dropped his burdens in a corner of the lounge; the girl added hers and slipped out of her coat. Quickly throwing it through the open door of the bedroom, she turned to Campbell:

'Coffee?'

'Please! One sugar, just a splash of milk?'

'Two minutes!' He smiled his thanks. Stevens, meanwhile, had disposed of his own coat; now, he waved the Constable to a seat, took the easy chair facing him:

'How can I help you further, Officer?'

'Well, sir - our investigation has become somewhat wider, since Mr Russell spoke to you last week. We now have confirmation of the drug-dealing which McKeenan was carrying on in the club, and we're hoping you might be able to give us supporting evidence. We have statements from one of your colleagues and one of the hostesses, implicating Mr Gidding in both the drugs and organised prostitution.'

Stevens was gazing at him, open-mouthed:

'Really? Who on Earth… no, I don't suppose you can tell me, can you? I think I can guess, though!' He laughed: 'I thought Gidding had got things sewn up so tight…! So did he, I expect! He's for his come-uppance, then, is he?' The girl had been watching, listening, from the kitchen doorway:

'About time! He's an evil-minded swine, Constable, I've been telling Aaron that for ages!' Stevens turned to her:

'You have, Katie. And you're not wrong, I've never argued that, have I?' He turned back to the policeman: 'She's been trying to persuade me to leave, give my notice in, for ages, ever since we got together.'

'Almost eighteen months now' she confirmed: 'I met Aaron there - but I didn't like the idea that you could get drugs openly in the bars. Or the things those poor girls had to do - you know?' Campbell nodded:

'We've known about that for a while, but we've never had the opportunity to nail Gidding for it - until now! Can you give us anything to support a prosecution, Mr Stevens?' The barman laughed again:

'Sounds as though my job's down the pan, anyway, doesn't it, if you put him in prison? What the hell, I can get work any time - I know the owner of The Dungeon, in Northampton, he's been after me to go and work for him for a long time! Looks like you've got your way, Katie!' He grinned over his shoulder at the girl, who came over, put her arms around his neck where he sat and kissed his cheek, her dark hair brushing his face. He slipped an arm about her, held her for a moment, smiled up at her as she let him go and turned toward the kitchen, where the kettle had begun to whistle. Looking back at the detective again, he said:

'I think I can give you what you want, Mr Campbell. I've been with Gidding since he took over the old police station, what, five years ago now? As long as Karl Jurgens. I've known about his involvement with what Roddie was doing, almost since he arrived - I was there in the bar when Gidding first spoke to him, although their discussions were quickly moved up to his office, away from the chance of being overheard. But - I think you're going to like this! - Monday, the day Sweeney's is usually closed, Gidding came here to see me. He wanted me to take over, become his pusher, with Roddie dead. He said he didn't have to be beholden to Roddie's supplier any more, that he could buy the stuff around here, there would be more profit in it for both of us that way.' The girl had returned from the kitchen, a tray in her hands - she stopped, looking down in horror at her boyfriend:

'You didn't tell me, Stevie! The arrogant *bastard!* Roddie not even buried yet, and he wants to carry on as if nothing's happened! Why didn't you tell me?' Stevens held a hand out to her; she put the tray down on the coffee-table between the chairs, took it in her own, as he said:

'I wanted to think it through, Kate. Oh, don't worry, there was no way I was going to go along with him - but you know what he's like. I couldn't turn him down, and stay on there, he'd have been on my back all the time, even if he didn't give me the sack. But it looks as if the decision's been made for me, doesn't it? I hadn't wanted to be on the dole for Christmas, which was why I was trying to string him along. But, what the hell, eh?'

Now, the girl was smiling down at him again. She perched on the arm of the chair, put her arms around his neck and kissed him soundly:

'We'll be fine, Stevie. We've got my salary - and you'll get a job, no trouble. I do love you, you dumb lump!' He kissed her back:

'So - are you going to marry me, then?' She pulled back in his arms, freed one hand to give him a clip round the ear:

'Of course I am, you stupid sod!' He drew her close again, grinning inanely over her shoulder at Campbell:

'You heard that, officer - can't get out of it now, can she?' Campbell shook his head, laughing but vaguely embarrassed at witnessing such a tender moment. The girl raised her head, gave the policeman a quick, apologetic smile before kissing her new fiancé once again, releasing him and getting to her feet:

'Now, talk to the Constable, Aaron, tell him everything, right? Let's see that evil sod in prison where he belongs!'

* * *

As Campbell was realising that he'd struck gold at the flat in Greenland, the Detective-Sergeant was coming to a similar conclusion in the interview room. Accompanied by DC Trent, he'd spoken to Alison Greening before collecting Lucy from her cell, told her of their intentions, and the deal on offer if her client would co-operate. The solicitor, smart in her dark green business suit and beige blouse, had reminded him that she had every intention, herself, of proving her client innocent of the charge; she had, however, agreed to encourage Lucy to give the police all the help she could.

And she had been as good as her word. Before the start of the formal interview, she had passed on his message to Lucy; after a brief discussion, the girl had agreed to tell them everything she knew:

'Whatever happens to me now, Sergeant, I wouldn't want to go back to work at Sweeney's, it would be… too difficult. Because of Roddie - and everything. I *didn't* kill him - and Miss Greening will *prove* that to you, eventually - but even so, I think I'll take Freya, and try and make a new start, somewhere else. So - I'll be a witness against Mr Gidding for you. For Emma's sake, if for no other reason! She was a great kid - and he talked her into being one of his 'hostesses', just because he wanted to screw her himself. Oh, the rest of us could cope with it, with *him;* but she was different, she was… a *nice* girl, you understand? Too good for him, too good to be making her living on her back - and she couldn't handle it, despite all her bravado, that's why she took to drugs, why they got such a grip on her….' Her voice trailed off. Rimmer found himself unexpectedly moved by her words; he reached across, gave her hand a quick squeeze where it lay on the table between them:

'I understand, Lucy. Now, what can you tell us about Mr Gidding?' She gave him a wan smile, glanced at Alison and drew a deep breath before speaking again:

'Elsa's told you all about how he ran the prostitution in the club, hasn't she? I can confirm all of that, how he recruited me when I was just a waitress there, told me how I could make a lot of tax-free money. When you're a single mum, with a baby to look after, any money you can earn is worth having, Sergeant, even… that way. I didn't keep diaries, records of what he took out of my earnings, the way Elsa did - but I can still stand up in court and describe how he went on.'

'That's excellent, Lucy - we'll take all that down formally, in a minute or two, get you to sign it. You're happy about that, Miss Greening?'

'I am, Sergeant. I can have copies of everything Lucy tells you, I assume? In case it's relevant to her defence on the murder charge?'

'You can, of course. Although… ' He shrugged, left his opinion unstated. Turning to Lucy again, he asked:

'Can you tell us any more about the drugs business? You've already told Inspector Russell that you knew he was in collusion with Roddie on that, haven't you?'

'Yes - I didn't tell him everything, though; I… hoped what he knew would be enough for him to find out who killed Roddie. I'm sorry - I suppose I should have told him all about it.'

'Did you know about Thomas's part in the business? That he was Roddie's courier?' She shook her head:

'Not really - I guessed he had something to do with it, but Roddie never said. And I didn't ask! But - he would talk about it with Gidding, when he came for his money. I suppose it was convenient for him, to be able to collect his cut from me, and from Roddie, at the same time; they would talk about things, quite openly. I imagine Mr Gidding thought he had nothing to fear from me knowing all about it - after all, everyone at the club knew, anyway. He must have thought that none of us would tell, because our own income depended upon the club - and without him, the club would be bound to close, wouldn't it?'

'I expect so, Lucy. Did they talk about it in front of your daughter, too?'

'No! I always made sure she was in her own room, or out playing with friends, when he was coming. Does she have to know all about this, Sergeant?'

'I'm sure we can do our best to protect her, Lucy - but it is bound to come out in court, at some stage.' The girl sighed:

'Yes, I suppose it must.' She held his eyes for a moment, then went on: 'All right - let me give you chapter and verse on their dealings, shall I? Got your pen ready, Constable?' She gave Trent a quick smile, which he echoed, raising his ballpoint in salute.

* * *

In his well-appointed office, Curtis Roseberry was contemplating the old adage that everything comes to he who waits. And, to cap it all, *now* he knew how someone had been able to sell drugs in Sweeney's nightclub without falling foul of the management!

The contact, through his well-protected network, from the club owner, had come as something of a surprise; but the prospect of supplying a new outlet, in a town where he had little trade at present, was a pleasant boost to his business. Gidding had even suggested he could provide the on-site sales team, thus avoiding Roseberry having to put any of his own people at risk. The Jamaican smiled happily as he leaned back in his soft leather chair, reached for the bottle and topped up his tumbler of Southern Comfort.

Had he been aware, however, of the net slowly closing in around Charles Gidding, he might have felt rather less self-content.

CHAPTER THIRTY-ONE

'Tell your Mum I could well be late tonight, okay?'

'Yes, Dad - still on that murder?' Daniel asked as he slid out of the car.

'Sort of, Dan. And Dan?'

'Yes, Dad?'

'I just happened to be near The Priors, okay? Picked you up because of the horrible weather. No need to tell her about what happened, is there?'

'Yeah, all right! Thanks, Dad!' The boy was gone, running through the cold darkness to the front door, fumbling for his key.

* * *

When he returned to the station, Russell was met by his Sergeant as he emerged from the stairway to the custody suite:

'You look like the cat that got the cream, Doug?' Rimmer's grin widened still further:

'You bet! I've got a statement from Lucy, not only backing up everything that the Jurgens girl told us, but with a lot of detail about Gidding's dealings with Roddie, too. The arrogant bastard was stupid enough to talk about it all in front of her! And now, with her testimony as well as theirs, I reckon we've got him neatly sewn up ready for Bedford Jail!'

'I think you mean we've got enough of a case to arrest him,

search his premises, get the financial boys at HQ to go through his books, and carry out a thorough investigation, don't you?' Rimmer's grin grew even wider:

'Amounts to the same thing, from where I'm standing, boss! Their stories should be enough to put him away whatever, I'd have thought!' Russell laughed, joining in his Sergeant's delight at the prospect:

'Could be, Doug, could be! But we'll let things take their course, shall we?'

'Yeah, of course! Shall we go and arrest him tonight?'

'I think so - a bit later. Has Steve reported in yet?'

'I spoke to him earlier, told him what we'd got from Elsa and her brother - he was on his way to see Stevens, then. You know, the barman?'

'Oh, yes. Not heard from him since?'

'Nah. I expect he'll call in any time, it's getting late!'

'Right. Come up to the office, Doug, let's go over things in detail. Darren's typing up Lucy's statement, is he?'

'Yeah. I've got a rough draft, here.'

'Good - let's see what you've got.'

The two took the lift up to the third floor and Russell's office. They were barely beginning to go through the draft statement, when a knock sounded at the door, and Steve Campbell put his head around the edge:

'Come in, Steve, join us. Take a look at what Doug's got from Lucy Cavendish!' Russell waved the DC into a chair. Campbell grinned at the Inspector, dropped several sheets of typewritten statement on top of the papers in front of his superior:

'I'll trump that, sir!' Russell picked up the sheets, glanced through them as he asked:

'What's all this, Steve?'

'Statement from Stevens, the barman, sir. He'll testify against Gidding; and he's really got the goods on him, too!' Russell looked up, askance at the Americanism:

'In English, preferably, Steve! But... ' He whistled softly: 'You're not wrong, either! Gidding has already approached *Stevens* to carry on in Roddie's shoes, Doug! With a local supply... Yes! We've got him, he'll have a job to wriggle out with all these witnesses against him. We'll pick him up shortly, Doug. Set the wheels in motion - I want a patrol car with us, for back-up...'

'Not expecting trouble, are you, boss?'

'Probably not - but let's play safe. We'll need two search teams, one for the club, one for his home - and alert HQ that we'll be wanting his records scouring thoroughly by their financial team. We still need to bring in Paddy Thomas, question him for anything he can add to our knowledge - and I'm betting he knows quite a bit! Do you want to send a car for him first, while we get the rest organised?'

'I'll do that. If they bring him in, the same car can come with us when we go for Gidding, hopefully.'

'That'll be fine, Doug.'

* * *

Less than an hour later, Inspector and Sergeant were in the custody suite to meet the two uniformed constables who were bringing Thomas in for questioning. The Irishman was quiet, cowed, wary - but when Rimmer introduced himself and Russell, he gave vent to loud protestations of innocence, declaring that he had no idea why they would want to talk to him. Russell gave him a grim smile:

'Mr Thomas? We're not charging you with anything - at least, not *yet*. I believe that you can provide us, if you choose to, with information which will be of considerable value to my investigation; whether you will face arrest and prosecution depends upon what you decide. Now, I have to go out for a while; we will be back to talk to you shortly. I suggest you use the intervening period to consider your options.' Thomas stared at him, obviously worried, as he turned away, leaving him to the attentions of the custody sergeant on duty.

As they returned to the ground floor, they were met by Chief Inspector Armstrong:

'David! Doug here tells me you're off to arrest Gidding?'

'That's right, sir. We've got enough evidence, sworn statements, to pick him up on suspicion of living off immoral earnings as well as conspiracy to supply illegal substances.'

'Right! Well done, I've wanted to see this for a long time. I've organised a search team to come with us - I assume you'll go to the house?'

'Yes, sir, I'd expect him to be there by the time we arrive, if he's following his usual schedule.'

'Fine! And there's a second team, ready to head for the club. I expect you want his office gone over with a fine tooth comb?'

'That's the idea, sir. And I've spoken to Wootton Hall Park, asked their financial investigators to get hold of his records, business and personal, and go through them for evidence of any undeclared income.'

'That's the ticket!' He glanced around as the two constables emerged from the stairway, beckoned them eagerly: 'Come on, Jackson, Dorman, we're all waiting for you!' Russell smiled at the senior officer's enthusiasm:

'Are you coming with us, sir?'

'You'd better believe it! I wouldn't miss this for the world!'

The uniformed Chief Inspector rode in the Jeep with them to Alderley Park Avenue; on the way, Russell filled him in on the evidence they held to date against the nightclub owner. Armstrong was soon chortling with delight:

'Sounds like he's facing a real rebellion in the ranks, doesn't it? Typical bloody bully - thinks no-one will have the nerve to stand up to him! I can't wait to see his face!'

Outside number 188, they pulled up; the patrol car behind, followed by the van with the search team. The three senior officers walked up to the front door, noting the presence on the drive of the white BMW, and rang the bell. The door opened, to reveal a short, mousy-haired woman, in slacks and a dark green top:

'Good evening?'

'Mrs Gidding? Is your husband home?'

'Yes, he is - who should I say's calling?' Russell smiled at her, held out his warrant card:

'D.I. Russell, Grancester CID…' Her face took on a troubled look:

'Oh, yes, I thought I recognised you. And this is your Sergeant, isn't it?'

'Sergeant Rimmer, Mrs Gidding.' He introduced himself: 'And this…' he stood aside to reveal the uniformed officer 'is Chief Inspector Armstrong.'

'Oh! So many of you? I'll get Chuck - please wait.' She hurried off inside; moments later, the solid figure of Gidding himself emerged from the dining room:

'Armstrong! What on Earth do you mean by coming here at this time, frightening my wife out of her wits?' The three policemen exchanged glances, none convinced that concern for his wife was really uppermost in the man's mind.

'Mr Gidding, so good to see you again! As I told you a while ago, this is Inspector Russell's enquiry - I'm only here as an observer.'

'Don't they let you out without a minder, then, Russell?' The small, deep-set eyes turned on the Inspector, who met them with an engaging smile:

'Sometimes, Mr Gidding, sometimes! Just now, I'm hoping to enjoy a little more of *your* company.'

'What do you mean?' The tone was suddenly suspicious.

'Charles Gidding, I am arresting you on suspicion of conspiracy to supply substances prohibited under schedules A and B of the dangerous drugs act; also, on suspicion of living off immoral earnings. You are not obliged to say anything at… '

'What bloody nonsense is *this?* For fuck's sake, Armstrong, tell this idiot to get real! *Me,* supplying drugs? And... And...' His bluster dried up in the face of the three men's implacable expressions: 'It's all fucking ridiculous!' he sounded suddenly less sure of himself. Russell continued where he had been interrupted, completing the official caution; Rimmer stepped forward:

'Now, if you'll come with us, Mr Gidding?'

CHAPTER THIRTY-TWO

The ride back to the station was notable for its silence. Every time he looked in the rear-view mirror, Russell was amused by the roguish sparkle in the Chief Inspector's eyes, the faint smile hovering around his lips - the result, he assumed, of the discomfiture of his back-seat companion.

At the police station, they ushered their captive down to the lower floor, saw him placed in custody and led away to a cell. They had left the search team at the house, beginning their usual efficient, systematic job; the second had been released, with the news of Gidding's arrest, to make their way to the club and begin a similar sweep of the offices, even though the searches of the previous week had revealed nothing there. But now, the target was different.

Armstrong, still chuckling over Gidding's fury at the turn of events, had left the two CID officers to their own devices, heading for his home in Oakfield and the supposed anger of his wife at his lateness. After a brief consultation, Rimmer led the Irish courier from his cell to an interview room, where Russell was waiting:

'Come in, Mr Thomas, sit down. Have you had a meal?' The man nodded, non-plussed by the officer's solicitude:

'Er - yes - thanks. They sent me somethin' in.'

'Sit down, please.' As he complied, Rimmer slipped two tapes into the recording machine at the end of the table between them; Russell took a seat next to the Sergeant, quoted the time and names of all three present for the sake of the record. He turned to their obviously-uncomfortable interviewee:

'Mr Thomas - we've asked you to come here because we think you have information regarding the supply of drugs to Roderick McKeenan, who was, until his death last week, selling them in Sweeney's nightclub in Midland Road. I should also tell you that we have arrested the owner of the club, Charles Gidding, for his part in supplying drugs in that establishment. Now, Mr Thomas, what do you know about all of this?'

The Irishman regarded him out of troubled eyes before asking:

'If Oi talk to yeh, what's goin' te happen te me?'

'That depends, Mr Thomas. My interest is in stopping the supply of drugs at the club, and putting those primarily responsible behind bars for a suitable period. If you can give me information, evidence, which will help me do that, it might be that I could persuade my superiors not to press any charges against you yourself - if your part in the supply was sufficiently minor, shall we say?'

'Okay, so - if Oi tell ye what Oi know, ye'll let me go, roight?'

'Possibly. If your evidence is useful to me. I don't believe you were directly involved in pushing the drugs locally; but I do know that you were acting as a courier, keeping Roddie supplied. It's his relationship with Gidding, their business relationship, you understand, that I want to know more about.' Thomas nodded, his eyes never leaving Russell's:

'What about - where Oi was gettin' the stuff? Ye'll want to know about that, too?'

'I do, Paddy. That's something I'm in the dark about, at the moment.'

'Okay - roight.' Thomas nodded, using the delay to think about what to say: 'Loike ye said, Inspector, Oi was just the courier. Oi'd pick the stuff up in London, in a bar down there - Oi didn't know where it had come from, a fella would just hand it to me, ye onderstand? Oi'd have a packet fur him, too, from Roddie - Oi guess that would be the money, wouldn't it?'

'Where was this bar, Paddy?'

'Big place, it was. Called the Hoighwayman, down the Tottenham Court Road, ye know where Oi mean?'

'I expect the boys in the Metropolitan Police will, Paddy.' Russell was aware of Rimmer regarding him with some amusement at his apparent acceptance of what they both knew was a complete fabrication. But it served his purpose to let the Irishman think he'd pulled the wool over their eyes - if he had information about Gidding!

'Let's talk about Roddie, shall we? And about Gidding. What can you tell us about them, Paddy?' Thomas paused to think once more - Roddie was dead, nothing he said could harm him now, could it? And he hadn't much liked the arrogant, bombastic club owner - if he gave them what they wanted, and this Inspector kept his word and let him go... As long as they didn't trip him up over the tale about where he'd got the stuff - but he seemed happy with it, didn't he...?

'Okay, Inspector, Oi'll tell ye what Oi can. Oi only met the guy, Gidding that is, a few times - at Roddie's flat, and once or twoice in the café, ye know, the one in Midland Road, not far from the station? He's a stuck-up bastard, thinks he rules the world, ye know? Treated me loike shit - and didn't treat Roddie much better, neither! Pleased enough te take his money, though! They'd talk about what he'd got to sell, how much they could charge for it, how much Gidding wanted out of it for keeping the local pushers off his back, keeping you guys confused, too.'

'So you can give me details of their transactions, amounts, percentages?'

'Oi can that! Whatever that jumped-up bastard thought of me, Oi'm not stupid, Inspector, and Oi've a good memory - especially when Oi've reason to remember someone!'

Russell glanced round at Rimmer, the smile spreading across his face:

'Okay, Paddy, let's have it!'

Forty-five minutes later, Russell returned to his office. Rimmer was in the CID room a floor below, typing up Thomas's statement ready for the Irishman to sign - complete with his hurriedly-made-up story of where he picked up the drugs he'd been bringing to Roddie. Russell smiled to himself - letting that go would ensure the continued security of DCI Callow's Ulster investigation, leave his targets unaware of their impending doom. Now, he had one last job himself, before he could go home for a late dinner; he reached for the telephone...

'Will you come with me, Lucy?' The girl looked up from where she was sitting despondently on the hard bench in her cell:

'More interviews, Mr Russell?' He smiled at her:

'Not exactly, Lucy.' He led her along the corridor, up the stairs and into the first interview room, waving her to a seat. He put his head out of the door, spoke to the constable on guard there:

'Will you bring in our guests, please?' He closed the door, stood to one side of it as she gazed up at him, puzzled. Then the door swung open again:

'Mummy!' Lucy spun around, a look of amazed wonder on her face; she leapt to her feet as the nine-year-old flung herself across the room and into her arms. In the doorway, Muriel Hepple regarded the two of them with a proprietorial smile; Russell beckoned her inside, quietly closed the door behind her. Beside the table, Lucy hugged her daughter close, then, gently disengaging the child's arms, held her at arms length:

'Let me look at you - Oh, Freya, I swear you've grown, even in a week! It's so lovely to see you...!' She drew her close again, held her in her arms. Over the russet blond head, she smiled up at the Inspector:

'Thank you, Mr Russell - thank you *so much!*' Her voice was a delighted whisper. He smiled back at her pleasure, as she buried her face in the little girl's hair, and turned to Muriel:

'I'll leave the three of you alone, Mrs Hepple - I can give you maybe half an hour, you understand?' She nodded, her austere face radiant with the reflected delight of the mother and daughter:

'You're not supposed to do this, Inspector?' He shook his head, grinning foolishly at the success of his machinations:

'Don't tell my boss, all right?'

'Never! And thank you - you don't know how much…' He waved her to silence, pointed to the child and her mother:

'Oh yes I do!' Her grateful smile followed him as he stepped out into the corridor.

CHAPTER THIRTY-THREE

For the second week running, David Russell found most of his weekend lost to his work. When the cases on hand were of a more mundane, low-priority nature, he could generally spend most if not all of the weekends enjoying the company of his family; but with Gidding in custody, awaiting interrogation, other witnesses and evidence in the case to be approached, studied, sifted, the job had to come first.

As he got up from the breakfast table on Saturday morning, he beckoned to his son, who looked up from the toast he was buttering with a puzzled expression.

'Your bicycle, young man!'

'What? Oh!'

'You'd better get it out of the back of my car, if you plan on using it today!'

'Yeah! I'd forgotten.' He followed his father out onto the drive, where a sharp frost had left the lawn and hedges sparklingly white. While Russell scraped the frost from the windscreen, the boy opened the tailgate and unloaded his bike, parking it close to the garage door. As he went to go back inside, his father called to him:

'Be careful, if you do go out on it today, right? The roads will be icy in places, I expect.'

'I will, Dad. Dad?'

'Yes?'

'I'm sorry - about Frankenstein dragging you in, yesterday. I know you're busy…' Russell grinned:

'That's okay - it was worth it, just for the laugh!'

'Yeah - I heard you, while I was waiting for you outside!'

'Listen to that man, Dan - he thinks a lot of you, you know?'

'Yeah, I know. He's pretty cool, for a teacher, isn't he?' Russell laughed:

'He is! I'll see you later, okay?'

'Okay - 'bye, Dad.'

The rest of Russell's day was spent focussed upon the various illegal goings-on which had been the stock-in-trade of Sweeney's nightclub and its proprietor. Gidding immediately refused to be interviewed without his solicitor present; and even when the man was on hand, the interviews were of little value to the police, with their suspect refusing to co-operate other than to stringently deny every accusation they laid against him.

Never-the-less, the case against him was growing stronger. Once his arrest had been announced, several other employees from the club had come forward to give statements, partly, Russell suspected, to try to save themselves from being implicated, even if the almost universal dislike in which the man had been held became more and more apparent as time went by. Late in the morning, Detective-Superintendent Wilson made an appearance, walking into Russell's office with a big smile on his round face:

'I gather you've got a result, David?'

'We have, sir. There're enough witnesses crawling out of the woodwork to put Gidding away with no difficulty at all!'

'That's excellent - HQ's financial group are going through his affairs, are they?'

'They're on the job as we speak, sir. I don't expect to get a report from them for a while, mind you.'

'No - that kind of investigation takes time, doesn't it?'

'Yes, sir. But the search team at the house have already come across a stash of notes, in the back of a bureau in his study - and bank books which might well refer to money he didn't want anyone to know about. I've passed them on.'

'And you can get a conviction on both charges, you think?'

'I'm sure we can, sir. Three of the 'hostesses' are prepared to go in the witness box, as well as other staff from the club, so I don't see how he can get away from the immoral earnings charge. And we've got a lot of testimony tying him in with the drugs business, from the barman he'd approached to take over after McKeenan's death to the man who brought the drugs over from Belfast.'

'You're not following through on the Belfast connection?'

'No, sir. I'm going to let Thomas, the courier, off with a caution - he doesn't know that we know about Belfast, spun us a cock-and-bull story about picking the stuff up in London, and I'm leaving it that way so as not to prejudice DCI Callow's enquiry over there. He's hoping to be able to wrap up the whole operation in one go, once they're ready.'

'Right. Good work, David. You've even got the Cavendish girl giving evidence against Gidding, I hear?'

'Yes, sir. I think, like the others, she's not sorry to see him go down - and helping us isn't going to do her any harm, even if she is convicted of killing Roddie.'

'You've nothing new on that, I take it?'

'No, sir. The case against her is unchanged, nothing has come to light to support her story.'

'Hmm. Can't say I'm surprised. But you've got another week before she's back in court, haven't you?'

'That's right, sir.'

'Well - I know you still doubt the evidence, David. See what another week brings - after that, I think you'll have to accept her guilt, come what may.'

'Very good, sir.'

'And David?'

'Sir?'

'Keep any illicit visitors in our interview rooms out of the public eye, won't you?'

As the Superintendent turned to the office door, it swung open in front of him, and Rimmer's head appeared around is edge:

'Boss! Oh, hello, sir!'

'Morning, Sergeant.'

'What is it, Doug?'

'I've just been to see Enid Hill - she's picked Gidding's picture out of the ones I took to show her.'

'So she can place him in the café, meeting Roddie?'

'Yeah - and Thomas. She's certain that all three met there at least once.'

'Great! That confirms Thomas's story nicely.'

'Doesn't it just!' Wilson was smiling:

'Excellent work, both of you! I'll leave you to get on.'

'Thank you, sir.'

* * *

After the excitement of the weekend, the following week seemed almost mundane by comparison. After being granted an extension of the time they were allowed for questioning the nightclub owner, Gidding finally appeared in court on the Tuesday morning, to be bailed to appear again after six weeks. In that time, the police hoped to be able to conclude their investigation into his affairs and brief the Crown Prosecution Service, ready for them to apply for the case to be referred for a full trial in front of a jury.

True to type, at the end of the hearing Gidding snarled at his barrister:

'Fine bloody Christmas I'm in for!' The lawyer's impatience showed in his face as well as his tone as he replied:

'Just be thankful they didn't oppose bail, Mr Gidding. You could have been spending the holiday in prison!'

'Huh!' He stormed out of the court, to be met and further

infuriated by the gaggle of press photographers who awaited him outside.

The nightclub remained closed: With most of the staff forming the prosecution case against its owner, there were too few left to run the place - Isaac Uris had joined the voices raised in accusation of his former employer, giving the police more information about his prostitution racket. The other manager, Frank Duffy, had apparently withdrawn from the fray - re-interviewed by Rimmer and Campbell, he had denied all knowledge of any illegal activities. Not that either policeman believed him - but they had enough witnesses that expending more effort on one recalcitrant one seemed unnecessary.

Apart from the man himself, one other was less than delighted at the news of Gidding's downfall. Curtis Roseberry had taken the information rather badly; his normal outward appearance of calm self-possession had escaped him momentarily, resulting in the need for the messenger, his right-hand-man Roy Winston, to take avoiding action as a heavy glass paperweight ricocheted from the wall close to his ear. His momentary anger submerged, Roseberry was now considering the future possibilities of Sweeney's - would the club remain open with Gidding out of the picture, and, if it did, could he return to the original plan of placing his own sales person in the premises in due course? For now, though, he was back to playing the waiting game.

* * *

As the dust of Gidding's arrest and charging began to settle, David Russell's mind returned to the case of Roddie McKeenan's murder. Still feeling uncomfortable with the idea of Lucy's guilt - or perhaps, the idea that he had missed something important - he was vaguely disappointed that nothing had come to light which supported his disquiet.

On the Wednesday, after Rimmer and the rest of his team had gone off duty, he again collected Lucy from her cell in person. After another all-too-brief half hour with her daughter and Muriel, he knocked on the door and re-entered the interview room where he had left them together. Sitting on her mother's lap, the little girl gave her a last, suffocating hug and kissed her; then, she got down and walked over to the Inspector, stopped looking up at him:

'Mr Russell?'

'Yes, Freya?'

'When're you going to let Mummy come home?' He bent his knees to come down to her level, not sure what to say, as she went on: 'Only - she hasn't *done* anything! And… it'll be Christmas, soon, and I don't want Christmas without her…' Tears sprang from the big emerald eyes and trickled down her cheeks. Lucy stood up and came to stand behind her child, her hands on the slim shoulders inside her thick, fur-edged coat. Russell found himself deeply affected by the little girl's sadness:

'Freya?' He reached out, held her gently by the upper arms as she nodded: 'I am still trying to find out exactly what happened to Roddie - I don't know everything yet, do you understand?' She nodded again; he went on: 'My boss in convinced that your Mummy is the one who shot him - but I'm not so sure. I want to know the truth - and I promise you, if I can prove that she didn't do it, I will. I don't know if I can - but I'll do my best, I promise.' The child nodded again:

'Mummy always says if we do our best, that's all we can do.'

CHAPTER THIRTY-FOUR

Through the brief minutes of his drive home that evening, David Russell was cursing his own stupidity. Still upset by the little girl's distress, he was none-the-less berating himself for his words to her - *Why can't I keep my mouth shut?* How could he have promised to get the child's mother off of the murder charge? *Never make a promise to a kid that you don't intend to make good!* He could hear his own mother's words, drummed into him when Daniel was still a baby. But then, he'd *actually* only promised to do his best, hadn't he...?

Four days. Tomorrow was Thursday; Lucy was due to appear before the magistrates again at ten-thirty on Monday. Four days - including the weekend - and then the PM would call a halt, order him to let it go, resign himself to the fact of her guilt. But he still couldn't quite convince himself.

Still distracted by his preoccupation, he didn't notice the tense atmosphere as he let himself into the cottage. In the kitchen, Sarah was sitting at the table with a colouring book, a frown of concentration screwing up her eyes as she busily worked on a picture of a circus clown. She looked up, a smile lighting up her face when she saw her father; he bent to hug her where she sat, kissing her forehead as she put her arms around his neck.

'Long day, David?' Tracy greeted him as she turned from the oven, closing the door after checking the casserole bubbling inside. He straightened up with a smile:

'Not too bad, Love. I've just had little Freya and her Grandmother in to see Lucy Cavendish again.'

'I didn't think visitors were allowed in Police cells?' He grinned guiltily:

'They're not!' She gave him a disapproving look as he asked: 'Where's Daniel?'

'He's in his room.' It was the tone rather than the words which alerted him to the fact that something was wrong; his heart sank: *Now what?* Tracy looked at him for a moment, then said:

'I'm in the doghouse, I'm afraid.' He sighed:

'What now?'

'Danny called, after school - he wanted to stop at that coffee shop down Market Street on his way home, have a Coke with his friends. I said no, so…' She raised her hands in a gesture of helplessness. Puzzled, he asked:

'Why didn't you want him to do that?'

'Well - last time they stopped there on the way home, he had a burger as well, upset his appetite and spoiled his dinner, later. And… it's only a few doors along from that amusement arcade…'

'You thought they might sneak in there?'

'Oh David! That sounds as though I don't trust him! It's just that… that whole area is a bit rough, isn't it? I'm always afraid of something happening to him…' He held her eyes as her voice trailed off, smiled his understanding:

'How many times do I have to tell you that what happened - *could* have happened - *wasn't* your fault?' His voice was quiet, gentle. Tracy's echoing smile was rather shamefaced:

'I know, Love, but…'

'But nothing! More to the point: He came home when you told him?'

'Oh, yes - he didn't disobey me, Love. But I'm not his favourite person right now.' She went on: 'Do you want to give him a call? Dinner's almost ready.'

'Okay.' He stepped out into the hall as Tracy told Sarah to put her things away and help Mummy to lay the table for dinner. Her voice, his daughter's cheery 'okay' in response, reminded him again of the distraught child he'd ushered from the Police Station a little time before, brought up the vision of her tear-stained face before his eyes. *Poor little beggar - what's her life going to be like, with her adopted Daddy dead and her mother in prison?* He shook his head, bringing his thoughts back to his own problems:

'Daniel - Dinner's ready!'

'Coming!' The answer echoed down the stairs. The footsteps which followed were slow and measured, as if the boy was reluctant to appear; but moments later he stepped into the kitchen, walked around and sat down at the table.

'Can you put out the cutlery for me, Danny?' He got to his feet again, even more reluctantly:

'I wish you wouldn't *call* me that!' His mother turned to him:

'I'm *sorry,* but it is your *name!'*

'My name's *Daniel! Danny* makes me sound like a little kid!' Tracy opened her mouth to snap out another retort, but Russell put up his hand to stop her:

'The knives and forks, Daniel?'

'All *right,* Dad, I'm going!' He just looked at his son. Daniel caught his expression, and the look on his face made the boy avert his eyes, realising he'd overstepped the mark. It was Tracy who went to reprimand him:

'Daniel! Don't you ever…'

'FOR HEAVEN'S SAKE! Both of you - will you *stop* it?' Mother and son both gaped at his uncharacteristic outburst; Sarah, in the act of setting out the placemats, looked ready to burst into tears. More calmly, he went on: 'I'm sorry, but I'm up to my neck at work, I've just had to cope with another family's problems, and I really can do *without* having to come home and act as mediator between the two of *you.'*

'Yes, Dad.'

'Sorry, Love.'

Silence reigned for few minutes, as Daniel set out the cutlery, and Tracy dished up the meal; Russell beckoned his daughter, gave her a hug to show he wasn't angry with her - a hug which became longer, tighter than he had intended, as the tear-stained face of Freya Cavendish rose once again in his mind. When they were all seated, no-one began to eat, all watching him as if afraid to start before he did. He glanced around, amused at their caution:

'Well? What are we waiting for?' He dug in to the sausage casserole and mashed potato, felt the relaxation around the table as the others did likewise. After a few minutes, Daniel raised the nerve to ask:

'Are you still having trouble with your murder case, Dad?' Russell nodded, chewing. He swallowed, replied:

'Yes, Dan. Mr Wilson - and Doug Rimmer, for that matter - are convinced that the girlfriend killed Roddie McKeenan. But I still don't feel happy about it. And now, I've promised the girl's little daughter that I'm going to try and prove she *didn't* do it!'

'Do you think you can, Dad?' It gave Russell an amused boost that his son's tone showed no doubt of his father's judgement of the matter.

'I don't know, Dan. All the evidence says that she did it; and I've got no-one else - well, no-one who fits the bill - who *could* have done it. Despite the fact that there were upwards of two hundred people in the club that night.'

'But if she *didn't*...?'

'Yeah, I know! One of my biggest problems is - I shouldn't be telling you this, so don't mention it to *anyone,* okay? Any of you?' Three heads nodded solemnly.

'The problem is, whoever shot Roddie was wearing gloves, right? Ladies gloves, and a small size, at that. They belong to Lucy, and she - whichever *she* it was - disposed of them in the bin in the ladies loo.'

'She?' Daniel asked.

'Well, it had to be a lady, because of the size of them.'

'Or a man with *very* small hands!' The boy grinned at his own flippancy. Russell snorted in amusement:

'Or a man with...' His voice trailed off; his son looked up at him, puzzled. Tracy and Sarah both turned to him, the little girl with a forkful of casserole halfway to her mouth, as he said slowly: 'Oh, Jesus Holy *Christ!*'

'DAVID!' But his eyes were on his son. Daniel gazed at his father, stunned at his blasphemous exclamation, and not a little scared, thinking he'd somehow rekindled his father's fury.

Russell sat, his mind working furiously. The boy's words had given him the nudge he needed - that elusive thought, which had got away from him when he'd been talking to Elsa Jurgens and her brother, had dropped into his hands. It *had* to be... but why? For goodness sake, *why?* His eyes came back into focus, to see his son gazing at him in trepidation:

'Dad? What've I *done?'* Daniel's frightened eyes followed him as he jumped to his feet, rushed around the table, came to stand behind the boy's chair. The elfin face screwed around, looking up as he put his hands on his son's shoulders; the teenager's startlement grew when his father bent and kissed him hard on his forehead:

'Dad!' Now, Russell burst out laughing, as Tracy asked:

'Whatever is the matter, David?'

'He said it! A man with very small hands!'

'Dad?' Daniel still sounded incredulous.

'Right in the middle of this case, Dan - a man with *very small hands!* How on Earth can I have been so *dense?'*

He cast a delighted look around his family, and hurried out into the hallway, grabbing up the telephone. But then he paused - they'd achieve nothing much tonight, he could as well wait and drop his bombshell on Doug in the morning. And that way, he'd have time to think through the implications, try and see beyond his immediate revelation to whether it might make some kind of sense... No, tomorrow would do; he went back into the kitchen, sat down and picked up his knife and fork:

'Well? Don't let your dinners get cold!' His wife and children looked at him as if he'd gone mad; but then, with a concerted shrug of their shoulders, went back to the business of eating.

CHAPTER THIRTY-FIVE

'Duffy? You're having me on!' The Sergeant's brown eyes reflected a feeling somewhere between despair and amusement. Russell shook his head:

'Never more serious, Doug.' He'd expected this kind of reaction, but still felt a vague annoyance at Rimmer's response.

'But… But…!' He'd never known his assistant stuck for words before.

'Look at the facts, Doug: His whereabouts for the few minutes when McKeenan was shot are unsupported by other witnesses - and his hands are small enough for him to have worn Lucy's gloves. If what she says is true, and she *had* returned the bag, and the gun, to her locker, he could have sneaked in there, taken it, met Roddie outside, shot him and then dumped the evidence in the ladies during the following confusion.'

'You sure? About his hands?'

'I think so. I shook his hand, remember, the day he came in here to be interviewed? And remember something else - he kept his hands in his pockets, while we were talking to him, didn't he?'

'Ye-ah, maybe - keeping them out of sight?'

'Could be.' Rimmer was still staring at him, flabbergasted by this new theory. He shook his head:

'What suddenly inspired you with *this* idea?'

'Something Daniel said, last night, just a flippant remark; but it made me see what I'd been missing. The ironic thing is, it's at

241

least partly *his* fault I'd missed it - these spats he's been having with his mother have been niggling at my mind, distracting me from concentrating the way I should.' Rimmer shook his head:

'Wait a minute - we've got a solid, cast-iron, unshakeable case against Lucy Cavendish - but now you want me to ignore that and work on the possibility that someone else who just might, possibly, conceivably, have been able to do it, is the *real* killer? On the basis of a chance remark by a twelve-year-old kid?' Russell held on to his patience:

'He's *thirteen.* And it would fit the evidence, Doug, don't you see?' The Sergeant sat in thought for a minute or so before answering. He looked up from his perch on the corner of the desk to where his superior stood, arms braced on its top:

'Okay, it *might* fit - the physical evidence, anyway. *If* you're right about the size of his hands - *If* we can show that he could have done all that in the time available - *If* he's left-handed - *If* he wore a second pair of gloves under Lucy's. But *why?* For Heaven's sake - what motive did *he* have, to kill McKeenan?'

Russell forced himself to relax, sat slowly down in his chair. He sighed:

'We need *two* motives, Doug. Why did he kill Roddie? And why did he try to frame Lucy?' The disbelief in Rimmer's eyes became more emphatic:

'*Exactly!* Frank Duffy's got no possible reason to do *either!* Why's it so important to you to prove Lucy's innocent, against all the evidence? Are you besotted with the girl, or something?' Russell was on his feet again, anger blazing in his eyes:

'*Sergeant! I* am still in charge of this enquiry, and we will continue to investigate *all* aspects of it until *I* say we've finished! And, in case it's escaped your attention, I have a wife and two children!' Rimmer jumped to his feet, standing almost at attention:

'Yes, sir - of course.' His tone said that he was already kicking himself for his remark. The cold silence held for almost a minute:

'Sir?' Russell just raised his eyebrows.

'Sir - I apologise, that was a stupid thing to say. I know it was completely unjustified, and...'

'Oh, sit down, Doug! Sorry I jumped down your throat, I know you didn't mean it.' He took his own advice, dropping into his chair with a sigh: 'We've got four days, if we include the weekend; after that, Mr Wilson's going to call a halt anyway. But - humour me, all right? Even if *you* don't believe it, let's take it seriously, check everything out and just see if it is a viable alternative. I want to go over all the eyewitness statements, see just where and when we can place Duffy during the relevant times. We'll need to talk to the man, go over his story, see if there are any inconsistencies...'

'Shall we bring him in for questioning?'

'No, I don't think so. I'd rather not give him any idea that we're on to him - can we find an excuse for talking to him again, without making him suspicious?'

'Dunno - probably.'

'Okay. I'd like to talk to the barman, Stevens - the Jurgens girl and her brother - the other hostess who was on the scene...'

'Petra Sandwell?'

'Yeah. And Lucy. This doesn't actually shift the time-scale of our efforts, Doug - whatever Duffy's motives, they have to have arisen in the period since Roddie moved to the town. Although I suppose we'd better look into his own background - it's just possible they might have met before, somewhere.' Rimmer had been jotting down notes; he nodded, looked up:

'Okay, boss. I'll get the file of statements, and put someone on checking Duffy's background.'

'What other loose ends have we got, from the last three years?'

'Well - Steve Campbell went over the records of that guy who was convicted for pushing in Sweeney's a couple of years back. He says there's nothing of any use to us, there, but I'll have him recheck in case it gives us a line on Duffy in any way.'

'Right - though I expect Gidding's defence will try to use it to show his opposition to drug sales in his premises, since he helped set the man up.'

'Yeah, bound to. The only other thing was the girl who died - we've been over the records, locally, and found nothing of interest, but we haven't spoken to the mother, or gone into it in any depth, to be frank.'

'Okay, Doug. We'll drive over and see the woman some time, just to tidy things up. Tomorrow, maybe. For now, let's concentrate on finding out if Duffy fits the bill as our murderer.'

'All right, boss.' Russell smiled:

'Not convinced, are you?' Rimmer grinned back:

'To be honest, no, sir! But, like you said - you're the boss. If you're right this time, I really *will* eat my hat!'

'You never *wear* a hat, Doug?'

'No, sir!'

* * *

Two hours later, with the aid of the witness statements and a ground-floor plan of the nightclub, Russell felt they were closer to agreeing the possibility of Duffy having murdered Roddie McKeenan:

'So Doug - putting all that together, and assuming that Lucy's telling the truth, we can guess that Duffy came down from his office about ten minutes before the shooting, via the stairs at the front right of the building. He checked quickly in the upper bar, then came down to the ground floor here' he pointed to the foot of the stairwell 'crossed the lounge floor to the bar' his finger followed the line 'and spoke to Jurgens, asking if everything was all right.'

'Jurgens says yes, fine, tells him Stevens is in the loo and will be back in a minute, turns back to his customers and goes on serving. Does he notice where Duffy went after their exchange?'

'We'll have to ask him, it's not clear in his statement. Roddie's in the bar at this point, and so's Lucy, both at the bar but well separated. Did Duffy talk to Roddie, asking him to meet him in the lane? Or had he already arranged that? Either way, Roddie goes out - Lucy follows him, and they row in the corridor. Duffy, meanwhile, has gone to the girls locker room and picked up Lucy's bag, with the gun and spare gloves.'

'Okay - Roddie goes outside, Lucy ducks into the ladies. Did Duffy see her go in there, I wonder?'

'If he'd intended to frame her all along, that would have played straight into his hands, wouldn't it? Given him the opportunity to plant the evidence there later. Anyway, he follows Roddie outside, shoots him... He must have realised that the odds were that someone would hear the shots and come running, mustn't he?'

'Maybe not - perhaps he hoped the body wouldn't be found until the morning.'

'Hmm - he'd have to work with the *possibility* that someone would hear, surely? In which case, would he come back in the same way? Or through the kitchens? Can you open that door from outside?'

'Yeah, you can!' Rimmer sounded as if he was becoming slowly more enthusiastic about his superior's theory: 'The corridor door is a pure fire door, opened with crash-bars - but this one' he pointed to the plan 'can be opened by anyone from inside, in an emergency, but also has a lock which will open it from outside. If you have the key.'

'And Duffy, as bar manager, would have a key!'

'I'd imagine so.'

'So - he lets himself in this way, watches the panic ensue when Stevens finds the body, grabs the first opportunity to dump the gun etcetera in the ladies, once Lucy's out of the way!'

'Yeah. Yeah, it could just work, boss. But how can we *prove* it?'

'That's the problem. Did Karl Jurgens notice where he went after talking to him? And remember the customer who was in the gents with Stevens - he said he thought it was the door of the ladies he heard slam. Maybe Stevens was wrong; maybe he *assumed* it was the outside door after finding Roddie out there, maybe on reflection he'll confirm the other man's statement? That would tend to confirm Lucy's story.'

'And all this depends on him wearing something over his hands to prevent *his* DNA rubbing off inside them. Would he have known enough to do that?'

'We have to assume he did, otherwise why do it? My bet's on a pair of those thin latex gloves people wear for mucky jobs - I've seen car mechanics in them, kitchen staff; did they use them in the club's kitchens?'

'Hang on…' Rimmer shuffled through the file, selected the search report from the premises, scanned it quickly: 'No mention of any among the stuff in the kitchen… but I seem to remember… yeah! In the storeroom, here' he pointed to the room in the corner between kitchen and bar on the plan 'they found materials left over after the redecoration last Spring, and there was a part-used box of them there! So he could have grabbed a pair - assuming he knew they were there.'

'From what I know of Duffy, I'd assume he knew where *everything* was in the place!'

'Yeah, right! If we had the actual pair he wore…'

'We'd be able to show that fact, if his DNA is inside them. Could forensic prove that he had Lucy's gloves on over the top? But we haven't got them, anyway, so that's idle speculation, isn't it?' Rimmer was looking thoughtful:

'Even if we *had* those gloves, it's barely enough for a defence argument, to throw doubt on the evidence against Lucy. I couldn't see a jury convicting him on that, could you?' Russell sat back, sighed:

'No, I guess not. If we had some kind of *motive*…'

'Lucy reckoned Duffy was sweet on her, didn't she? Would he have killed Roddie to get rid of him?' Russell thought, shook his head:

'Doesn't fit. Why wait three years, if he was so besotted with her to kill for her? And remember, it was common knowledge that Roddie was leaving her; all he had to do was wait to have his chance with her - it would be crazy to gun the man down *then.*'

'I suppose so. But what other reason could he have had for killing him?'

'And trying to frame Lucy, don't forget that.' Rimmer sat in thought for a moment:

'Look - I agree that we can put the sequence of events together so that Duffy *could* have killed him, and planted the evidence against Lucy. But - it just doesn't make any *sense!* If he had no reason for doing it... All right, it's plausible, but the evidence still makes a lot more sense if *Lucy* held the gun; that way, every little piece of the jigsaw fits in place, you have to agree, sir?'

'Yes, I know, Doug. But - we *have* the case against Lucy, spending a little time following up this as an alternative won't change that; unless it pays off, somehow. So let's try, okay?' Rimmer shrugged:

'Sure - like I said, you're the boss!'

'Come on - let's get some lunch, then we'll talk to some of these people again.'

CHAPTER THIRTY-SIX

Over a quick snack and a coffee, the two detectives planned their afternoon:

'Doug, you take Duffy, okay? It'll keep the approach to him low-profile, if you and a DC talk to him rather than me - is anyone free to go with you?'

'I don't know, sir. Steve's on tracing back his background, and we don't want to take him off that, do we? And Darren's on something else, since we locked Gidding up.'

'Oh - right. See if you can find someone, although I suppose it wouldn't matter if you went on your own at this stage. I'm going to talk to the Jurgens', see if they can remember any more about his movements that night - but I might have a word with Terry first, see if forensic can help at all.'

'Okay, sir. How do you want me to approach Duffy?'

'Oh, just tying up loose ends - you could ask him about the girl who died of an overdose, perhaps, let him think we're looking for a connection to Gidding and Roddie. Yes - take a picture of her, hand it to him, you should get a look at his hands, and see which he uses to take it.' Rimmer chuckled:

'Yeah - that'll tell us what we need to know, won't it?'

'Should do, Doug. And go over his story, watch for any inconsistencies, right?'

'Will do.' The Sergeant swigged the dregs of his coffee, got to his feet.

As Russell stood up, a uniformed constable at the next table rose as well:

'Sir?' Russell turned to him:

'Yes, Andrew?'

'Sir - er... I'm off duty, now, I was just grabbing a quick coffee before going home. I, er... couldn't help overhearing what you and Sergeant Rimmer were saying: If you need a volunteer, I wouldn't mind going with him - as long as you can square it with Mr Armstrong?'

'I don't want to keep you from your rest - what about your next duty?'

'Oh, I'm off for a couple of days, sir, so that wouldn't matter.' Russell looked at his Sergeant:

'What do you say, Doug?' Rimmer grinned:

'Welcome aboard, Constable Dorman! Have you got a change of clothes with you?'

'Of course, sir! I'll go and slip into civvies, shall I?' Russell gave him the nod, and the keen young officer hurried away as he turned to Rimmer:

'Eager, isn't he?'

'No bad thing, boss.' The Sergeant shared his superior's high opinion of the young man: 'I'll be pleased to have him along.'

'Okay, Doug. I'll see you later - I'll have a word with Strongarm, make sure he's okay about us using Andrew for an hour or two.'

After a moment's thought, the Inspector made his way down to the basement lair of the division's forensic department, where he found Owen poring over a binocular microscope. He tapped him on the shoulder, to be rewarded with a startled lurch:

'Afternoon, Terry.'

'Dave! Bugger, you made me jump! You shouldn't creep up on people like that.'

'I was hardly creeping, Terry! Can I help it if you switch off from the real world?' Owen laughed:

'I suppose not, boyo! What can I do for you, then?'

'Well - I'm still on the McKeenan murder, Terry. And I've got a new suspect.'

'You have?' The forensic Sergeant's voice betrayed a sudden interest, reinforced by the sparkle in his blue eyes.

'Yeah. Remember what you said a while ago, that someone *could* have worn a second pair of gloves inside Lucy's leather ones? I reckon that's exactly what did happen - and I think Frank Duffy's our man.'

'Duffy? He was the manager or something, wasn't he?'

'That's right; the bar manager. He's an ex-jockey, stands about five foot not-very-much, and he's got pretty small hands. Small enough, I reckon, to have got her gloves on, even if it might have been a bit tight.'

'Ah! And he could have been on hand to do the deed, could he?'

'He could. Doug's checking that side of things out right now.'

'And you want to know if the evidence as I see it supports that idea, right?'

'Right!'

Owen sat back in his chair, entwining his fingers behind his neck as he arched it back. The spectacles, perched on his bald pate, slipped off, to fall on the floor behind the chair:

'Oh, damn! That's always happening!' He got up, retrieved them and put them on after polishing the lenses with a tissue from the bench, sat down again.

'I see no reason for it *not* to fit, Dave. We're assuming that this fellow grabbed her bag, with the gun in it, and a pair of her gloves, used them to kill McKeenan, with the intention of framing the girl? That would account for them all being found together... So okay, the physical evidence doesn't rule him out, given that your theory is right. But I can't see that it'll put him in the hot seat, either. Have you got any other evidence against him? Witnesses? Circumstantial? What about motive - why would he have done it, rather than the girl?' Russell's expression turned glum:

'That's the big problem, Terry, I don't know. If I could come up with just *one* piece of hard evidence which showed him as the killer, I could bring pressure to bear - it's a pity your boys didn't think to keep the contents of the bins from the club, we might have got our hands on the other gloves!'

'Bins?'

'Yeah - I'm guessing that he threw the latex gloves, or whatever they were, in one of the waste bins, probably in the kitchen, so that they weren't found with the gun and other things. But I gather you didn't hang on to any of that?'

'No-o, not the kitchen bins; didn't seem relevant, at the time...' Owen sounded thoughtful, the Welsh in his voice coming out as it did in times of excitement or deep cogitation: 'But - I *have* got the contents of the bin from the ladies, the one they were found in, naturally.'

'You have? Can I take a look?'

'Sure! Hold on, the whole bin's in the store, somewhere, I'll go and find it.'

Owen went out, the thoughtful look still on his round face. Russell felt the glimmer of a fresh hope: Perhaps it was just possible they had the clue he needed! Common sense would dictate that Duffy would have hidden the latex gloves somewhere different from Lucy's - but the man had been under great stress; however cold-blooded his attitude to killing Roddie might have been, he'd been under pressure, with perhaps a matter of no more than seconds to be in place to observe the aftermath of his actions - maybe, just maybe...

A couple of minutes later, Owen was back, carrying the tall swing-bin, completely encased in a large, sealed plastic bag. The lop-sided grin on his face, along with the tangled grey tonsure around his bald head and the white lab-coat, reminded Russell of the man's nick-name; the Mad Professor placed the bin down on a nearby bench, pushing other things to one side to make room, and unsealed the bag, folding it down:

'We've got the gun, the girl's bag and gloves, under lock and key, of course. But everything else is still in here, pretty much as it was found. You want to look through it?' Russell nodded eagerly; Owen found a pair of thin latex gloves, threw them to him with a grin:

'These are clean ones - don't get 'em mixed up with any from in there, or we'll have *you* in the dock!' Russell laughed, pulling them over his hands. He began to remove items from the bin, carefully laying them out on the bench in order: An occasional spent lipstick; other discarded items of make-up; a broken watch-strap; they exchanged amused glances at the appearance of a pair of lacy knickers; and tissues by the handful. And then, from near the bottom:

'Bingo!' Russell looked up at the watching forensic Sergeant as he extracted a pair of latex gloves, to all intents and purposes identical with the ones he himself was wearing. The twinkle was back in Owen's eyes:

'You'll want those checked for DNA, will you?'

'How soon? For a result?'

'Monday, maybe?'

'How about tomorrow?' Owen blew through his teeth:

'No chance! I'll try for Saturday, shall I?'

'Please, Terry. I'd like to have the court release Lucy at the hearing on Monday, if this pays off, and I'd need to have Duffy in custody by then.'

'Right-o, Dave, I'll do what I can, okay?'

'Okay - and thanks, Terry!'

On his way to Oakfield, Russell felt a swell of hope. Maybe, at last, things were coming together - if Duffy's DNA was inside those gloves, he was one step closer to proving his theory. But, he reflected, it was only a small step - the man could easily admit wearing the gloves, but claim it had been for some other purpose, unless he could show that he'd had Lucy's leather ones over the top, somehow. And, as everyone kept pointing out, he had to have a motive for the manager to have both killed McKeenan *and* set out to frame Lucy Cavendish. The physical evidence, if Owen came through, might be enough to cast doubt on the case against Lucy, but it didn't look strong enough to convict Duffy in front of a jury...

'Oh, come in, Mr Russell!' Elsa Jurgens greeted the Inspector as she opened the door to him. He followed her into the living room, took one of the easy chairs at her wave:

'Would you like a coffee? Karl will be down in a minute - I'm afraid we're still on night-work time, I've not been up long myself!'

'Thank you, I'd love one! Police canteen coffee tastes like mud, and that's all I've had all day. How are you both getting on, with the club closed?'

'Oh, fine!' she called through from the kitchen 'we're still getting paid, until things get sorted out, so that's handy - even if it's only our basic salaries; you understand?' He smiled to himself, aware that with no clients for her 'other services', the girl had lost the larger part of her income. She went on:

'We've been talking about going back to South Africa, once this affair is all over, setting ourselves up out there. We've still got family there - and it would be nice to get away from all the memories here.' She came back into the room, carrying two mugs of steaming coffee:

'It's only instant, I'm afraid. We're going to ask Lucy to come with us, as well - it would be better for her, I'm sure, after all that's happened; and Freya would have a fresh start that way, without the reminders of Roddie, and... all this; you know?' He nodded, sympathetically:

'In a way, that's why I'm here, Elsa. I think I have another possible suspect, who just might have shot Roddie, and I think you and Karl might be able to help me see if I'm right.' The girl was gazing at him, a delighted smile on her face, hope sparkling in her bright eyes:

'*Really?* I told you! Didn't we tell you, Lucy didn't kill him, all along?' He grinned, catching her enthusiasm:

'I'm a long way from *proving* anything! I need you to cast your mind back to that night again, try to remember… Oh, good morning, Karl!' The girl's younger brother had appeared in the doorway, clad in a bathrobe, looking slightly bleary:

'Morning, Inspector - Hi, Else. Thought I heard voices - is there any coffee?'

'Kettle's hot, kiddo, help yourself. Hey, guess what? Inspector Russell thinks he knows who *did* shoot Roddie!'

'Yeah, I gathered. Let me get a drink, I'll come and join you.'

A couple of minutes later, the young man was seated beside his sister on the settee, a mug held between his hands as if to warm them on it. He looked a trifle more awake, now:

'So - what do you want from us, Inspector?'

'I need you to go back to the night Roddie was shot - what do you remember of Mr Duffy's movements, that night? He came down, to check on the bars, and the cellar, is that right?'

'*Frank Duffy?* You think Fluffy killed him? Why in the blue blazes would *he* do it?' Elsa sounded astonished. Russell was beginning to tire of everyone latching on to the big flaw in his theory:

'I don't know *why,* that's my biggest problem - I was hoping you two might be able to give me an idea on that score, as well!' He looked from one to the other, to see both shaking their heads:

'I don't think he *liked* Roddie, particularly' Karl said slowly 'but I can't see any reason why he'd kill him. Oh, I know he was the one there who really was opposed to drugs, but he just kind of ignored all that, pretended it wasn't happening. If he'd felt that strongly, he might have shopped him to your colleagues. Perhaps? But…' He shook his head again. Elsa chipped in:

'He *was* rather taken with Lucy, once - but… that doesn't make sense, does it? If Roddie wanted to leave her, he'd only to

wait; even if he still felt the same way, and I don't think he did...'
Russell sighed inwardly, one of his hopes dashed:

'Let's go back to that night, can we? What do you remember of his movements, Karl - you spoke to him, didn't you?'

'That's right. He came down - it would have been a few minutes before it all happened. He came over to the bar, asked if things were okay; I said yes, fine; I told him Aaron was in the loo, he'd only be a minute or two. It was busy-ish; I had customers waiting, so I went to look after them. I didn't notice him again until afterwards - he came up to me, asked what was going on, where Aaron was - he went out to the corridor when I told him we'd heard shots outside.'

'Did you see where he came *from,* the second time he approached you?' The young man thought for a moment:

'I'm not *certain* - but I think he came from that side of the lounge, from somewhere by the corridor door. Which is a bit odd - if he'd come up from the cellars, he'd have come out from the kitchen... But then, I suppose he could have gone across, taken a quick look at the fuss going on before he came over to me.'

'Okay, Karl. When he spoke to you the first time; both Lucy and Roddie were still in the bar?'

'Yes - I'd been chatting a bit with both of them. They weren't together, you understand - she was to the left, near the end of the bar, on a stool...'

'That'd be *your* left?'

'Yep - towards the corridor and the toilets, to the right if you look from the front. Roddie was towards the far end - in fact, he was right beside where Fluffy came to the bar, now I think about it...'

'Did he speak to him?' Karl regarded him thoughtfully:

'Not at first - but... I have the impression, now you ask, that he turned to him as I went to serve the folk who were waiting. I mean, they knew each other, of course, so I suppose it would be natural that he'd say hello, at least.'

'You've no idea what might have been said?' Jurgens shook his head:

'No, sorry, Inspector.'

'Okay, thank you, Karl. You were at your table, with the customer, at that time, Elsa?' He turned to the girl. She nodded:

'That's right - I didn't notice Mr Duffy then, at all. I only saw him later, after I'd met Lucy coming out of the ladies, and she'd dashed out to Roddie; he came up behind me in the corridor, asked me what was happening. I told him Roddie'd been shot, and he went off out into the lane.'

'How did he seem, when you told him? Surprised? Shocked?' The girl giggled:

'Not really! Annoyed, more like - but that would be typical of the man. A murder would upset his tight-run ship, wouldn't it?'

CHAPTER THIRTY-SEVEN

It was almost four o'clock when David Russell left the house, the darkness of the winter evening already closing in. He contemplated driving over to Greenland and talking to Stevens, but opted to return to the station to compare notes with Rimmer and Campbell: The former should be back from interviewing Duffy by now, and the latter should have at least a preliminary outline of the man's background.

He parked the Jeep in the station car park, and made his way up to the CID office. Steve Campbell was on the telephone, but, catching the Inspector's eye, beckoned him over; Russell took the seat in front of the DC's desk, waited for him to finish his call:

'How's it going, Steve?'

'Okay, sir. I've got enough to do 'This is your Life' for Duffy, anyway!'

'Just don't expect me to play Michael Aspel, okay?' Campbell grinned:

'No, sir!'

'Give me the quick version, can you?'

'Right. As we knew, he used to be a jockey, quite a successful one without being among the big names - he was born in Suffolk, and lived in Newmarket while he was riding. I can't see that there's anything relevant to our case in all this, but still... He packed it up sixteen years ago - he had an accident, quite a bad one, a fall, and the horse fell onto him apparently, smashed his right arm and shoulder pretty badly. He was in and out of hospital for almost a year, while they rebuilt his shoulder, and under a physio for a long time after that - but from what I can gather, he'd lost his nerve as a result, and never went back to riding, at least, not competitively.'

'So he moved over here when?'

'About that time. He'd got some money behind him, and there was an insurance settlement from the accident; he bought a pub in Pitsford village, you know, by the reservoir? Ran that for a few years, but didn't make a go of it; then Gidding offered him a job. He's been working for him ever since.'

'Any family?' Campbell grinned again:

'He *was* married, for a time. But, reading between the lines, I doubt if it stood much chance - people I've spoken to describe him as being difficult to get along with. This was over the period of his accident - I gather she nursed him through it, but then threw him out once he was back on his feet, so to speak!'

'Doesn't surprise me, having met the man! What about the wife? Ex-wife, I should say?'

'Haven't traced her, as yet - I was concentrating on him. They had a cottage in a village outside the town, and I assume she stayed on there at first, but there's another family living there now. I hadn't followed her trail - do you want me to?'

'We'd better, just for the sake of completeness - but later, perhaps. Whatever his motive for killing McKeenan, it has to derive from the time after they were both in Grancester, surely? And that's the most important thing for now, Steve. Were there any children?'

'Not that I'm aware of - again, I haven't really pushed that question, sir. There doesn't seem to be any possibility of the two having met until Roddie moved here three years ago, so I've been focussing more on Duffy's time here. Like I said, the pub didn't work out; Gidding had been working for other people as a bouncer, but then he set up the old Locomotive nightclub, in the premises just up from the railway station - you remember that?'

'Yeah, sure!'

'Well, he took Duffy on as a barman. The pub was sold to one of the big breweries, and he moved to a house in the town, then bought the apartment in Northampton a few years later. He stayed with Gidding - I gather the two of them got on quite well, at least as employer and employee - and became the bar manager when Gidding moved to the old police station.'

'Right. McKeenan had been in the UK for about nine-ten years; so Duffy had been here in the town all that time. And no hint that they might have met until Roddie moved here too?'

'No, sir, not that I've found. And since then, their relationship seems to have been a kind of polite but arms-length affair. Neither seems to have liked the other, but I can find no source of any real animosity, so far. I take it that's where you'd like me to keep digging?'

'Please, Steve. As I said...' He broke off, as Rimmer and a plain-clothed Andrew Dorman entered the office and headed toward them 'we should follow up things like the ex-wife as well, but that's a lower priority - we'll come to that if it looks like we can place him in the frame as Roddie's killer. Hi, Doug, Andrew!'

'Hi, boss!'

'Hello, sir.'

'How did you get on with Duffy?' Rimmer laughed:

'Surprisingly well! We found him at home; he's got this rather plush apartment in Kingsthorpe, you know? I convinced him we were only filling in background, asked him about the pusher they helped to set up that time, then showed him the picture of Emma Verdon, asked him about her. Anyway, he got quite chatty after that, so I let him ramble; he was telling us about the pub he used to have, even about his days in horse-racing, and his accident - seems he gave up riding after a bad fall at Cheltenham.'

'Felt safe, on his own territory, probably!'

'Yeah, I'd guess so.'

'So? What about his hands, Doug?'

'Ah - well, you were right on that score. They're quite small, and very slender, so I'd agree he could almost certainly have got Lucy's gloves on, even if the fingers might have been a bit short for him. But the bad news is, he's right-handed: I was watching him all the time; and he took the picture with his right hand when I gave it to him.'

'Damn!'

'Sir?' Russell turned to the young Constable:

'What is it, Andrew?'

'I've been thinking about that, sir. His accident - it was his *right* arm that was damaged?'

'Yes - pretty badly, from what Steve here tells me.'

'Well, sir, I was wondering…' The young man broke off, drew a deep breath before plunging on: 'My brother broke his arm once, his right arm. And while it was in plaster, he tried to teach himself to write with his left. He never got very good at it, but then they took the plaster off after a few weeks…' he trailed off again; Russell looked with sympathy at the pain on his face as he described the memory - Philip, Andrew's older brother, had died at the age of twelve, and the anguish of that loss still had the power to hurt the boy who had been his devoted shadow. None of the other officers had ever heard him refer to his brother before, in their working environment; Russell nodded slowly:

'So, you're suggesting that Duffy might have done the same, while he was incapacitated?'

'Yes, sir.' The Constable had recovered his composure: 'He had a lot longer with his right arm out of commission, if I understand things right; so maybe he'd time to train himself to use his left hand for most things, if you see what I mean?'

'You could well be right! Duffy's the kind of obstinate character that might well do just that - I don't see him as the type to just sit back and do nothing, do you, Doug?'

'No, sir!'

'And, if he was already on bad terms with his wife, that would drive him to be as independent as possible, too, wouldn't it?' Campbell added.

'Well, maybe my brilliant theory isn't quite down the tubes after all!' Russell sounded more cheerful.

'There's something else, sir?' Dorman was encouraged by the success of his first idea.

'Yes?'

'When Sergeant Rimmer gave him the photo, of the girl? He went, sort of, very quiet, for a moment, sat looking at her - and there was a sort of blankness in his eyes. You noticed that too, Sarge?' Rimmer looked at him, then at Russell; then he grinned self-consciously:

'I did - but, to tell the truth, I didn't think anything of it, just put it down to a reaction to seeing a picture of her again, knowing she was dead.'

'That could be all it was, sir - but I had the feeling that there might have been something between them, you understand? I mean, there was nothing I could put a finger on, but...'

'Yes, I see.' Russell considered the idea: 'He comes across to me as a bit of a womaniser, don't you agree, Doug?'

'Yeah - maybe a not very successful one, though! I mean, Lucy didn't want to know, did she? Perhaps he got the same response from this girl.'

'Maybe - but he still could have had a fancy for her, couldn't he?'

'Yeah, okay - but what would that have to do with him shooting Roddie?'

Russell smiled, shrugged his shoulders:

'Nothing, I imagine!' He looked around at his companions: 'Carry on the good work, Steve. Andrew, you'd better get off home; and thank you for your help today.'

'Any time, sir!' The young Constable left them.

'Come up to the office, Doug, let's go over things.'

Up in his own office, Russell slumped into his chair; Rimmer, as ever, perched on a corner of his desk:

'What did you get from the Jurgens', boss?'

'Well, Karl's memory of Duffy's movements that night would fit in with the idea of him killing Roddie. And he *thinks* Duffy spoke to him after he came to the bar to see if things were running all right; he says he was right next to him at the bar, and turned to him as he, Karl that is, went back to serving a customer.'

'Asking him to meet him out in the lane?'

'Possible, certainly. If Duffy is our man, I think he must have laid his plan in a general way, but then waited until he saw an opportunity to put it into action - he had to avoid the risk of Lucy having an alibi, for example. But *that* night, Roddie was there, on his own and approachable; and she was sat at the bar, alone, too, so it was reasonable that she wouldn't be able to prove conclusively that she couldn't have done it. You see what I mean?'

'Sure. He couldn't have pre-arranged to meet Roddie, in case Lucy was alibi'd at the time in question, right?'

'Right. So, so far, we can't prove that he did it - but we've not ruled him out, either. Especially if young Dorman is right, and he had trained himself to use his left hand when required. I'll get Steve to contact the doctors, and his physiotherapist, they might be able to confirm that idea. Maybe his ex-wife, too, she'd know, surely?'

'You'd think so.'

'Oh, Doug - another thing! It turns out Terry still had the rest of the contents of the bin, the one we found the gun in - and in there, pushed down near the bottom, we found a pair of latex gloves!'

'You did?'

'Yeah! Might be nothing to do with it, of course, but he's going to get them checked for DNA traces on the inside, see if we can prove who wore them.'

'Have we got a sample of Duffy's?'

'No. If we can put together enough of a case otherwise, we'll get one and have them compared.'

'Can we do that, anyway?'

'I don't want to tip our hand to him too soon. We're starting to show that he *could* be our murderer - if we had some kind of *motive,* a sensible reason why he had a grudge against the two of them, I'd chance bringing him in for questioning, perhaps.'

Silence fell for a minute or so, while they pondered that difficulty. Then Russell got to his feet again:

'Come on, Doug - let's go and talk to Stevens. Give him a call, see if he's home, will you?'

'Right!' Rimmer reached for the telephone.

CHAPTER THIRTY-EIGHT

'Come in, gentlemen, take a seat! My fiancée is still at work, but she'll be home soon.' Stevens greeted the two detectives at the door of his apartment.

'Coffee? Or something stronger?'

'Coffee would be fine, Mr Stevens, thank you.'

'Right-o, give me a moment!'

A few minutes later, he was back from the kitchen with a tray bearing three mugs and a steaming cafetiere, which he set down on the coffee-table between them.

'How are things, Mr Stevens?' Russell asked.

'Fine, thank you! As I expect you know, we're still getting paid by Sweeney's, until the present situation is sorted out, so that's good - and of course, we've still got Katie's salary as well. But - I had Mrs Gidding on the phone today!'

'Not trying to alter your testimony about her husband, I hope?' Stevens laughed:

'Far from it! She seems quite unperturbed at the idea that he's going to go to prison for a good long time - I've an idea they've tended to lead almost separate lives for quite a while, anyway. No, she's got ideas of taking over the lease on his premises, keeping the place open, but changing it around pretty drastically. And she wants me to stay on, and run the bars for her.'

'Oh? Not Mr Duffy?'

'I don't think she likes him very much! She wants to turn the

264

ground floor into more of a restaurant, and convert the dance floor upstairs into a kind of events and conference room.'

'Really? Sounds like a more acceptable kind of operation, from our point of view!' Stevens laughed again:

'I'm sure it does! Anyhow, I'm sure you didn't come to ask about my future prospects - what can I do for you?'

'My call today has to do with the murder of Roddie McKeenan, rather than the case against Gidding, Mr Stevens. I want you to think back to that night, and try to answer a few questions for me.'

'Sure, if I can.'

'You were in the gents' toilet for the few minutes immediately before the shooting?'

'That's right - as I told you in my statement, I'd gone for a pee, exchanged pleasantries with that customer who was in there at the same time - you found him, did you?'

'We did - and his statement pretty much agrees with yours. You hadn't seen Mr Duffy come down into the ground-floor lounge, go up to the bar?'

'No. He must have got there just as I left the room, from what Karl told me afterwards. I didn't see him at all; not until later, when he pushed his way out into the alley, just about as the first police car and the ambulance arrived.'

'So you know nothing of his movements over that time?'

'No, I'm afraid not. Why the sudden interest in Fluffy, of all people?'

'I'd rather not say, at this stage, if you don't mind. When you were in the toilet, you heard Lucy Cavendish and Roddie talking in the corridor outside?'

'Yes - again, that's all in my statement. I *knew* her voice, but couldn't make out the words; and I'm pretty sure it was Roddie, but I wouldn't be absolutely certain.'

'That's fine. Then, after they'd parted, you heard a door slam?'

'Yes, I did.' The man's voice was beginning to sound puzzled at this reiteration of his testimony. Russell reached his point:

'Would you be certain of which door that was, Mr Stevens? You told us before that you thought it was the outside door, at the end of the corridor - but the other man who was with you in the toilet thinks it was the door to the ladies, next door.'

'Oh! Well now… Let me think…' Stevens sat back, a frown of concentration on his face. After a moment, he looked up again:

'To be honest, Inspector, I'm not certain, now. I thought at the time it was the other door, but now you ask… Maybe, because of what happened afterwards, I thought it must have been that door - I'm not sure I'd want to stand up in court and say, either way.'

'Do you think it possible that you would be able to decide if we were to recreate the situation?'

'What, stand in the loo while someone slams the doors, do you mean?'

'Exactly. Would you give it a try?' Stevens shrugged:

'If you like - I'm not sure it would help, after all this time, but I'll give it a go if you want.'

'Thank you, Mr Stevens. It's getting late, now - could we meet you at the club tomorrow, in the morning? We can try our experiment with the doors, and go over a few other things with you at the same time?'

'Yes, I don't see why not. It might even be easier to remember, in the right surroundings; what time?'

'Can we say nine o'clock? I have a lot of other things to do tomorrow.'

'Sure! I'll come down when Katie sets off for work.'

'Good! We'll see you then - and thank you for the coffee!'

* * *

As they got out of the Jeep in the police station car park, Russell told his Sergeant:

'You might as well get off home, Doug. I'm just going to have a quick chat with Lucy, then I'll be away for my dinner, too.'

'Okay, boss - see you in the morning.'

'Yeah - meet me here, about half past eight, we'll get down to meet Stevens for nine. 'Night, Doug.'

''Night, boss.'

'Hello, Lucy.' The girl looked up as the custody sergeant opened the cell door for Russell:

'Hello, Inspector.' He crossed the cramped confines of the cell, sat beside her on the bench:

'How are you?' She shrugged, giving him an ironic smile:

'As well as can be expected, I suppose!'

'That's a girl! Keep your spirits up.' She regarded him with wary surprise:

'What's happened?' He smiled at her:

'I think I'm beginning to understand what happened that night, Lucy.' Her eyes grew wide:

'You *believe* me? That I didn't kill Roddie?'

'I'm… beginning to see an alternative; I won't put it more strongly than that. If you'll bear with me, for a day or two, maybe I can show who else might have shot him.' She gazed at him for a moment, then drew a long, shuddering breath, let it out as a deep sigh, bright tears of relief glistening in her emerald eyes. He held up a cautionary hand:

'Don't get too excited! I can't prove anything, yet - and the case against you is still a strong one. But - I told you before - I want the truth, not an easy conviction, so I'm going to go on digging as long as I can.'

'Thank you, Mr Russell!' Her voice was barely audible.

'Now - I need your help. Can you think back to that night? Just before… everything began to happen, you were in the lower bar, right?' She nodded:

'Yes, that's right. I'd come back down after my… client left. I put my little bag back in the locker, went and sat at the bar

267

for a drink, where I could see Roddie at the other end.'

'You didn't go to join him?'

'No. We weren't supposed to spend time talking to our own friends - I was still at work, remember. But I *did* want to talk to him again, so I was waiting for an opportunity, watching for him to make a move - that was why I followed him when he went out.'

'Okay. I know we've covered this before - but now, I need you to think: Did you see Mr Duffy come into the lounge?'

'Yes.' She sounded puzzled by the question: 'He came across from the front stairs, went up to the bar, beckoned Karl over. He would always check on the bars, every now and then through the evening, so I suppose that was what he was doing then.'

'Where was he, at the bar? In relation to yourself, and Roddie?'

'He went to the far end, away from where I was - the stairs are over that side. He was right beside Roddie, I remember.'

'What was Roddie doing?'

'He was just sitting, on a stool. He had a drink, lager I think, on the bar in front of him.'

'So - Duffy spoke to Karl - then what happened?'

'Oh - Karl went back to the customer he'd been serving; there were one or two more waiting, I think. Mr Duffy went off towards the kitchen - I guess he was going to check the cellar, the stairs down are through the kitchen, you know?'

'Right - Did he speak to Roddie, at all?' She gave him an odd look, nodded slowly:

'Yes, he did… That was strange… Oh, he would always say good evening, or whatever, he's always punctilious about being polite, even to people he doesn't like!'

'Like Roddie?'

'Like Roddie!'

'So why was it strange?'

'Well - that night, they talked for a minute or two. Roddie seemed surprised, to judge from the way he reacted… Fluffy was doing the talking, I think... Then, I saw Roddie nod; and Frank turned away to go to the cellar.'

'What did Roddie do next?'

'He sat for a moment - then he emptied his drink, got up, and walked out. I followed him, because I thought he was going to the loo, and I'd be able to catch him alone in the corridor.' Russell nodded:

'And when do you remember seeing Mr Duffy again, later?' She shook her head:

'I don't, to be honest. I was too upset to notice anyone... You understand?'

His smile was sympathetic:

'Of course. Thank you, Lucy! I'll leave you to rest, now - but I will want you to repeat all that for a statement in the morning.'

'Yes, of course - is all this important, Inspector?' He grinned at her as he got to his feet:

'Oh, yes!' Suspicion dawned in the girl's eyes:

'You think... You think *Frank* killed Roddie? But *why?* Why would he? I mean, he didn't *like* him, but that's not a motive for murder, surely?'

'That's the question I need to answer, Lucy.'

'Can I tell Alison about this? She's coming to see me tomorrow.'

'As your solicitor, she'll get all this information in due course, anyway. So I don't see why not - she's bound by confidentiality rules, so I've no fear of it getting out before we're ready.'

'Thank you, Mr Russell - and thank you, for believing in me.'

He gave her an encouraging smile as he left the cell.

CHAPTER THIRTY-NINE

'Damn! This really is all beginning to fit together, isn't it?'

'Yes, Doug.' David Russell had just brought his assistant up to date with Lucy's information, as the two drove to the closed and shuttered nightclub: 'If only I could see *why* Duffy would do it - he must have held some kind of really deep grudge against them both, to kill one and frame the other.'

'Yeah, that's what worries me, boss. Oh, it's all possible - but my money's still on Lucy, to be honest with you.'

'I know. All we can do is tie up all the loose ends, wait for Terry to find out if there's a DNA trace from those gloves - that's going to be the decider.'

'And you've got until Monday!'

'Yeah, don't remind me!'

Stevens was waiting for them by the front door of Sweeney's. He let them in with a pass-key, and the three made their way to the side corridor, and the gents toilet; there, Russell and the barman went inside:

'I was standing here, washing my hands, when I heard the door, Inspector.'

'Right - Doug, will you go and open the outside door, and then slam it shut?'

The Sergeant did as he was bid, closing the toilet door first; Stevens shook his head, uncertainly. Rimmer put his head around the door:

'Any good?'

'I'm not sure, Sergeant. It *could* have been that door I heard - can you try the other one?'

'Okay.' He closed the gents door again, and moments later they heard the bang from the ladies, next door. At this, Stevens eyes brightened up; as Rimmer looked in once more, he said:

'Can you try that again? Not quite so hard - just let the spring mechanism shut it, this time.' Rimmer nodded, went to comply. And now, when the ladies door closed with an audible thump, Stevens nodded:

'Yes! That's what I heard, I'm almost certain. I *might* be wrong - it's quite a while ago, now - but if I had to choose, I'd say that was it.'

'*Not* the outside door, at the end of the corridor?' Russell confirmed.

'No. If you notice, there was a kind of rattle from that one as it shut - the crash-bars, I expect - and I don't remember that, from the night Roddie died. I think I must have taken it for granted that it was *that* door I heard, because it was closed when I went to see what had happened outside.'

'When you found Roddie, in the alley?'

'Yeah.'

'The outside door was *closed,* when you went out?'

'Yes, I'm sure. I had to bang the crash-bar to open it.'

'But you didn't *hear* it close - if you're right, and it was the ladies door you *did* hear?'

'That's right...' Stevens sounded puzzled: 'But... Roddie wasn't in the corridor when we came out of the loo, so he must have been outside. And if he hadn't closed the door...?'

'Someone else did! You'd make a good detective, Mr Stevens!' Rimmer had rejoined them from the ladies. The man laughed:

'Oh, no! I'm quite happy selling booze, thank you very much!'

'You've already answered most of my questions, Mr Stevens - just one more thing: Would you have any idea if Mr Duffy might have had some kind of grudge against Roddie, and Lucy? Something really serious, at least in his eyes?'

'I haven't, Mr Russell. Oh, he didn't like Roddie much, most people knew that - but I assume you're asking if he had a motive for killing him? Do you think *he* did it?'

'It's a possibility we're looking into, Mr Stevens - but I'd be grateful if you didn't tell anyone that, at least for now!'

'Okay - I guess!'

'What now, boss?' They'd left the barman after seeing him relock the club, and were on their way back to the station.

'We've done pretty well all we can, as far as confirming Duffy's movements, I think. Terry won't have anything on the gloves until tomorrow, he reckons - we might as well fill our time by tackling the last of our loose ends.'

'Such as?'

'The girl who died, last year - let's go and talk to the mother. You can drive, and I'll use the restful journey to think about why Duffy killed Roddie McKeenan!'

'Okay!' Rimmer laughed.

They stopped off at the police station, to make sure of the woman's address; then, the Sergeant driving, set off for Newmarket.

Little more than an hour later, after an easy cruise Eastwards along the A14, they reached the town, and found their way to the neat little bungalow on the outskirts. The front door opened to Rimmer's knock, revealing a small, grey-haired lady as neat as the bungalow in her appearance:

'Good Morning - you must be the policemen from Grancester?'

'Yes, Ma'am. Sergeant Rimmer; and this is Inspector Russell.' The two showed their ID's; they had radio'd ahead, to get clearance from the Cambridgeshire force to conduct an interview on their territory, and to make sure the lady would be home.

'Come in, won't you? I'm Mary Verdon - but you knew that, didn't you?'

They echoed her welcoming smile, followed her into a smart and spotless living room, where she waved them into two cottage-style armchairs:

'Would you like some tea, after your journey?'

'Thank you, Mrs Verdon, that would be very nice.' She smiled again, bustled off into the kitchen, to return a few minutes later with a laden tray.

'Now - what can I do for you?' She asked as she poured tea into three bone china cups.

'We need to talk to you about Emma, Mrs Verdon. I'm very sorry to bring it all up again, I know how painful it must be for you.' She nodded, sadly:

'It is, Inspector - but you have a job to do, don't you? Why, though, is it important, after all this time?'

'We are investigating a lot of what went on at the club where she worked, Mrs Verdon.'

'I see.' She sighed: 'It was that place which killed my daughter, Inspector. She only went to work there as a waitress, but they talked her into doing... terrible things! I didn't *know,* she never told me - I only found out afterwards, how she had been earning so much money there. I suppose, I should have known something wasn't right... But, perhaps I didn't *want* to know...' Russell nodded sympathetically:

'How did she come to be working in Grancester, if you lived here?'

'She had gone to St Bride's School, you know, the girl's boarding school near Kettering? Her father wanted her to have the best education she could - and he lives near there, now, of course. He paid all her fees, her expenses, while she was at school; and, to be honest, it suited me, really. I couldn't have done so well for her, on my salary, and he could see more of her without the two of us having to meet. She came home to me for the holidays, and the odd weekend in term, but he could see her, other times.'

'You aren't on good terms with her father?' The woman smiled, shook her head:

'No, Inspector! I should never have married him! But then, I wouldn't have had Emma, would I? And, even now she's gone, I wouldn't have wanted *not* to have had her - you understand?' Russell nodded again, as she went on: 'He's an arrogant, self-opinionated man - everything had to be *his* way, you know? I didn't have the words then, but now I suppose you'd call him, what's the term - a control freak!'

'She stayed over there, after finishing school?'

'Yes - I wanted her to come home, go to the college here, perhaps, but she wanted the freedom of earning her own money, like so many kids that age. *He* got her the job; but then it all went wrong...' She let her voice trail off, suddenly close to tears. Russell reached across, took her hand in his:

'I'm really sorry to come here and upset you, Mrs Verdon. Am I right to assume that Verdon was your maiden name?'

'That's right, Inspector; I went back to it after the divorce.'

'Can you tell me - what's your ex-husband's name?'

She raised startled eyes to his: 'But - you said, you were investigating all about that club - I thought you knew that! You *must* know, surely?' Russell shook his head, but a smile was hovering around his lips; Rimmer looked up from the notes he was scribbling, puzzled.

'Inspector - My ex-husband is the manager there! My married name was Duffy!' Russell couldn't prevent his grin spreading from ear to ear. Rimmer gaped in amazement:

'You mean - *Frank* Duffy...?'

'Got it in one, Doug!'

'But... How... Dammit to hell, I will! I'll eat *your* hat!'

CHAPTER FORTY

'You knew! You bloody-well knew!' David Russell threw his head back and laughed:

'I didn't! I swear to you, Doug, I didn't. Oh, I'd wondered about the double link to Newmarket; the girl's mother, and then Duffy's background - but I had no idea she'd turn out to be his ex-wife! Not until she was talking about her ex-husband, and the description began to sound awfully familiar!'

The two were in the car once more, returning to Grancester, Rimmer again behind the wheel.

At the bungalow, the embarrassed Sergeant had apologised for his startled outburst, to the amusement of their interviewee. Russell had explained their suspicions about Frank Duffy's part in the death of Roddie McKeenan, and the attempt to frame Lucy Cavendish for his killing; he had gently pushed the woman for details of her family's internal politics:

'Whatever I thought of him, whatever my problems with him, Frank thought the world of Emma. She was his little girl, come what may! He insisted on paying for her education, as I told you - and he could afford it, after all. And I think he was pleased that she decided to stay in Grancester when she left school, even though that was mostly due to him saying he could get her a job.'

'But that job was what killed her?' Russell had coaxed; Mary Verdon sighed:

'Oh, it was! But he never meant that to happen, I'm sure - he only meant for her to get a start, earn a bit of money, then probably get a better job somewhere else. He was furious, I know, when they talked her into being a 'hostess' - and then, when she started taking drugs…'

'No-one at the club, in the town, for that matter, knew that he was her father?'

'Oh, no! I think that was her doing, mostly - she was happy enough to take his money, let him find her a job, but her attitude to him was always… ambivalent, that's the word. I'm afraid that was probably my fault, Inspector - she'd grown up with my side of our arguments, my view if him, so it wasn't surprising, maybe, that she never quite trusted him, didn't want to be known to everyone as his daughter. He may have resented that - but he didn't let it show, not to her. And, I suppose, he might not have wanted people to know he'd wangled a job for his own daughter because he was the manager, you know?'

'Of course. How did he take it when she died?'

'O-oh!' The woman's sigh had spoken of her own grief, but she replied: 'Very badly, Inspector, as you might expect. At her funeral, he told me - that was the only time he and I have had anything like a conversation, for years! - he said he knew who was to blame for her death, and he'd get even with them.'

'Did he tell you who he meant?'

'Oh, yes! They were there - he pointed them out. I wasn't sure he knew what he was talking about; Emma had told me about them, she said they were her friends! The girl, especially - she'd given Emma a home, for quite a long time, until she could afford that flat in Northampton. But *he* blamed her, for getting Emma involved in - you know what I mean. And, he said the man had been supplying her with drugs, got her addicted to them, so he was responsible for what happened to her.'

'Not an unreasonable argument, perhaps?'

'Pshaw! Emma was a head-strong girl, if she didn't want to

do something, she'd soon tell you so. If she did… *what* she did, she knew what she was getting into, or at least thought she did. Although, maybe it was… harder, than she expected. Lucy, her friend, told me that that was why she'd used drugs; she told me they'd tried to stop her! Do you really think that Frank did all that? Killed the young man, and tried to blame it on Lucy?' Russell had nodded:

'I'm as sure as I can be, Mrs Verdon.' She held his eyes, the sorrow deepening in her own:

'He was a part of my life, Inspector - he still is, I suppose, in a way. But if he really did those terrible things… You'll want me to give evidence against him, will you? Tell everyone about what he thought of those two young people, how he blamed them for Emma's death?'

'If you feel able to?' She hesitated, then nodded firmly:

'All right, Inspector. That poor boy deserves justice - and his girl has suffered enough, hasn't she? I'll do what you ask.'

'Thank you, Mrs Verdon. Just one last question, and we'll leave you in peace - after your husband's accident, you looked after him?' She gave a quick bark of a laugh:

'Only until he could fend for himself! I'd have left sooner, but I couldn't leave him stranded, could I?' Russell smiled, went on:

'During that time, he tried to learn to use his left hand more?'

'He did. Always cussed and self-reliant, he had to prove he could manage on his own! He got quite good, to be fair - couldn't write that well, left-handed, however hard he tried, but he could do most other things. If he wanted to.'

'Thank you, Mrs Verdon!' Russell's smile became even wider.

* * *

Back in Russell's office, as the winter night closed in outside, an air of triumph prevailed:

'You got your motive, in the end!'

Russell grinned at the Sergeant:

'Yeah! All we need is for Terry to match his DNA with those gloves, and we're home and dry. We can show that he had the opportunity and the motive; and the means were right at hand, for the taking.'

'Do you want to go and arrest him tonight?' Russell considered:

'Let's leave him 'til the morning. Once we hear from Terry, if he's got a good trace from the gloves, we'll bring him in for questioning, get a sample for comparison. Without that, the case is still a bit shaky.'

A companionable silence fell for a few minutes, until Rimmer spoke:

'Sir?'

'Yes, Doug?'

'I owe you an apology - you were right all along, weren't you? I mean, you never trusted the evidence against Lucy Cavendish, from the start...' Russell shook his head:

'No, Doug - I could so easily have been wrong! I just had that crazy feeling that we were being manipulated, even though I couldn't see how. And the trouble Duffy went to, to frame her - he must have studied up on forensic science, and even then tried to second-guess things. Like using his left hand - could he have *known* that analysis of the residues on the gloves would prove the killer to be left-handed, or was he just trying to cover all eventualities?'

'Perhaps he'll tell us?' Russell laughed:

'You never know! And he might just be the type to want to crow about how clever he is, even if it does help to get him a life sentence!'

'Right!' Russell looked up at the clock:

'It's likely to be a long weekend again, Doug - and I think we deserve an early night, don't you? I'm off home - see you in the morning.'

'Okay - see you then, boss.'

''Night, Doug.'

* * *

The next morning, David Russell's first call was on Lucy, in her cell. The news that the young girl she had befriended had in fact been Frank Duffy's daughter left her close to speechless:

'What? You're joking! I don't… Why? Why didn't she *tell* me?'

'It seems she wasn't too proud of the fact, from what her mother tells us. And she wanted to be seen to be making her own way, if I read things correctly.'

'Yes… Yes, that sounds like Emma, for sure…'

'Anyway, Lucy; if one more piece of forensic evidence I'm waiting for comes through, I have a case I can take to court. Your next appearance in court is on Monday - it looks as though I'll be able to ask the magistrates to release you, if the Crown Prosecutors agree we should offer no evidence against you.'

'Oh, Mr Russell…' The girl swayed on her feet, her face hidden in her hands; he stepped over, held her by the shoulders. She smiled into his eyes:

'Can we tell Freya? And Muriel?'

'I'll let them know. We have to wait for the court to release you from their remand, you understand?' She nodded:

'But at least, they'll *know!* It'll put their minds at rest - thank you, Mr Russell!' He gave her shoulders an encouraging squeeze, and left her to relax in the knowledge that she would soon be free.

The rest of that Saturday passed in a flurry of office-bound activity, a collating of facts, a tying-together of threads, until by mid-afternoon Russell found himself looking at the substantial framework of a case against Frank Duffy. Its backbone was the revelation of his motive for both the killing and the framing of Lucy Cavendish, the supporting skeleton their reconstruction of his movements on the fatal night, based upon the various eye-witness statements. Even minor subtleties, insignificant in themselves, added their fractional weight to the whole; his observed reaction to the photograph of the girl they now knew to be his dead daughter; and his reaction also when Elsa Jurgens had first told him of the shooting of Roddie McKeenan:

'I mean, you'd expect at least *some* expression of surprise, even if he couldn't stand the man and didn't care if he'd been hurt or killed! Surprise at the event, if you see what I mean?' Rimmer had seen the significance of the point as soon as Russell repeated the girl's words to him.

And answers to other questions posed during the last twenty-four hours were coming in; each one providing yet more support for their hypothesis. Steve Campbell had contacted the physiotherapist who had treated Duffy after his accident, and the woman had confirmed Mary Verdon's statement that he had indeed trained himself to use his left hand:

'Oh, yes, Officer! He's a stubborn character, had to do what he could for himself, come what may. He was far from being fully ambidextrous, you understand, but by the time he had full use of his right arm again, he had learned to write competently with his left hand, and perform a good many functions which normal right-handed people would find quite difficult' she had told him when he tracked her down to her post at Bedford's South Wing Hospital.

Detective Superintendent Wilson had looked in at one point:

'Finally got your new suspect in the McKeenan murder, then, David?'

'Yes, sir. It turns out Frank Duffy was the father of the girl who died of a drugs overdose last year - and he blamed him and Lucy Cavendish for getting her into both that and prostitution at the club.'

'So I hear. Good work, David - you were right all along, to doubt the case against the Cavendish girl, weren't you?'

'Seems so, sir. Duffy had put a lot of effort into framing her, planning it all out and then grabbing the chance when it offered to put it into practice.'

'Mmm. Very good. Any word from DCI Callow in Belfast?'

'I had a message earlier, sir - he's traced most of the outlet routes into England, and should be closing them all down, with the Irish operation, in a week or two.'

'Excellent! Nice Christmas present for them, eh?'

Just after three o'clock, the door of Russell's office burst open and the forensic Sergeant swept in, his lab-coat flying behind him, the eyes behind his spectacles gleaming:

'Dave! You want the good news first?' Russell looked up from his desk; Rimmer turned with a grin as his superior asked:

'What's the *bad* news, Terry?' The Mad Professor responded with a laugh which might have tended to support doubts of his sanity:

'That's the best bit! There isn't any, it just gets better! Your gloves - the latex ones, right?'

'Yes?'

'Good, clear DNA trace from them. No match on the database, but just get me a sample to compare, boyo!'

'You're on, Terry - how quick can we get a comparison done?'

'I'll do you a preliminary, myself, but you'll not get a final one from the lab until Tuesday, probably. If we get the sample today.'

'So, what's the *better* news, Terry?'

'Well - I sent one glove off to the contract lab, kept the other one here, right? I decided I'd see what I could find on the outside surface - and guess what? It's contaminated with traces of the chemicals which are used in the preparation of leather, and the mix is exactly the same as I found in Lucy's gloves; the ones with the powder residues on!'

'Really? Bloody good work, Terry!'

'Yeah, well - it was good that that pair of gloves were quite new, if they'd been worn a lot the chemical content would have dissipated, and I probably wouldn't have got the result.'

Russell got to his feet:

'Come on, Doug - it's time we brought Duffy in for questioning. I'll have that DNA sample for you within the hour, Terry!'

'Good show - I'll be down in my dungeon, okay?'

CHAPTER FORTY-ONE

Sunday morning saw the grey, depressing weather take a turn for the worse; showers of rain and sleet swept in on a bitter North-Westerly wind, keeping indoors all those who had no urgent need to venture out. Except, of course, teenage boys, to whom weather of any kind was something of an irrelevance.

Daniel Russell had set off after breakfast, against his mother's urging, to cycle to his friend Jacko's house in the next village. Sarah was playing quietly in her room, accompanied by Becky Ransome, the little girl from next door; David Russell gave his wife a peck on the cheek:

'I'll try to be home as soon as I can, Love.'

'You have to go in, on a day like this?' He smiled:

'I do! We need to interview someone again - I'll be as quick as I can.'

The previous night, true to character, Frank Duffy had stuck obstinately to his story, insisting that he had been in the cellars during the vital moments when McKeenan had been shot. On the following morning, his attitude had become even more aggressive, after a night in the discomfort of a police cell:

'For goodness' sake, why are you asking *me* about all this? It's perfectly obvious to any *sensible* person what happened!'

'What makes you say that, sir?' Rimmer was quietly polite.

'Oh, for crying out loud! Lucy and McKeenan were having a

282

fight, everyone knew that! He wanted to dump her, and she was getting very emotional about it. She must have lost her cool, shot him in a fit of anger - she's got quite a temper!'

'It's possible, sir - but evidence we have suggests otherwise?'

'What evidence? He was shot with *her gun,* for Christ's sake!'

The two detectives exchanged glances at this outburst; Russell turned back to the man and said quietly:

'What makes you say that, Mr Duffy? We've never released details of the murder weapon to the press, have we, Sergeant?'

'No, sir, we haven't.' Duffy stared from one to the other:

'But... It's *obvious,* surely? He was shot, and she had a gun...' there was a glint of panic in his eyes.

'And where does Emma fit into that scenario, Mr Duffy?'

'Emma...?'

'Your *daughter,* Mr Duffy. The girl whose death you blamed on McKeenan and Miss Cavendish.' He held the Inspector's eyes for a moment, stubbornly frantic; but his collapse, when it came, was complete. He folded forward over the edge of the table, dropped his head onto his arms and began to sob uncontrollably.

* * *

After the wild wetness of the day before, Monday dawned bright and cold, a hard frost sparkling on the lawn and hedges as David Russell looked down from the bedroom window. His mood was buoyant - today would see Lucy freed by the court, her innocence of the killing of her lover finally established by the real murderer's confession. Breakfast was over; Tracy was getting Sarah ready to take her to her nursery class at the village school, and Daniel was getting his books together as his father came down again into the kitchen.

'I'll drop you at school today, Daniel' Tracy suggested to her son. She'd been making a special effort to call him by his full name since their last row.

'No need, Mum, I'll cycle as usual.'

'Oh, Dan! Look at the weather - the roads will be like skating rinks after all that rain!'

'I'll be all right! I'm always careful, you know that!'

'Go and put your coat on, Sarah, there's good girl. Let your father run you in then, if you'd rather?' She addressed the boy again.

'It's all right, Mum! We're going on to Snow's after school, to work on our history project, and it'll be awkward if I haven't got my bike.'

'You could walk, couldn't you?'

'Oh, Mum! That'd take *forever!*'

'Do as I ask, Daniel, please?' He gave a deep sigh, carried his school bag out into the hallway, pulling the door to behind him. Tracy raised weary eyes to her husband, who smiled at her:

'I'll see you later, Love.' He kissed her on the cheek.

'Yes - have a good day at work, Darling. Home for dinner tonight?'

'All being well!' He stepped into the hall, ruffled his daughter's hair in fond farewell:

'Be good, sprout!'

'Bye-bye, Daddy!' He opened the front door, then paused and looked around:

'Where's Dan?'

'He went, Daddy.'

'Where, sweetheart?'

'To school, Daddy.' He checked outside, turned back just as Tracy emerged from the kitchen:

'Where's Danny?' He held up a hand to calm the storm as he said:

'He's left for school.'

'What? On his bike? After I *specifically* told him not to?' He nodded, saying in order to reassure her, to appease her anger:

'He'll be all right, don't worry - he *is* a sensible kid, he won't take any risks.'

'I know - but…'

'Leave it for now, Love. I'll have a word with him tonight, okay?'

'Oh, all right! You'd better go, too. See you later.'

'Bye, Love.'

In the Jeep, as he waited to turn right onto the road into town, a bright red Jaguar sports car passed in front of him. Harvey Williams was a well-known local eccentric; an ex-RAF officer, he still sported a bristling handlebar moustache. Owner of the old manor house in Great Thornwood, the neighbouring village, the XJS was his pride and joy; even on this bitter but bright morning, he had the roof down.

Russell smiled as he turned out, following the red soft-top at a little distance. For all his flamboyance, the elderly air-commodore was driving with great restraint: *That much power must be difficult to handle in this weather!* He watched the sleek vehicle as it slipped in and out of his field of view, on the bends and rises of the road in front of him.

* * *

Mum was right! Within a quarter of a mile, Daniel was beginning to regret his haste in disobeying his mother's instructions; the road surface *looked* okay, but several times he'd felt the tyres trying to slide from under him, kept his balance with some difficulty. *I'll be all right once I get past the bypass...* Thinking ahead, he knew that the road would be safe once he entered the town - they obviously hadn't been able to grit this little-used stretch yet. The worst bit, he knew, would be the dip just before he passed under the dual carriageway, where this road ran downhill past the entrance to the old quarry, now their local Country Park - it was sheltered, so the sun couldn't get to the frost, and the steepness would make it treacherous.

He breasted the rise, saw the long slope stretching away before him. Stopping pedalling, he let the bike coast - even so, it began to pick up speed, slowly at first, but faster and faster as the gradient steepened. *Too fast!* He tried applying the brakes, gently; then a little harder, as it seemed to have no effect. And suddenly, he was out of control, the back wheel no longer gripping the road, sliding away from him towards the verge… He could hear a car behind him, looked desperately over his shoulder…

* * *

Harvey Williams was enjoying himself. It was a grand morning, the sun low on the horizon, frost sparkling on the hedgerow, the air so clean and sweet. Perhaps people did think he was crazy, driving around with the top down in December - he didn't care!

The Jaguar was a joy to handle, as always. Fifteen years old, he had it maintained regardless of cost by the local dealer; despite all that power under his right foot, it was so sensitive, so controllable, even on a slippery surface! He breasted the rise on the approach to the town, let the agile beast cruise past the entrance to the park; there was a kid on a racing bike, travelling in front of him: *That looks tricky, with those narrow tyres in this weather!* He hesitated, thinking to stay behind the boy, but then decided to pass: *If he falls off, better behind me than in front!*

Just as he pulled out to pass, he realised the kid was in trouble, the bike no longer travelling in a straight line but slewing sideways. He tried to go wider, give him room; but then he felt the car's back tyres slipping, the deceleration of the engine as he lifted his foot enough to break them loose on the icy surface. As the rear came round, he tried to steer out of the skid, without success - he heard the bang, as his rear wing hit the bicycle, fought the car to a halt on the wrong side of the road, almost facing the way it had come…

* * *

David Russell saw the Jaguar vanish out of sight on the downslope towards the Grancester bypass. Breasting the rise himself a few moments later, he realised instantly that something had happened; the car was just coming to rest, facing him, on the other side of the road: *He's lost it!* It didn't look to be serious; his first thought, perhaps incongruously, was to hope that the car wasn't damaged; it was a beauty, and everyone knew how proud the man was of it.

He drove cautiously down, came to a halt a few yards short of the now-stationary sports car. Getting out of the Jeep, he walked over to where he could see Williams sitting in the driving seat, looking shocked; A plumber's van and a couple of other cars were pulling up, having appeared from the other direction.

'Mr Williams? Are you all right?' The man gave him a jerky nod:

'Yes - yes, I'm fine! How's the boy?'

'Boy?'

'The boy - on the bike! I hit him, I heard the bang…' He put his hands over his mouth, dragging the moustache down, a look of horror in the eyes he turned on the Inspector. Russell looked around, puzzled; then, for the first time, he saw the bicycle wheel protruding from below the rear of the car. He raised his eyes to look farther afield, saw a textbook lying spread-eagled like a dead bird on the tarmac, an exercise book close to his feet; he bent to look closer: On its cover, in a neat, rounded hand surrounded by incomprehensible schoolboy hieroglyphics, he read:

Form 2A - Physics Theory

Daniel Russell

The plumber, out of his van, skidded to a halt as the man standing by the car turned unseeing eyes on him. All thought in Russell's brain had locked solid, his whole consciousness drowned out by the silent scream which was echoing through his entire being:

DANIEEEELLL!!!

CHAPTER FORTY-TWO

Doug Rimmer was annoyed with himself. He felt lost, unfocussed, far from his usual positive self: *Pull yourself together, Douglas!*

He was sitting in his superior's otherwise-deserted office, looking across at the empty chair behind his desk. The two court hearings had gone much as expected - Duffy had been remanded in custody for a month, and taken away to Wellingborough prison, while enquiries progressed; and Lucy Cavendish had been duly released from her remand, to the delight of a waiting Muriel Hepple who, with little Freya, had been in the public gallery primed for the expected result. But now, with that excitement over, he had come back to the station, dreading to hear more of the morning's other events.

Entering from the car park, he'd made his way up in an empty lift, met only one constable in the corridor who'd merely greeted him with a subdued 'hello, Sarge'. He was desperate to know what had happened to Daniel Russell - but at the same time, terrified of hearing the worst. He knew his Inspector's family, had visited the old cottage many times with his own wife, Julie, felt a great affection for his superior's children - the bubbly, cute little girl, and the lively, intelligent boy.

First reports, before he'd had to leave for the courtroom, only said that he'd been in a road accident; the traffic car which had been first on the scene had confirmed that the boy's bicycle had gone under Williams' Jaguar, but no more: The XJS was a big, heavy car - if the kid had gone under it, too, what chance would he stand?

He should go and find out, he owed that to Russell; but still, a fear of being told the man's son was dead kept him motionless. If he hadn't heard, maybe it hadn't really happened...

Screwing up his resolve, he forced himself to get to his feet, step towards the door. But before he could open it, it swung towards him, and the Inspector came into the room, looking haggard, moving without his customary vigour. He passed Rimmer, and slumped into one of the chairs in front of his own desk:

'Hello, Doug.' He sounded so tired!

'Sir - what are you doing here? Can I get you something? Coffee? God, you look terrible!' The words slipped out before he could stop them. Russell looked up, amusement overlying the shattered look on his face:

'Always ready with a cheerful word, eh, Doug?'

'Sorry! I mean...' Russell waved a hand to silence his apology, leant forward, elbows on the desk, and put his face in his hands. Rimmer stood over him, looking down with his concern mirrored in his eyes, feeling helpless and ineffective; Russell breathed slowly, deeply, four times, five, six, before raising his head again:

'He's all right, Doug - he's going to be okay.' Rimmer gaped, surprised but so gloriously relieved:

'Okay?' He echoed, stupidly. Russell gave him a thin smile:

'He's going to be fine. He's broken his left arm, and his collarbone, cracked a couple of ribs - but he's going to be fine!' Recovering himself, Rimmer sat down in the chair next to his superior, reached out a hand; Russell took it in his own, gripped it in grateful understanding:

'It seems the back of the car hit him as it skidded, knocked him off his bike, threw him onto the verge. We didn't spot him at first - I thought...' he broke off at the remembered horror of that moment: 'I thought he'd gone under the car. It was the guy from the plumber's van that plucked up the courage to look; and he wasn't there! Even then, it took us a few minutes to find him, he was almost underneath the hedge. They're keeping him in hospital, overnight, just to make sure there's nothing else wrong - Tracy's with him, now, although he's still out from the anaesthetic.'

'Oh, thank God! I'm so pleased he's all right…'

'I know, Doug.'

Silence fell for a minute or so, then Russell spoke again:

'I'm not stopping, Doug…'

'I should think not!'

'I want to get back to the hospital. But, so's I know - everything went off okay this morning?'

'Oh, sure - Lucy's gone home with her family, and Duffy's on his way to Wellingborough. What about the Old Bailey, sir?'

'Oh, I'll have to go, Wednesday, but the word from Mr Steadman is that they'll probably put it back - it's going to be a long trial, and starting it so close to Christmas could cause problems. If they do, I'll take some time off, to be with Tracy and the kids while Dan's getting better.'

'I should think so too! Now, bugger off back there, look after your boy - and give him my best wishes, right?' Russell laughed:

'I will, Doug! And thank you. You'll bring Mr Wilson up to date with everything?'

'I will - now get going, we can manage without you for a day or two!'

* * *

Lunchtime, the next day, saw David Russell sitting quietly by his son's bed in the private room in Grancester's small but efficient General Hospital. The boy was sleeping again, his body taking its own steps to promote its recovery alongside the efforts of the doctors; Tracy had gone to collect Sarah from nursery class, would bring her in to see her brother when they'd had a little lunch, trying to keep the little girl's routine as normal as possible.

He turned to look out of the window; outside, the sky was an unbroken blue, the sun bright, the frost giving an almost supernatural clarity to the air sparkling across the adjacent rooftops: *Thank you, God, for such a beautiful world - and for the life of my son.* He turned back, to find the boy's eyes on him from his pillow:

'Awake, Dan?'

'Yeah.'

'How are you feeling?'

'Okay, I guess.' Daniel reached out with his right hand; his father took it in both of his, held it gently.

'Dad?'

'I know.'

The companionable silence stretched out, man and boy each lost in their own thoughts. Russell looked down at the boy, who lay quiet, his eyes half-closed:

'Dan?'

'Yes, Dad?'

'You know what was the worst moment of my life?' Daniel grinned:

'Yesterday morning - thought you'd got rid of me for a while, didn't you?'

'Don't even joke about that!' But he laughed at the boy's irrepressible humour before replying:

'Not then - last year. The day you went up to the park, you remember, to meet that man Evans? I got home from work, and your mother told me where you'd gone; I *knew* what that man was, Dan! I think I broke every law in the book in the time it took me to drive there from home. I could have stopped you, if I'd any idea you'd even met him - all the way there, I was afraid... I *knew* I was going to find you somewhere in those woods, dead. And it was all my fault!'

Daniel looked up at his father, his hazel eyes wide with sudden understanding:

'It didn't *happen,* Dad - I'm okay!' Russell nodded, smiling. He went on:

'You remember how your mother was, that day? How she took charge of us, when we got home, packed you off to the bathroom, looked after us? What you *don't* know is that later, when you and your sister were safe in bed, she broke down, crying on my shoulder because of what could have happened to you, because she blamed *herself* for not stopping you from cycling up there. She still does, Dan. You understand?'

'You're saying that that's why she doesn't like me going off on my own, with Snow and Jacko?'

'She's afraid that sometime, something *will* happen to you, that's right.' Daniel fell silent, gazing down at his plaster-encased left arm, thinking about his father's words; Russell watched his son, knowing he had understood the implications of what he'd said. He spoke again:

'We don't always get things right, Dan. Nobody taught us how to be parents, any more than they told you how to be a kid - babies don't come with instruction manuals!' The boy looked up, chuckling at the image of a new-born child with a handbook clutched in its tiny fist. His father smiled down at him, carried on:

'So if we get things wrong, sometimes, it's not because we're being cussed, it's because we're having to make this up as we go along, just like you!' Daniel grinned:

'We're a bunch of amateurs, aren't we?'

'We are, Dan.'

This time, the silence lasted for a while, before Russell returned to his theme:

'If it seems like all we want to do is clip your wings and keep you on the ground, it's not because we're being difficult on purpose - it's because we're so afraid that you'll get hurt if we let you fly alone, too soon.' He felt his son's grip tighten on his hand; and a voice spoke from the doorway:

'But what's the use of wings, if you can't fly?' Father and son looked around, startled:

'How long have you been listening?' Tracy laughed:

'Long enough!' She stood aside to let Sarah push past her. The little girl rushed over to her brother and went to give him a hug, but her father redirected her to the other side of the bed, away from the boy's injured arm and shoulder. Tracy followed her daughter, more slowly, reached down to take her son's hand where he held his sister in his good arm:

'I think we should make an agreement with Daniel, don't you, Dad?'

'What do you suggest, Mum?' Russell sounded amused.

'I think it's time we let him make a few of his own mistakes - after all, he made a good start at that, yesterday, didn't he?' Daniel grinned ruefully:

'Don't remind me, Mum!'

'Don't worry, I will! If we let you show your independence a bit more, make some of your own decisions, will you *promise* that you'll always let us know where you are, and who you're with? And *listen* to our advice, even if you don't *take* it all the time. All right, Daniel?'

'All right, Mum! Thanks - I know I was very stupid, yesterday. I'll try not to be so pig-headed in future. Hey - I love you, Mum.' She gave him a loving smile, bent to kiss him over his sister's head. There was a twinkle in the boy's eyes as he asked:

'Does that mean we can go down the GPS, in future?' His parents exchanged loving but exasperated looks:

'As long as you're careful - and remember that some of the people there may not be as trustworthy as you three are!'

'Yeah! Thanks - and I promise, we'll keep to ourselves, okay?'

'Okay, Dan.' Russell reached down to ruffle his son's hair. Daniel smiled up at him:

'Dad? That day, at the park?'

'Yes, Dan?'

'After... you know? You sat me in the car, ready to bring me home - you remember what I said?' Russell looked down into his son's smiling eyes; he could hear those words in his mind, the quiet, shocked voice saying *I love you, Dad.* He replied again as he had then:

'I love you too, Dan.'

CHAPTER FORTY-THREE

Christmas morning, in Glebe Farm. Freya Cavendish sat on the floor of Muriel Hepple's living room, surrounded by the most wonderful array of presents she'd ever had. Her mother watched her, love for the nine-year-old radiant in her face:

'Well, Freya? What do you think is the best present, this year?' Granny Moo asked her, not expecting any sensible answer. The little girl looked up, her expression quizzical; she gazed around at the clutter of gifts, then up at her mother. She got up, went to her, threw he arms about her neck:

'Having Mummy home for Christmas!' Lucy hugged her daughter tight, held her so that she wouldn't see the sudden tears running down her cheeks.

* * *

In Bevington village, Sarah Russell had done almost as well for presents; she, too, was squatting on the floor, bemused by the wonderful things around her. Daniel was grinning fit to bust, admiring the new bike to replace the one wrecked in his accident; his ribs felt almost normal, now, just a small cast still supported his left arm, and most of the stiffness was gone.

'One more, Dan?' His father held out a package to him, in Christmas paper. He took it, puzzled; it was heavy, and round, and felt as if it was full of something liquid. He tore off the paper:

'What on earth?' He held a five litre tin of yacht varnish in his hands: 'Dad?' Russell was trying not to laugh at his son's expression:

'Follow me!' He led the dumbfounded boy to the front door, took him outside. Tracy followed, grinning; Sarah looked as puzzled as her brother. Russell opened the garage door, waved Daniel inside; he stopped short, his mouth hanging open, looked back at his father:

'Dad?'

'Well, what do you think of her?' 'She' was a small clinker-built sailing dinghy, sitting on her own two-wheeled trailer. A big blue ribbon was tied around her, amidships, the bow on top of her stowed mast.

'She's… beautiful, Dad! Is she really for me?'

'You said you wouldn't mind trying sailing for real, some time! She'll need a bit of fixing up, first, mind - she belonged to an old chap who sailed her on the lake in the park, but he's had to give up because of ill-health, hasn't been able to look after her properly for a while…'

'Hence the tin of yacht-varnish?'

'Right! I thought you and the terrible twins could get her rubbed down and revarnished over the next little while, until the weather's good enough to try her out. The harbour-master of the club said he'll show you how to handle her, when you're ready.' Daniel walked slowly around the little boat, his expression saying that he still didn't believe his eyes. His father said:

'You can work on her here in the garage, okay?' He looked up, his eyes shining, as his mother asked:

'Do you like her, Daniel?'

'Oh, wow, Mum…!'

'We could have got you a modern, fibreglass one - but we thought you'd prefer a real wooden boat. She's called Petrel - but you could change that, I suppose, if you wanted to?'

'No - Petrel's fine! Oh, Mum, Dad…!' He looked past them,

at the hard frost sparkling on the grass of the lawn: 'Only you two would have got me a boat, when everywhere's frozen solid and I can't try her out!' Their laughter echoed from the garage out into the street.

* * *

Mid-afternoon, and the doorbell of Old Laundry Cottage rang. Tracy got up from the armchair where she'd been relaxing with a glass of wine while the turkey sizzled to itself in the oven, out in the kitchen:

'That'll be Doug and Julie.'

'You've got their Christmas cake ready for them?'

'*Yes*, David!' she told her husband. Minutes later, the Sergeant and his wife were with them, raising their glasses to the holiday around the kitchen table while Daniel and Sarah eagerly opened yet one more present each. Tracy opened a cupboard, lifted out the cakeboard from inside:

'I promised to bake you a Christmas cake - just don't blame me, all right? This was *his* idea!' She nodded at her husband. Rimmer took one look at the cake and burst out laughing:

'Keeping me to my word, then, boss?'

'You said you'd eat my hat, Doug!' A sprig of holly was stuck jauntily in the marzipan hat-band of the chocolate-iced fruit trilby. Rimmer raised his glass in acknowledgement, and asked:

'Ready to return to the fray, after Christmas?' Russell nodded:

'Yes, Doug. This break has been great, and I've been able to help Daniel keep up with his studies…' A chuckle passed among the grown-ups at the boy's theatrical groan: 'But I shan't be sorry to be back!'

'We'll be glad to see you back, boss. I had a call from D.C.I. Callow, by the way - they've wrapped up that whole drugs operation, got pretty well all of the English outlets at the same time.'

'They did? That's excellent!' Russell caught the look in the two women's eyes: 'We'll be in trouble if we talk shop today, Doug, better change the subject!'

In the midst of their amusement, the doorbell rang again:

'Who on earth can that be?'

'I'll go.' Russell left them with their drinks, opened the front door:

'Lucy! What brings you here?'

'Hello, Mr Russell. I'm sorry to disturb your Christmas, but it was Freya's idea.' Her hands were on the little girl's shoulders.

'Come inside, please!'

'We mustn't stop, Muriel will have dinner ready soon - but Freya wanted to say something to you.' Russell got down on his haunches in front of the child:

'What is it, Freya?' Her expression was serious, but she smiled at him:

'I wanted to say thank you for my present!' He looked puzzled, said gently:

'But Freya - I didn't *give* you a Christmas present, sweetheart.' The little girl nodded vigorously, her russet blond hair glowing in the sunlight, her green eyes shining:

'Yes, you did - you gave me my Mummy back!'

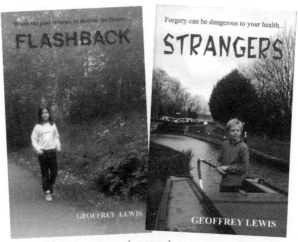

(see over)

If you have enjoyed *Winter's Tale*, you will want to read the first two David Russell novels, *Flashback* and *Strangers*.

These titles may be ordered from any good bookshop.

Just ask for
Flashback by Geoffrey Lewis   ISBN 0-9545624-0-2
Strangers by Geoffrey Lewis   ISBN 0-9545624-1-0
published by SGM Publishing.

For a full up-to-date list of David Russell novels,
please write to:

SGM Publishing
20 Alexandra Road
Gravesend
Kent
DA12 2QQ

Tel: 07792 497116
info@sgmpublishing.co.uk

The first David Russell novel
Published 2003

A ten-year-old girl is missing, on her way to visit a friend after school. Absconded or Abducted? D.I. David Russell is drafted in to begin the background investigation.

As it becomes clear the child has been taken, the events of that Friday evening are slowly unravelled, despite a lack of firm evidence. Red herrings are laid to rest; at last, suspicion begins to focus upon one man; and then another little girl disappears. Everyone thinks she has run away - but has she?

The second David Russell novel
Published 2004

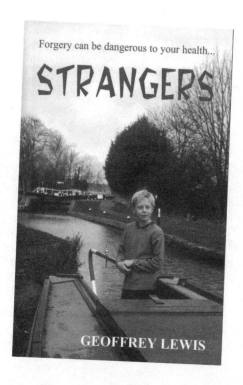

Forgery can be dangerous to your health...

STRANGERS

GEOFFREY LEWIS

The Metropolitan Police have smashed a major counterfeiting gang - but the ringleaders have escaped. And Ron Walker has a problem: How do you protect your family when it is being threatened by a cold, soulless killer?

As the forgers try to re-establish themselves in the provinces, David Russell's investigation becomes a race against time, both to convict the men and to save Walker's grandson from the fate which is stalking him on the idyllic highway of the Grand Union Canal.

What Goes Around,
Comes Around ....

CYCLE

Geoffrey Lewis

ISBN 0-9545624-3-7
Publication date 23 February 2005

CYCLE

Another David Russell novel from Geoffrey Lewis

The callous murder of a schoolboy has lain unsolved for twelve years: D.I. David Russell remembers the case - he was a youthful detective sergeant at the time.

A routine enquiry from India betrays a tenuous link with the boy's death. The connection seems insignificant, a matter of only casual interest; but as more information comes to light, Russell begins to realise that his curiosity has led him to a startling but unprovable conclusion. What he doesn't know is that the killer is back in town - and his own eleven-year-old son has met and befriended the man...

Cycle takes the reader back to David Russell's days as assistant to D.I. Keith Foreman, in the old Victorian police station of Grancester, and, latterly, brings him and the newly-promoted D.S. Doug Rimmer together for their first major investigation. Although only to be published as the fourth David Russell story, it effectively forms the first chapter of their continuing partnership, and provides a deeper insight into Russell's relationship with his son.

Cycle is scheduled for publication on 23 February 2005.